Mara couldn't tear her gaze from Mr. Jakeman's.

He looked at her so straightforwardly and so… kindly. But no! She couldn't trust how a man looked at a woman. Her husband, Klaus, had looked at her so charmingly when he'd courted her.

"I—"

Before Mara could refuse the honor, Liza spoke up. "Aw, come on, Mrs. Hoffman, I bet you're the best dancer. Please let me see you dance."

"I— Very well," she finished instead, and with a trembling hand, reached out to the farmer.

He was a tall, large man, and she felt like a piece of fragile porcelain being embraced by a clumsy giant. But as they began moving to the music, she was surprised at how deftly he led her. She thought of his fiddle playing. The man certainly was musical.

Now his hands held her surely by the waist and hand. Her hand rested lightly on his broad shoulder, her fingertips feeling the slight roughness of his wool coat. She felt protected, as she hadn't been since her father was alive.

Books by Ruth Axtell Morren

Love Inspired Historical	Steeple Hill Single Title
Hearts in the Highlands	*Winter Is Past*
A Man Most Worthy	*Wild Rose*
To Be a Mother	*Lilac Spring*
"A Family of Her Own"	*Dawn in My Heart*
A Gentleman's Homecoming	*The Healing Season*
Hometown Cinderella	*The Rogue's Redemption*
	The Making of a Gentleman
	A Bride of Honor

RUTH AXTELL MORREN

wrote her first story when she was twelve—a spy thriller—and knew she wanted to be a writer. There were many detours along the way. She studied comparative literature at Smith College, taught English in the Canary Islands and worked in international development in Miami, Florida.

She gained her first recognition as a writer when her second manuscript became a finalist in the Romance Writers of America Golden Heart Contest in 1994. Ruth has been writing for Love Inspired Books since 2002, and her second novel, *Wild Rose,* was selected as a Booklist Top 10 Christian Novel in 2005.

Ruth and her family live on the down-east coast of Maine. Ruth loves hearing from readers. You can contact her through her website, www.ruthaxtellmorren.com, or her blog, www.ruthaxtellmorren.blogspot.com.

RUTH AXTELL MORREN

Hometown Cinderella

Love Inspired

Recycling programs
for this product may
not exist in your area.

TM LOVE INSPIRED BOOKS

ISBN-13: 978-0-373-82904-0

HOMETOWN CINDERELLA
Copyright © 2012 by Ruth Axtell

THE INN AT HOPE SPRINGS
Copyright © 2010 by Harlequin Books S.A.

www.LoveInspiredBooks.com

Printed in U.S.A.

Dear Reader,

In 2012, Love Inspired Books is proudly celebrating fifteen years of heartwarming inspirational romance! Love Inspired launched in September 1997 and successfully brought inspiration to series romance. From heartwarming contemporary romance to heart-stopping romantic suspense to adventurous historical romance, Love Inspired Books offers a variety of inspirational stories for every preference. And we deliver uplifting, wholesome and emotional romances that every generation can enjoy.

We're marking our fifteenth anniversary with a special theme month in Love Inspired Historical: *Family Ties*. Whether ready-made families or families in the making, these touching stories celebrate the ties that bind and prove why family matters. Because sometimes it takes a family to open one's heart to the possibility of love. With wonderful stories by favorite authors Linda Ford and Ruth Axtell Morren, an exciting new miniseries from Regina Scott and a tender tale by debut author Lily George, this month full of family-themed reads will warm your heart.

I hope you enjoy each and every story—and then come back next month for more of the most powerful, engaging stories of romance, adventure and faith set in times past. From rugged handsome cowboys of the West to proper English gentlemen in Regency England, let Love Inspired Historical sweep you away to a place where love is timeless.

Sincerely,

Tina James
Senior Editor

To Oreo, our dear little Maine coon cat, who wasn't with us long, but made a lasting impression on our hearts. And to all those who've lost a beloved pet.

* * *

Weeping may endure for a night,
but joy cometh in the morning.
—*Psalms* 30:5b

Chapter One

Eagle's Bay, Maine
October 1884

Mara Keller didn't need the hymnal in her hands to sing. She knew the words by heart. "'Crown Him with many crowns, The Lamb upon His throne.'"

Dietrich fidgeted beside her. She placed a hand on her son's head, smoothing down his dark silky hair.

"'Awake, my soul, and sing of Him who died for thee.'"

She couldn't help but glance at the gentleman who stood on the other side of her son. He had a deep, melodious voice, not what she'd expect in a farmer. He was a large man, and despite his broadcloth suit, he seemed more suited to corduroys and a flannel shirt. Her gaze strayed to the hand holding the hymnal within her view. As she thought, it was large and rough-looking, the back lightly sprinkled with rusty-red hair the same shade as the hair on his head.

He had a strong profile. His cheeks were cleanly shaven, which surprised her, since most of the men in this farming community sported bushy side whiskers or beards.

She gave an imperceptible shake of her head at her own inattention to the music, and turned back to face the front of the church. Her musician's ear cringed slightly as a wrong note was struck on the organ. The robed men and women sang lustily but their voices were untrained. It made the farmer's voice to her left all the more agreeable to her ears.

The final notes echoed in the small wooden church as the last verse of the hymn came to an end. The rustle of people putting away their hymnals and sitting down on the wooden pews filled the room for the next few moments. Mara gently closed her own hymnal and set it soundlessly in the back of the pew in front of her before sitting down. She glanced at Dietrich to make sure he was putting away his book—he'd insisted on holding his own instead of sharing hers. He was forever forging ahead determined to do everything for himself.

"Good morning, everyone," the minister said, taking his place behind the pulpit. "It makes my heart glad to see all of you here today."

As he began the announcements, Mara settled back and smoothed down the merino wool of her old black dress. Once it had been the height of fashion but it had seen many winters. It would have to do, however, for the months remaining of her mourning period—for both her father and her husband.

For the one she felt such sorrow, and for the other nothing but a numbing relief.

Her stepmother nudged her sharply on her other side. Mara raised an inquiring eyebrow to Carina, whose nostrils flared in displeasure. With a jut of her pointy chin she indicated Dietrich.

Mara quickly turned to see what her six-year-old was up to. His hands rested on his lap but his legs swung vigorously, causing a slight noise each time the toes of his boots banged against the pew in front of him.

Mara touched him lightly on his arm and he looked up at her, his brown eyes wide in inquiry. How much he resembled his father in moments like these. With a gesture of her hand she indicated his feet, and after a few seconds he stopped moving them. Blowing out a loud sigh, he shifted on the pew.

"Make sure you greet Eagle's Bay's newest resident, Mrs. Mara Keller."

Hearing her name from the pulpit, Mara looked forward with a start.

The minister glanced at her with a benign smile. "She has lately come to live with us from the faraway capitals of Europe."

The color rose in her cheeks as people turned to stare at her. It was her first Sunday at the church, and she dreaded what her stepmother would say after the service during their ride home. *Most unseemly of you to be calling attention to yourself like that* would be a good bet, accompanied by a sniff.

"As some of you may know," the minister continued, "Mrs. Keller is the daughter of the late Mr. Robert Blackstone, a gifted painter who made Eagle Bay his residence in the latter years of his life. Mrs. Keller is gifted in her own right as a musician.

"She has suffered the recent bereavement of her husband, an acclaimed pianist. We are so happy to have you with us, ma'am, though we regret your loss, which made your return to our hamlet possible."

She smiled wanly, shrinking from the curiosity she saw in people's eyes. If they only knew the reality of her existence in Europe. But she'd become so adept at keeping up a front that it had become second nature.

"Well, now that I've given you the particulars on our latest resident, you can save yourselves the trouble of reading about it in the *Weekly Chronicle*."

As the congregation laughed, the parson turned to other announcements.

"Mama, was that you he was talking about?" Dietrich whispered loudly.

She bent close to his ear. "Yes. Now, hush, dear, so others can hear the minister."

He nodded and turned back to face the front. Mara sat back and caught the eyes of a girl craning her neck around the tall farmer on Dietrich's left. The girl's greenish-gray eyes stared at her, her pale pink lips slightly parted. She wore two long braids, a shade redder than the gentleman's. Clearly, the two must be related, perhaps father and daughter.

When Mara smiled tentatively at the girl, who appeared in her early teenage years, she snapped her mouth shut and disappeared once more behind the gentleman. Mara glanced toward his face to find him looking at her.

He, too, had light-colored eyes, though his were more gray-blue. Washed-out, she would call them. Yet he was looking at her kindly enough. He held her gaze a second longer before bowing his head slightly.

He had the ruddy complexion of someone who spent time out of doors. The color in his cheeks seemed to deepen just as he turned away. Mara wondered if he were shy. Possibly a farmer trying to be friendly but who wouldn't know what to say to her after the minister had built her up so much. Reverend Grayson meant well, she was sure, but from the little she remembered of this isolated part of the coast of Maine, she could well imagine that she would soon be friendless if everyone was intimidated by her reputation. How little they would realize how much in need she was of a friend and of a place to call home.

As the minister gave the Scripture reading of the morning, she opened her Bible on her lap and turned to it.

Minutes later, the fidgeting on her left increased. Mara tried to ignore it, but as it grew worse, she resorted to tapping Dietrich's arm from time to time. That only served to still his movements for a few seconds before they began again. She repressed a sigh. Dietrich had always been active. She remembered his hard kicks when she'd carried him in her womb. As a boy of six, he had trouble sitting through an entire church service.

She focused on the preacher's words. He was talking about facing the trials of life. Her own life seemed to have been nothing but trials since she'd become an adult. She let her mind wander to those carefree days of her youth, when she'd been beloved by her father, and she'd kept house for him until…he'd married Carina.

As she pulled herself from these reflections of the past, Mara realized she hadn't felt any movement from Dietrich in several minutes. She turned her gaze sideward and stopped in amazement at the sight of her son's attention glued to the gentleman's hands.

They were folding a piece of paper into an intricate shape. She stared spellbound at the sight of such blunt fingers handling a delicate piece of paper so lightly and deftly. In moments, the clear figure of a bird emerged from the workings of his quick creases and pleats.

She blinked up and once again caught the man's gaze. This time he gave a brief smile before focusing on the paper in his hand. With a final adjustment, he handed the bird to Dietrich.

She studied the man's profile a few seconds longer, noting the straight nose and wide forehead beneath hair that was slicked back, evidence of his morning ablutions, yet which didn't succeed in taming its curl. Her glance strayed downward past the deeper reddish hair of his sideburns and along the firm jawline to the defined curve of his chin.

Once more, she caught a telltale shade along his cheekbones and she realized she was staring. Was he conscious of it? Quickly, she looked back down at her Bible.

Dietrich turned his paper bird around and around in his

hands. Mara settled back against the pew and listened to the preacher's message.

When she next sensed restless movement at her side, she barely glanced over before she glimpsed the farmer's hand handing the boy a small sheet of paper from between the pages of his Bible. Dietrich immediately began to fold it. When he had succeeded in folding it thoroughly but making nothing that appeared like a bird, he looked up at the man, who took it and smoothed it out on his own Bible. Then he began with the first fold. He undid it and handed it back to Dietrich. As soon as Dietrich had copied it, the gentleman took it and proceeded with the next fold. Fold by fold, he guided Dietrich in producing his own paper creature.

When they were thoroughly engrossed in this endeavor, Mara let out a soft sigh and turned back to the sermon. Bless this man, whoever he was, for keeping Dietrich occupied. It was the first time she had been able to give her full attention to a sermon in a long time.

As soon as the minister dismissed the congregation, everyone stood and began to greet one another as they shuffled their way out of the cramped space between the pews. Gideon stood and eased the stiffness from his legs.

"May I have this, sir?"

He glanced down at the young boy looking up so earnestly at him. The first thing he noticed was the boy's accent. British? Not quite, he judged, although he'd heard an Englishman's accent only once.

"Of course you may, son." He resisted the urge to ruffle the boy's dark hair. The next instant, an elegant gloved hand was extended toward him. He raised startled eyes to the lady who had sat beside the boy during the service, and with whom he'd crossed glances a time or two.

He swallowed and quickly extended his own hand, feeling the heat rise in his face, unsure how to address such a fine lady as he remembered the words of praise Reverend Grayson had given her.

"Thank you, sir, for helping to keep my son quiet during the service."

She had a soft voice, very pleasing to the ear, and an American accent, unlike her son. His discomfort grew. Hadn't the preacher said she'd lived in Europe? "That's quite—" He was forced to clear his throat when his voice came out like a frog's croak. "That's quite all right, ma'am."

She was a beautiful woman, with porcelain skin and dark hair combed neatly into a knot under her small bonnet. Her black outfit reminded him further of Reverend Grayson's words. A surge of compassion rose in his chest for the young widow with a boy to raise. He tried to remember what else the minister had said about her. Something about her being a musician or her husband one?

"Dietrich gets restless easily. It's very hard to keep him still during a church service."

Dietrich. The name sounded foreign. German? "That's natural," he said, wanting to reassure her. She seemed so out of place, like an exotic creature, in their small, rustic church. "I remember how it was when I was a tyke." He glanced down with a smile at the boy, who was pretending to fly the bird. "Young boys aren't supposed to be quiet and sit still, isn't that so?"

Dietrich stopped the paper bird in mid-flight and looked hesitantly from him to his mother as if not sure how to answer.

An awkward pause ensued. The lady gave a short, nervous-sounding laugh. "I apologize for the long introduction Reverend Grayson gave. It puts me at a disadvantage, I'm afraid."

He drew his eyebrows together, trying to fathom her meaning when she smiled a bit and said, "I'm sorry. I don't know whom I'm thanking."

"Oh—yes, I beg your pardon." What a clodhopper she must think him, not even knowing how to introduce himself. "My name's Gideon Jakeman. I own a farm up the road a piece from Mrs. Blackstone." That's when he realized he was still holding her hand. His face flooded with color and he released her hand as if it were a live coal. "I'm sorry—"

Her laughter sounded as sweet as a running brook in spring. "Not at all. I'm pleased to make your acquaintance, Mr. Jakeman."

At that moment, Mrs. Blackstone peered around Mrs. Keller. "What's keeping you, Mara? Really, we must be going. The roast will be dry as leather." As usual, Mrs. Blackstone sounded aggrieved. Gideon wondered what it must be like for the younger woman to dwell with the older widow who was known to be difficult.

"Yes, Carina."

"You know how crowded it gets at the entrance," she said with a sniff and a nod to Gideon before turning around and pushing her way forward.

"Yes. I shall be with you directly." By neither look nor tone did Mrs. Keller betray any displeasure. When she turned her large eyes—blue, he noted, fringed in black lashes—to him she smiled once more. "It was a pleasure to make your acquaintance, Mr. Jakeman." Her gaze strayed to his side and she waited as if expectantly. It took Gideon a few seconds to realize his daughter stood there. "Oh." He swallowed, realizing again how socially inept he was. He'd forgotten all about Lizzie. "This is my daughter, Lizzie—Elizabeth," he amended. "But everyone calls her Lizzie. Elizabeth was her mother's name, but we called her Elsie—" He stopped, realizing how confusing his introduction had become.

But Mrs. Keller didn't seem to notice. She was already extending her hand to his fourteen-year-old daughter with a warm smile. "How do you do, Lizzie?"

Lizzie seemed as dumbfounded as he felt with Mrs. Keller's ladylike ways. She quickly bobbed her head, her cheeks looking as red as frost-tinged apples.

"Well, I must be going." Mrs. Keller smiled again at Gideon, a smile which succeeded in touching him all the way down to his toes, and took a step back. "Thank you again for your help with Dietrich."

"Anytime, ma'am," he managed before she turned and took a step away.

"Wait—" he called, a sudden thought pushing aside all the rest.

She glanced back, a finely arched black eyebrow lifted, a half smile of inquiry on her lips. "Yes, Mr. Jakeman?" she asked when he said nothing.

He coughed, feeling his face warm, mentally cursing the fact that he was enough of a redhead to turn beet-red at the merest provocation.

"I just thought—we're neighbors. My farm's the one just before Mrs. Blackstone's. If you ever want to send Dietrich down my way, he's welcome." Gideon glanced down at her son, who was looking at him round-eyed as if he'd proposed going to the moon.

Gideon smiled to reassure him. The boy smiled back. Gideon met the woman's glance again. "I'll keep him busy over there." At the slight frown that formed between her eyebrows, he quickly amended, "I mean, he'll find plenty to do." Did she think he meant to put the boy to work?

Before she could say anything, the boy turned to her. "Oh, Mama, please, may I?" He started tugging on her arm, his voice rising.

Gideon put a hand on the boy's shoulder, quieting him instantly. "Simmer down, son. Let your mother have a chance to think it over." Dietrich nodded and looked at his feet. Gideon gave his shoulder a gentle squeeze before turning back to his mother.

The frown eased from her brow. "Thank you, Mr. Jakeman. That's very kind of you. But I wouldn't want Dietrich to be in your way."

His lips tugged upward. "Oh, he wouldn't be in the way. I can show him a few things if you don't mind his getting his hands a little dirty." The boy's hands were as white as a young lady's. He was a good-looking lad, a lot like his mother, with her slim build.

"No, of course not," she murmured.

"Ever milked a cow, Dietrich?"

The boy shook his head, sending his straight hair flying. "No, sir."

"Well, we shall see," Mrs. Keller said. "Thank you for your offer, Mr. Jakeman."

With a nod, she took her son by the hand and moved off toward the aisle.

Gideon stood looking after her until an acquaintance from the pew behind him slapped him on the back and greeted him. He shook away his distraction and focused on the kind of conversation he was comfortable with—the purchase of a new mare and the butchering of a hog.

Mara guided the horse and buggy into the barn after letting Carina off at the kitchen doorway, glad for the stillness in the large, shadowy interior after the tiresome ride home. Carina never seemed to be satisfied with anything she did. This noon it was Dietrich's behavior in church, and her stepmother's harangue still echoed in her ears.

Dietrich jumped down from the buggy. "Mama, let me unhitch Jacob."

"Very well." She allowed him to undo the traces as she unbuckled the straps of the harness. Carina allowed her use of the buggy only when she went along. But she did expect Mara to put it away when their handyman wasn't around.

As they led the horse to the stall, Mara told her son, "I'll give him some oats and you start brushing him down."

The two worked quietly awhile. "Mama, that man in church was nice."

"The one who made the lovely paper bird for you? That was Mr. Jakeman." She remembered his offer for Dietrich.

"Yes. I kept it in my pocket." He paused in his brushing and fished it out. "Oh, Mama, it's crushed."

Mara went over to his side of the stall and took the flattened paper. "We can plump it up, I think." She folded out the creases as she spoke and tried to reshape the bird as best she could. "There, that doesn't look too bad."

He took it but didn't say anything.

"Let's put it over here until we're finished." She set it on a barrel then went back to brushing down the horse's haunches. "There now, we'll give Jacob a blanket. The days are certainly getting cooler."

When they had set everything to rights in the barn, the two shoved closed the barn door then walked through the woodshed which connected the barn to the house. With each step closer, Mara's spirits fell a notch at the thought of what awaited her inside. With a sigh, she pushed open the door to the kitchen.

Her stepmother turned from the cookstove. "The meat is drying out and the beans are getting cold."

"I'm sorry. It took us a bit longer than I expected. Come, Dietrich, let's wash our hands."

As quickly as she could, she donned an apron and took over at the stove. As soon as she did so, Carina took her own apron off and headed to the dining room to sit down. Mara swallowed back her annoyance.

Since Mara had arrived at her father's old house, her stepmother had relinquished all household tasks to her, making it plain she expected Mara to earn her keep. The fact that her father had left her half the house didn't make up for the fact that Mara hadn't a penny to her name.

The meal was a silent one, as were most in this cold, dingy house. The only sound in the dining room was the ticking of a clock over the mantel and the occasional sound of cutlery against a plate.

"Young man, chew your food with decorum."

Mara glanced at her son and saw him quickly swallow the lump of food in his mouth. She smiled encouragement to ease the sharpness of Carina's words to him. To take her attention off him, she said, "The minister gave a fine sermon."

Carina's fork paused halfway up to her mouth. "Grayson? He's so long-winded, it's a wonder half his congregation doesn't nod off midway. Those pews are so hard, it's inconsiderate of him to go on so." Her eyes narrowed on Dietrich. "That reminds me, you'd better learn to keep quiet during service, young man. I could hardly hear the preacher for your banging your feet against the pew. Goodness, Mara, haven't you taught your son anything?"

Mara clenched her teeth in renewed anger. Carina hadn't yet called Dietrich by his given name. *"Dietrich—"* she stressed the syllables "—finds it difficult to sit still for too long…just the way some adults do," she couldn't help but add.

Mara regretted the words as soon as they were out. Carina narrowed her eyes at Mara until she felt she'd skewer her if she could. "Well, I never! I would hardly compare an ill-behaved boy to an elderly lady with a bad back."

"I beg your pardon. I didn't mean any offense." Why hadn't she just kept quiet? The words of the sermon on bearing suffering had flown out of her mind as soon as she'd left church, it seemed. Now poor Dietrich would bear the brunt of Carina's wrath all afternoon. She searched around in her mind for something to take her stepmother's mind off her remark. "That gentleman beside us was very nice."

Carina's eyes narrowed. "Gentleman? What gentleman? Don't tell me you're encouraging gentlemen with your husband not yet cold in the grave."

Mara drew back at the sharp words. "Of course not!"

"May I remind you that you are still in mourning for your father, if not for your husband? I don't know what the practices are over there in those foreign parts for widows, but here in New England, a widow is expected to be chaste and sober."

Mara choked down the mashed potatoes in her mouth, and immediately felt her stomach clench in knots. How long would she have to put up with this woman? What had her poor father endured? And now Mara, for she had no money to go elsewhere.

"I need to know which gentleman you were speaking to in order to put a stop to any gossip that starts."

Mara drew herself up. "I did nothing to start any gossip."

Carina sniffed. "All it takes is for an unmarried woman to talk to a man and the whole hamlet knows about it within days."

Mara set down her knife and fork on the edge of her plate. "I simply introduced myself to the gentleman sitting on the other side of Dietrich."

"What a forward thing to do, introducing yourself to the first man you meet!"

"He was patient with Dietrich and I wanted to thank him."

Carina thumped her forefinger against the tablecloth. "If you'd exercise some firmness with your boy, he wouldn't fidget so much in church."

Mara stared at the remaining food on her plate, praying for grace to keep her tongue still.

Before she could say anything, her stepmother tilted her head and pursed her lips. "As I recall that was Gideon Jakeman sitting by you." She made a contemptuous sound, between a cackle and a snort. "Gentleman! That's a good one!" She laughed some more. "A farmer, that's what he is."

She turned a scornful eye on Mara. "You're wasting your time on that one! More'n one widow around here has tried to catch him."

Mara stared at her stepmother's quick turnaround from accusatory to smug.

"He's a widower, all right, but not the kind you'd want to set your cap for, you with your fine ways."

"I have no intention of setting my cap for anyone."

Carina fixed her dark eyes on her in a way that always made Mara feel her malevolence like a viscous black syrup. "It might not be a bad idea for you to begin looking around at the widowers. I don't know how long you can keep on here without contributing to the cost of the household."

With an effort, Mara pushed her plate away and stood. "I intend to go to town tomorrow to seek employment. I will give you a portion of my wages as soon as I obtain them."

"Employment! Why, whatever can you do for wages? I warn you, I'll have nothing disreputable that would reflect badly on your poor father's name!"

"I assure you, I would never shame my father's name!" Mara's voice shook with feeling. She pushed her chair to the table, gripping its back. "I intend to offer music lessons, perhaps deportment to young ladies—"

Another nasty cackle erupted from Carina's lips. "Deportment! I doubt you'll find anyone in these parts willing to pay good money to put on airs the way you do."

Mara picked up her half-empty plate and left the table. She would keep her temper for Dietrich's sake if nothing more.

"Mama, may I be excused?"

She turned back to her son. "Eat your turnip, dear." If he didn't clean his plate, it would mean more carping.

He made a face. "Do I have to?"

"Yes, you must."

He ran his fork through the mashed vegetable until Carina said sharply, "Don't play with your food, boy! You heard your mother. Now clean your plate and be off with you."

He gave the older woman a frightened look and quickly obeyed. As soon as he'd gagged down the vegetable he stood and looked at his mother. Mara nodded. "You may be excused."

Dietrich ran into the kitchen and Mara followed more slowly. "Mama, may I go to Mr. Jakeman's house?"

Mara bit her lip. She didn't know the man, or how far away he lived. "Down the road a piece" could mean a mile or more in these parts. "We only just met him, dear."

"But Mama, he invited me."

"I know that, but I need to go with you the first time."

Dietrich began to pout. Mara set down her dish and stood before him, lifting his chin. "I'll take you soon, but today you're to stay in the yard. Understood?"

Dietrich's gaze took on the mutinous look she was so familiar with in his late father's eyes. "But Mama—"

"I'm sorry. If you won't obey me, you'll just have to stay in your room."

He looked down. "All right, but it's not fair."

She turned him around and gave him a gentle push toward the door. "I'll take you soon. Now, go put on your jacket. It's chilly outside."

When he'd left the kitchen, Mara turned wearily back to the dining room to finish clearing the table.

As she stacked the dirty dishes onto a tray, Carina sat back with a satisfied sigh. "There've been two or three women in the hamlet who've set their eyes on Gideon in the years he's been widowed, but he hasn't given them a glance. He pretty much keeps to himself—he and that gangly redhead daughter o' his."

Mara kept silent, preferring to ignore her stepmother's

criticism. She never seemed to have anything good to say about anyone. The last thing Mara needed was to have Carina accusing her of setting her eye on the poor gentleman who'd helped keep Dietrich amused this morning.

"That homely daughter o' his keeps house for Gideon." Carina sniffed as she lifted her coffee cup. "I'm sure she wouldn't welcome any strange woman into her father's life." She gave a contemptuous snort. "I shouldn't want to see the inside of that house! A fourteen-year-old for a housekeeper!" Another sharp laugh punctuated the statement.

Mara lifted the tray, intrigued in spite of herself. "His daughter keeps house for him?" It reminded her of her own life with her father before he'd married Carina.

"The girl lords it over him. She wouldn't let him look at another woman even if he had any inclination to do so." Carina's mouth twisted in a contemptuous smile. "More's the pity for you. Jakeman's quite a prosperous farmer. He owns the acreage up the hill past the Tate land. We go by it on our way to town."

Mara remembered the man's words and his offer for Dietrich.

Her stepmother took a sip of coffee. "It's one of the largest pieces of land in Eagle's Bay. But you wouldn't know it to see him or that girl o' his. Always dressed in work clothes and standing behind a plow." She shook her head. "I can't see you setting your sights on the likes o' him, not with all your 'European' ways!" She said the word as if Mara had brought home some new way of living.

Sorry she'd shown any interest in the man, Mara lifted the heavy tray and headed back to the kitchen. She'd vowed never to marry again and she intended to keep that promise, even if she had to scrub floors for a living and save every penny until Dietrich reached manhood.

"Remember, I don't want any gossip started, you hear?" Carina called behind her. "I've been living in Eagle's Bay a good many years and never been the object of shame. Just because your father saw fit to leave you part of this property doesn't mean you can do as you please."

Mara escaped into the kitchen, banging down the tray and causing the china to rattle. "Tomorrow I shall look for employment," she vowed under her breath. She would have to get out of this house before she did something she'd regret!

Chapter Two

⌒

Gideon sat in the buckboard with Lizzie at his side. The two rode back from their weekly trip to town. The maples along the road were brilliant with red and yellow, the dirt road covered with their shed leaves, the fields beyond the stone walls golden yellow.

"Who's that, Pa?"

He squinted against the late-afternoon sun at the woman far ahead of them on the gently undulating road. Her long black cloak billowed out behind her. Despite her satchel, she walked straight.

"Isn't that the lady from church?"

"Could be." He flicked the reins and the mare picked up her pace.

It was quite a clip to town, almost four miles, and the stretch to the hamlet was up and downhill.

When the buckboard was within twenty feet of her, she finally slowed her pace and eventually stopped as he drew Bessie abreast of her.

It was indeed Mrs.— He strained to recall her name, remembering only that it had sounded unfamiliar to these parts.

He lifted a hand to his straw hat. "Howdy. Need a lift back?"

"That's kind of you, Mr. Jakeman, but I haven't far to go. Thank you all the same." The black ribbons of her bonnet tied beneath her chin fluttered in the breeze. Her cheeks were tinged pink, her eyes bright blue.

"You got at least a couple miles to go," Lizzie said. "Here, you can ride beside me. There's plenty of room for three." She scooted over on the seat, patting the empty place beside her.

The lady said nothing, looking from Lizzie to the seat. Why the hesitation? Was it because it was only a farm wagon? Was it too dirty a conveyance for her?

Finally, with a small smile, she said, "Very well, that's very kind of you."

"No trouble at all, ma'am." Before he could make a move to get down to help her, the lady clutched the rim of the wagon and swung herself up.

"I'm much obliged to you."

"I thought it was you from way back," Lizzie said, satisfaction in her voice. "We were also in town taking some apples to sell and buying some supplies." She indicated the sacks behind them in the wagon.

"You have sharp eyes," the lady said.

"You live at Mrs. Blackstone's?" Lizzie asked once they were on their way again.

"Hush, Lizzie. I'm sure Mrs.—er…" He could feel himself flush as he struggled to remember her name. His skin grew even warmer at the thought of her first name, which he did remember. Mara. It was a pretty-sounding name.

"Keller," she supplied quickly as if reading his mind. Then she laughed. "I would have been very surprised indeed if you had remembered my name."

He shook his head with a chuckle, relieved the woman

wasn't offended. "I should have after all Reverend Grayson said about you on Sunday."

"Oh, my goodness, I was quite mortified with such a long introduction. I was afraid everyone would think I was a proud person too far above the likes of anyone around here to talk to."

"Oh, no. Reverend Grayson always likes to welcome anyone new. 'Course, there's rarely anyone new here," Lizzie added.

"Well, I'm glad he didn't put you off then."

They rode along in silence a few minutes.

"Were you walking from town?" Lizzie asked.

"Yes."

"Don't you have a horse and buggy?"

"Uh—no. That is, Mrs. Blackstone does. That's my step-mother. But I don't take it out."

"Why not?"

The widow gave what sounded like a nervous laugh. "My, aren't you full of questions?"

"Leave the lady be, Lizzie," Gideon said.

Lizzie fell silent, and Gideon felt bad to have had to admonish her like that. He knew her naturally pink cheeks were deepening in color, and she'd probably clam up the rest of the way home. But he'd sensed the lady hadn't been comfortable with the question.

"Oh, that's all right," Mrs. Keller said. "I didn't mean to scold. I was just too embarrassed to confess I'm not a very good driver. I've only just been learning again since I arrived last week."

"You don't know how to drive a buggy?" Lizzie's voice rose in wonder.

"Well," she said with another small laugh, "I've been living in the city for so long, where I never had—or needed—my own carriage."

"Is it true you've traveled to all those places Reverend Grayson talked about?" Lizzie asked.

Gideon glanced sidelong at Mrs. Keller in time to catch her nod.

"How'd you manage that? I've never even been outside of Eagle's Bay, though Pa here took the steamer to Boston once, didn't you, Papa?"

He merely nodded, keeping his focus on the mare, uncomfortable with the attention.

"I used to live near Boston and then went there after leaving home," the lady said.

"You left home?" There was shocked awe in Lizzie's voice.

"Yes, to study music at the conservatory there."

"How did you get to Europe from Boston?"

"I continued my studies in Vienna and there I met my future husband. He was a pianist and toured all over Europe, performing at the different concert halls."

"A pianist?"

"Mmm-hmm. He played the piano. He was also studying at the conservatory."

"What'd you study there?"

"Piano and violin—and voice."

Gideon listened as Lizzie kept plying Mrs. Keller—he vowed he wouldn't forget her name again—with question after question.

The lady didn't seem to mind, but he'd have to have a word with Lizzie afterward about minding her own business. But he hesitated to say anything more now. He didn't like to shame his only child in public. She was too shy by far, something that came from having lost her mother so young, he often thought, and then felt guilty for not having remarried to provide her with a female companion. But Lizzie had been adamant that she didn't want just any woman living with them. And Gideon had never met anyone he'd felt the way he had about Elsie.

Besides that, he was intrigued with the newcomer and was just as curious as Lizzie. Mrs. Keller's life sounded like something out of a storybook.

"Where all did you live?"

"Well, let's see. Most recently, I have been living in Paris."

"Paris. Did you have to speak another language?"

Mrs. Keller had a very pleasant laugh. Soft and low, like a summer rain on leaves. "Yes. They speak French in Paris. Let's see, before that, we lived in Vienna awhile. There we had to speak German, which came easily for my husband, since he was originally from Germany. I had studied it in school, so it wasn't long before I could converse easily with the people."

"And where else did you live?"

"Hmm. Milan—that's in Italy—for a while, but mostly we traveled, staying only a few weeks in the capitals. London, Frankfurt, Rome, Madrid. We were even in St. Petersburg a few times. That's in Russia."

"Russia!" Lizzie's tone was filled with awe. "How did you keep it all straight in your head?"

Once again she gave her melodious laugh. "It was a bit daunting at times, I have to admit. But each city is so distinct in its architecture—the buildings, that is. And, in the language, of course, the food, even many times the dress, in more subtle ways."

"Did your little boy go with you everywhere?"

She was silent a moment, causing Gideon to glance over at her.

"By the time he was born," she said slowly, "my husband had fallen ill and our traveling days were over. Dietrich has only lived in Paris."

"I'm sorry…about your husband, that is," Lizzie said softly.

"That's all right." Once again, Gideon glanced her way to gauge her reaction. He knew what it was to lose a spouse. She revealed little by her words or tone. Her face had a shrouded look.

"It must be nice to have been so many places," Lizzie said with a sigh.

"It…has its advantages and disadvantages."

Gideon couldn't help but look over a third time. Had she experienced some hardship while she'd been abroad? If her boy was now six or seven, that meant that her husband had been an invalid a good many years.

She looked so self-possessed that it was hard to tell what she might mean. Her manner of dressing, though obviously that of a lady, was unadorned and almost severe, so that, too, gave little away.

"Tell me, Lizzie, do you like music?"

It sounded to Gideon that the widow wanted to change the subject. Her voice had brightened and she'd turned slightly to face his daughter. A second later, her glance rose to meet his. Feeling his face flush, he quickly faced the horse again.

"Oh, my, yes," Lizzie answered immediately.

"Do you play any instruments or sing?"

"Aw, no. But I like to sing, when I'm washing the dishes or ironing the clothes, don't I, Pa?"

"What? Oh, yes, you certainly do." Lizzie had a nice voice. But he didn't say so aloud, afraid Mrs. Keller would think he was boasting about his daughter. He remembered hearing the widow's singing voice during church. Probably no one in all Eagle's Bay sang as good as she did, not even those in the church choir.

"And Pa sings and plays the fiddle real good, don't you?"

Gideon kept his eyes fixed on his horse.

"Does he, indeed? Well, I know he has a fine voice, so it

doesn't surprise me if he should also play a musical instrument."

At her first words, Gideon's glance shot to Mrs. Keller. As if sensing his glance, she met it over his daughter's head. "I heard it in church," she continued, addressing Lizzie as if he wasn't there. But the twinkle in her deep blue eyes told him otherwise.

He couldn't help a quirk of his own lips upward.

"Well, you certainly seem to be a busy girl," Mrs. Keller said, bringing the conversation back to Lizzie, for which Gideon could only be thankful. "Do you attend school?"

"Yes'm. When it's in session. Papa insists on that."

"School is important. What other things do you do?"

"Well, I keep house for Pa, o' course. And then there're sociables now that winter is coming. There's singing at those, and dancing," continued Lizzie. "I like to watch from the sidelines. Are you going to be at the cider pressing on Saturday? There'll be some fiddling and dancing for sure. You can hear Pa play then."

"I don't know. I hadn't heard anything about it. I wonder if Mrs. Blackstone will be attending."

"She generally hires someone to pick her apples and gets some of them pressed into cider for the winter," Gideon said.

Both females turned to him as if surprised to hear him speak. He cleared his throat, embarrassed. "I reckon she'll be by."

"Where is this cider pressing held?"

"At the McClellans'," Lizzie answered before Gideon could say anything. "They're real nice folks with a big farm and orchard. They're kin. Sarah McClellan is Papa's cousin on his father's side, ain't she?"

"Yes, that's so."

"They set up the cider press and everyone brings their jugs or barrels. It's always such fun."

"Well, perhaps I shall see you there."

"I hope so."

About a half mile from the Blackstone place, as they were approaching their own place, Mrs. Keller turned to him. "Please, Mr. Jakeman, could you drop me off here?"

He raised his eyebrows in surprise. "It's no trouble for me to turn into your place."

"I…" She hesitated and he wondered at her sudden discomfort. "It would be best if I…if I came in alone."

He frowned then slowly nodded, realizing it probably had something to do with Mrs. Blackstone. Without a word, he pulled over along the side of the road and brought the wagon to a stop. This time, he quickly handed the reins to Lizzie and jumped down.

Mrs. Keller was already descending the wagon when he reached her side. But he took her elbow and helped her the remaining way.

"Thank you," she said, sounding breathless, her free hand going to her bonnet.

He let her arm go and stepped back. Feeling as tongue-tied as a boy, he watched her grip her satchel in one hand and turn to Lizzie. "It was very nice conversing with you. I hope we may do it again sometime."

"Oh, sure. Come over to the farm anytime." Lizzie looked over at him. "We can always bring you to town if you'd like, can't we, Pa?"

He gave a quick nod. "Certainly, anytime."

"Thank you," she repeated. "That does remind me, Dietrich, my son, has been wanting to visit, and I promised I'd bring him by as soon as I had a moment."

"Bring him by anytime," Gideon said before Lizzie could respond.

Mrs. Keller smiled at him, a smile that warmed him to the depths of his heart. Before he could examine his reaction, she addressed them both. "Well, I'd better be on my way. Mrs. Blackstone will wonder where I am. Good day to you, Mr. Jakeman. Thank you for the lift."

Gideon touched the brim of his hat as she walked by him.

He returned to his seat and turned into their gate. Lizzie waved to Mrs. Keller. "Be seein' ya."

"I hope so."

When they were beyond her hearing, Lizzie said, "She is such a nice lady, don't you think so, Pa?"

"Yes, very nice." He appreciated her having been so patient with Lizzie, talking to her as if she were an adult. He preferred thinking about that than about his own reaction to her.

"I wonder why she didn't want us to bring her all the way home?"

"I 'spect she wanted to enjoy the nice fall weather."

Lizzie jutted out her bottom lip, considering. "But she could enjoy it just as well from up here."

"Maybe she needed some peace and quiet."

"Did I talk too much, Pa?" came her immediate reply, her voice full of concern.

He tugged at one of her braids. "Not a bit."

"She sure sounds like she's led an interesting life."

As they drew up to their barn, he halted the wagon. "Yes, indeed. You know, you have to watch your questions sometimes. Not everyone wants to tell you their life story the first time they meet you."

"I'm sorry, Pa. I hope she doesn't think I was being nosy."

"I'm sure she just thought you were being friendly. But next time, slow down the questions some. Let her be the one who volunteers the information."

"Yes, Pa. I hope we see her again." She brightened. "Maybe she'll be at the cider pressing."

"Yes…" Already, he was trying to suppress the spurt of nervous anticipation at the thought—and trying to figure out why he was feeling so nervous.

As he tended the mare, he mused on the strange life Mrs. Keller had led, changing residence every year.

The one time he'd been up to Boston, he'd hated living in the cramped building wedged between the others along the street. Everything had seemed noisy and dirty.

He shook his head. Well, to each his own, he'd always heard. Walking back to the house, he wondered how the widow was going to take the quiet and solitude of Eagle's Bay, especially once snow set in.

He looked across the rolling fields dotted with gray boulders and edged by dark fir trees. Far to the east the inky blue sea looked cold and intense against the paler sky. He couldn't imagine a better existence, but for a city person? And living with Mrs. Blackstone? He didn't know the older widow well, but the little contact he'd had gave him the impression of a bitter, exacting woman who never smiled.

With a final shake of his head, he turned to enter the house.

Lizzie was already in the kitchen, stirring up the fire. "I'll have some biscuits in the oven in a jiffy. Thought I'd fry up some o' that salt pork and have the beans from this noon."

He walked over to the sink and pumped some water. "Sounds fine to me." He wished Lizzie could have more time with other girls her age, but she always seemed content keeping house for him. He grabbed the cake of soap she'd made and began to lather up his hands.

"Want a cup o' tea?"

"Sure. Take the chill off. I can make it for us both."

"You just sit, Pa. I'll have it steeping in a moment. The water's almost boiled."

While drying his hands, he watched his only child fill the teapot.

"I can't believe a body can live so many places the way Mrs. Keller has."

It was clear the widow had made as great an impression

on his daughter as she had on him. "No. It's hard to imagine, all right." He remembered more of their conversation. "You wouldn't like to take some music lessons, would you? Perhaps she'd give you some."

Lizzie swiveled around from the counter. "What—me?" She laughed, her face suffusing with color. "Aw, no."

"Why not?"

She just shook her head and replaced the lid on the pot.

He wished he could give her more, but she always seemed content. It had been years since Elsie had died and he wondered sometimes if Lizzie still missed her. They rarely talked of her.

"Here's your tea."

He took the cup with a "Thank you," and sat at the table with the newspaper, determined to focus on the local headlines. He had no business thinking about the beautiful young widow who'd lived in so many cities as if he were a young man again.

Chapter Three

Mara held her seat as the wagon wheels rumbled along the rutted road. Beside her, Carina held the reins. Dietrich sat on Mara's other side, holding a string in his hands and pretending it was a pair of reins. He bounced in his seat more than the bumpy ride warranted.

As they neared the McClellan farm where the cider pressing was being held, Carina eyed the many wagons and buggies already parked along the dirt entry and yard. "I knew we should have arrived earlier. I hope we won't have to wait out in the cold too long for our cider."

"I can wait if you'd care to go inside."

"I feel a chill coming on. I knew I shouldn't have ventured out tonight." It was still late afternoon but the sun was already sinking behind the dark horizon of fir trees.

Carina brought the wagon to a stop beside some others and allowed a local farmer to take the reins and help her down. "Thank you, Charlie."

"Howdy, Miz Blackstone. Glad to see you out today."

Carina turned to Mara. "I'm going inside then. You see to the bushels."

"Yes."

Dietrich jumped down from the wagon and Mara followed

more slowly, relieved at being left alone, although not looking forward to unloading all the bushels of apples she'd just had to load.

Dietrich was already trying to unlatch the back of the wagon. "Mama, it's stuck."

"That's because you can't quite reach it." She let down the back and began to drag one of the bushel baskets forward.

"I can help you take one of those." The farmer named Charlie reached over and took up a bushel of small, tart apples and swung it onto his shoulder. With an effort, Mara dragged another bushel basket by its handles.

"Come, Dietrich, you take one handle, and I'll take the other just the way we did at home this afternoon."

He did as she asked, and the two carried the heavy basket which swung awkwardly between them. They walked slowly toward the barn, where she saw others gathered. The load was heavy. Her arms ached from the afternoon's hauling.

"Here, let me take that." Before she could protest, a strong pair of arms reached for the basket.

Dietrich relinquished his side immediately. "Watch out, Dietrich—" Before she could say anything more, he'd run off. Mr. Jakeman, however, grabbed the basket before it could fall.

"Th-thank you, Mr. Jakeman." The tall farmer had appeared behind her as if out of nowhere. Mara brushed back a wisp of her hair, feeling suddenly self-conscious. Telling herself it was due to Carina's awful insinuations about setting her cap for him, she took a step away from him.

Mr. Jakeman only nodded and in a few long strides was at the barn, setting the basket beside some others on the straw-covered barn floor.

Mara went to fetch another basket. When she turned, Mr. Jakeman was at her side. With only a mumbled "Excuse me," he took the basket from her.

She tried to protest. "That's quite all right, I've got this one."

"These are too heavy for a lady."

She couldn't help a short laugh. "You'd be surprised the things I've carried." If he could have seen her picking the apples and loading them onto the wagon this afternoon!

He gave her a quick look and said no more but took the basket from her, nevertheless. She looked after his broad back with a bemused smile at having found gallantry in the most unexpected quarter. Her smile faded. She hardly remembered what gallantry was like—nor did she trust it.

Remembering her son, she scanned the barnyard. Where had he gone? Several children were running around. With a sigh of relief she spotted Dietrich among them. The next second her breath caught as she watched him tag along after some older boys. She bit her lip, hoping he wouldn't get hurt. Would he fit in? He wasn't accustomed to being around other boys. But it would be so nice for him to have some companions.

"Mrs. Keller! You came!"

With a smile Mara turned to the excited girl skipping toward her from the house. "You look pretty this evening."

Lizzie's two red braids were tied with dark blue ribbons. Her flowered dress was a becoming shade of navy blue against her pale skin.

"Aw, you don't have to say that."

"Of course I don't, except that it's true."

The girl twisted her hands in her skirt and Mara said no more, realizing the gawky girl was truly embarrassed. "Would you like to show me where I ought to go, since it seems your father is not allowing me to carry any of the baskets?"

Lizzie gave a careless wave. "Oh, he's used to heavy work. Come on, I'll show you the cider press and then we can go indoors where the ladies are. They're setting out the food."

"Oh, that reminds me. I brought a cake. I hope it's all right." Suddenly, she felt unsure of herself. Would they like a *Sacher torte?*

Lizzie's eyes lit up. "Oh, I'm sure everyone will like it. May I see?"

Mara led her to the wagon seat and retrieved the cake basket she'd stowed underneath.

"It looks delicious. Such dark chocolate. Let's set it in the kitchen first and then I'll show you around."

With a deep breath, Mara followed the girl who seemed so at home. This would be her first social foray into the world of Eagle's Bay, a small community her father had chosen to get away from city life and paint its physical wonders of rocky coast and turbulent sea.

Would they receive a woman who knew little of country life and felt bruised and battered by life's circumstances?

Gideon chewed on a piece of hay as he stood in a semi-circle in the roomy barn. The apples had been pressed and the men had loaded the various barrels and jugs into the appropriate wagons.

As more of the guests moved toward the house, he heard laughter and music spill out from the doorway. When he entered the warm parlor, he glanced around, looking for Lizzie but didn't see her anywhere. With a shrug, he headed toward the heavily laden tables set against one wall.

"Hello there, Gideon. Come, let me fix you a plate." Sarah, the hostess and his first cousin, beamed at him. She took an edge of her ruffled apron and wiped her perspiring forehead.

"Thank you, don't mind if you do. Everything sure looks good."

"Everyone's brought her best dish, I'm sure." She took a plate and began heaping up food for him.

He thanked her again and took the plate to a corner of the room where he stood alongside a fellow farmer from the neighborhood. Soon he saw Lizzie entering from the kitchen area with a large tray of cookies. Behind her followed Mrs. Keller, carrying a cake.

The two smiled and spoke to one another as they set down their platters. Lizzie, instead of coming over to him, hurried after the widow when she returned to the kitchen.

Another man nodded to him. "Evenin', Gideon."

"Evenin', Mike." The men continued eating, standing and watching the crowd in the room.

He spied Mrs. Keller's young son darting in and among the adults with some other boys.

"Here, take a mug of this fresh cider." One woman handed each of the men a cup of the frothy amber drink. "Let me take that empty plate from you," she told one of them, "unless you'd like to fill it up again?"

The other man patted his belly. "I couldn't fit another swallow. Delicious, though."

Gideon handed the woman his plate with a smile and took a sip of the tangy, sweet cider. Though some would prefer it a few weeks from now when it had a chance to ferment, for him there was nothing like fresh-pressed cider.

Soon, a group of men took out their fiddles and headed for a corner of the room. "Come on, Gid, did you bring your fiddle?"

"Yep. It's in the wagon. I'll fetch it in a bit."

Young people formed lines down the middle of the room. Tapping his foot to the lively beat of "Turkey in the Straw," he glanced around once again, expecting to see Lizzie reappear at last. She always liked to listen to the music.

Sure enough, she soon emerged from down the kitchen way. She turned her head, laughing at what someone had said to her. Mrs. Keller appeared behind her again, this time with her son at her side.

When she smiled, she looked so appealingly lovely. He shook his head as if to clear it of such a notion. He hadn't looked at a woman in that way since Elsie had died. To have such a thought about a lady like Mrs. Keller was unseemly.

The room with its press of people and woodstove going in one corner felt too warm.

Lizzie came over with a small plate. "Pa, have you tried some of Mrs. Keller's cake?"

He shook his head.

"Good. I brought you some. It's delicious. I asked her for the recipe."

He took the plate and fork offered to him. The cake was a rich dark chocolate with a dollop of whipped cream on top. A burst of sweet jam surprised him as he chewed the bittersweet chocolate. "It's good," he said slowly, savoring the intense flavors. His glance drifted across the room until he spotted the widow.

Lee Sanderson, the handsome, dark-haired blacksmith, approached her. Lee had been widowed only a year. A wisp of distaste curled in Gideon's belly at the thought that the widower was already looking for a replacement. He chided himself immediately. He of all men knew how lonely that first year was.

Although she seemed friendly enough, Mrs. Keller gave a small shake of her head and what appeared a regretful smile, and the man wandered off.

Had she turned down an offer to dance? Of course, she was still in mourning. Gideon continued looking at the widow, his taste buds once again assaulted by the sweet mix of apricot and chocolate.

He felt a surge of compassion for the still-young lady. Despite her severe black gown and kindly air, she shone like a queen in the crowded parlor. What could she possibly find in common with the plain folk of Eagle's Bay?

He remembered her father, an artist of some renown who had settled in this area from Boston. He had kept pretty much to himself. Everyone had been surprised when in a short time, Mrs. Blackstone—Mrs. Flynn then, who'd only been widowed a short time—had married the famous painter.

Funny how Gideon didn't recall Mrs. Keller then. Well, he'd been in his early twenties, married and busy starting out, so he hadn't paid much attention to his neighbor "from away."

How long would such a sophisticated lady like Mrs. Keller stay this time, if she had hardly made her presence known the last time?

Mara stifled a yawn as she watched the dancers. Her feet were tired from standing against the wall, her muscles ached from carrying the bushels earlier. She'd been up since dawn, baking the cake and picking apples.

For a while she amused herself listening to the fiddle players. As his daughter had said, Mr. Jakeman did indeed play. Even though they were simple tunes, she admired the way he gave his heart and soul to the music as his bow skipped along the strings.

Lizzie gave her father a smile and quick wave and moved to stand beside her again. "He liked your cake. What did you call it again?"

"Sacher torte," she said with an effort to appear light-hearted. But the truth was she felt more alone in the crowded room than she did at home with one of the books off her father's shelf. For a while she'd made friendly conversation with the ladies as they set out the dishes on the table, each woman commenting on each other's specialties.

Dietrich tugged at her hand. "Mama, may I go outside?"

"I think it's too cold and dark." She motioned to some children across the room. "Why don't you go and play with those children?"

He looked to where she pointed then bent his head, shaking it.

"I sure love to watch people dancing."

Mara looked at Lizzie in surprise. "Why don't you dance?"

The girl's cheeks reddened. "I couldn't dance."

"Why ever not? How old are you now?"

"Fifteen in a few months."

Mara said nothing but continued watching the girl.

"Excuse me, ma'am, would you like to have this dance?"

She turned to a gentleman addressing her. "Oh, thank you, but I'm not dancing this evening. Thank you just the same." She'd never expected to have anyone ask her to dance tonight. It had been years since she'd danced. So far, three gentlemen had approached.

The dancers finished the set and started forming another.

As Mara divided her time watching the dancers and talking with Lizzie, she noticed the longing in the girl's eyes. "Would you like to learn how to dance?" she asked on an impulse.

Lizzie turned her head slowly and stared wide-eyed at her. "Me?"

"Yes. Everyone has to learn sometime. I was about your age when I had my first dancing lesson. Our instructor was an old lady, who scared me half to death she was so strict." She smiled in recollection. "But she taught me to waltz. Wouldn't you rather I taught you than someone like that?"

Lizzie laughed. "Well, I guess so. Could you really teach me?" Her voice sounded wistful. "I'm real clumsy."

"I'm sure that's nonsense." She considered the crowded dance floor. "I have an idea. Why don't we go outside? I wouldn't mind a breath of fresh air. It's grown quite stuffy in here."

She looked around for Dietrich but he was no longer at her side. He must have gone off with the children.

Gideon pulled at his collar, feeling the perspiration begin to roll down his neck. He'd lost interest in the company since Lizzie and Mrs. Keller had disappeared. He set his fiddle down on a nearby chair and spoke to one of the other players. "I'm going to take a short break, if you don't mind."

Grabbing his jacket from a peg, Gideon made his way to the front door. The clear sharp night was a welcome relief. He glanced up at the sky, pitch-black with a multitude of shining stars. The vastness above him always made him sensitive to the presence of the Almighty.

With the sounds of laughter and fiddle music ebbing behind him, he strode toward the woodshed.

He could have walked through the kitchen to reach it, but he preferred the coolness of the night air.

A number of the older men, whose dancing days were over, congregated in the woodshed with their pipes. The smell of tobacco mingled with the spicy smell of seasoned firewood which lined half the shed from floor to ceiling.

"You sell your corn yet, Gideon?"

He nodded, leaning against the chopped, stacked firewood and folding his arms across his chest.

"What kind of price did'ya fetch at Wilson's?"

He told them and a number of the men commented on the fluctuating price over the preceding months.

"I'm taking the boat out tomorrow with the tide. Need to put down a few more herring and cod 'fore the winter sets in."

They discussed the arrival of a schooner in town the day before.

Feeling a bit restless, and wondering whether Lizzie was

ready to leave yet, Gideon finally straightened. "Well, I expect I'll be going on home soon."

"Good to see you, Gid."

With a few more farewells, he wandered back outside. Instead of returning to the house, he stood a moment. The October night hit him like a bracing swallow of cold, filling his lungs and invigorating him. There'd be frost again tonight. He said a silent prayer of thanksgiving, feeling at peace.

He crossed the dirt drive and looked in the barn, checking on Bessie. "We'll get you home soon," he whispered, giving the mare an apple.

Exiting the barn, he slowed his steps, enjoying the stillness and feeling in no particular hurry to reenter the parlor. As he approached an ell of the house, he heard some scuffling and a giggle. He frowned, thinking it sounded like Lizzie.

His steps slowed, and he leaned forward to peer around the corner.

Light from the parlor only half illuminated the yard. A couple of the parlor windows had been opened a crack to let in fresh air. The sounds of a waltz floated out into the night air.

Lizzie stood in front of Mrs. Keller with her arms held out from her sides.

"All right, now you need to let yourself move in time to the music and follow my lead. If you look at me, I'll let you know which way I'm going to turn next. Let's begin again."

"I feel so clumsy."

"Nonsense." Mrs. Keller took one of Lizzie's hands and bowed over it slightly. "May I have this dance, Miss Jakeman?"

"Yes, sir, I'd be honored." She ruined the effect by breaking out in giggles once again.

Gideon folded his arms and stayed put where he was, his

body half-hidden by the corner of the house. Well, if that didn't beat all. His Lizzie having a dance lesson. They had dancing schools in town, groups of young people who got together regularly with a dancing master, but she'd never wanted to go, always disdaining any suggestion of such accomplishments.

"Now, none of that silliness, Miss Jakeman," Mrs. Keller chided in a schoolteacher's tone. "The waltz is a serious dance." She took one of Lizzie's hands and held her lightly at the waist, and the two began to move in time to the music.

"That's right. Very good," she said softly from time to time. Lizzie stumbled a few times but Mrs. Keller didn't allow her to stop and quickly led her into the next step.

Suddenly Lizzie's gaze looked directly across at her father. Before he had a chance to step back into the shadows, his daughter's face broke into a smile. "Look, Papa, I'm dancing." The next second she stumbled over Mrs. Keller's feet.

Mrs. Keller quickly let go of Lizzie and whirled around to face him. Gideon had no choice but to emerge from his hiding place, embarrassed at being seen.

Chapter Four

"Mr. Jakeman, I— We didn't see you there." Mrs. Keller stepped back a pace, her hands clasped in front of her.

"I beg your pardon. I didn't mean to startle the two of you."

"Did you see me waltzing?" Lizzie stuck her hands out and began to imitate the steps by herself. "One, two, three... one, two, three. Just like Mrs. Keller taught me. It's not so hard once you know how."

"Yes, you did nicely," he said softly, still amazed at how ladylike his daughter had appeared and how formal the words *Miss Jakeman* sounded. One of these days that's what she'd begin to be called. He cleared his throat and scuffed the toe of his boot in the dirt. "I didn't know Lizzie was interested in dancing."

"I think every young woman wants to be ready when a young man asks her to dance."

He stared at Mrs. Keller's soft tone. "Yes, I reckon so." He shoved his hands in his pockets, wondering if he should leave. Had he spoiled it for them? Before he could decide what to do, his daughter touched him on the arm. "Papa, why don't you dance with Mrs. Keller so I can see how it's really supposed to look? I've never seen you dance, Papa, not since I was a little girl. You haven't forgotten how, have you?"

He swallowed, feeling caught like a rabbit in a snare. His daughter's face shone in anticipation and he didn't have the heart to deny her wish. His glance strayed to Mrs. Keller. She was looking at him but he didn't have a clue how to read her thoughts. Was she disgusted by the idea of dancing with a lumbering farmer? She'd turned down everyone else who'd asked her to dance. Would it be disrespectful, seeing she was still in mourning?

"It's all right, Lizzie. Let your father be," Mrs. Keller said quietly.

"But Pa is a good dancer. Don't you want to dance, Mrs. Keller?"

"My dancing days are over," she said with a smile which seemed sad to Gideon.

"But you don't look old, Mrs. Keller."

She chuckled. "Thank you, Lizzie. Perhaps I feel old inside."

Gideon knew exactly what she meant. The deepest sadness that a person carried was the one least visible to the world. Perhaps she mourned her late husband the way he mourned Elsie.

As the strains of a new waltz drifted out the window, he took a step toward her, holding out his hand. "If you'd do me the honor of this dance, Mrs. Keller?" he said with a bow.

Mara couldn't tear her gaze from Mr. Jakeman's. He looked at her so straightforwardly and so…kindly. But no! She couldn't trust how a man looked at a woman. Her husband, Klaus, had looked at her so charmingly when he'd courted her.

"I—"

Before Mara could refuse the honor, Lizzie spoke up. "Aw,

come on, Mrs. Keller, I bet you're the best dancer. Please let me see you dance."

"I— Very well," she finished instead and with a trembling hand, reached out to the farmer.

He was a tall, large man, and she felt like a piece of fragile porcelain being embraced by a clumsy giant. But as they began moving to the music, she was surprised at how deftly he led her. She thought of his fiddle playing. The man certainly was musical.

Now his hands held her surely by the waist and hand. Her other hand rested lightly on his broad shoulder, her fingertips feeling the slight roughness of his wool coat. Her other hand was ensconced in his, her palm against the smooth calluses of his, her fingers brushing against the sparse, springy hairs on the back of his hand.

Klaus had been a much smaller man. Around him, she had felt like the stronger one. But now she felt protected, as she hadn't been since her father was alive.

The thought brought her up short and she almost stumbled. She gripped his shoulder. He must have felt it because when she looked his way, he inclined his head toward her. She quickly looked away. She couldn't quite see over his shoulder so she fixed her gaze on the dark weave of his suit. Everything was a blurry darkness anyway.

The fiddles played a Viennese waltz.

Little by little, she began to relax as she allowed the music to fill her. All the cares of her present life faded and only the music existed. It brought back happier times, when life was joyous and...fun.

Her partner led her so surely, she hardly felt the uneven ground beneath her feet. His hand on the small of her back was like a steady support.

Suddenly, a boy's cry rent the night air. She stopped in midstep. "That sounded like Dietrich!"

Mr. Jakeman didn't let her go immediately. Instead, gripping her lightly, he looked beyond her to where the cry had come. Then loosening his hold, he took her by the elbow, guiding her in that direction. As they approached the area, a boy's angry cries rose amidst the sound of laughter and jeers.

They rounded the house and in the darkness made out a ring of boys circling a smaller boy.

As soon as she saw it was indeed Dietrich, she broke away from Mr. Jakeman's hold and rushed forward.

"What is going on here?"

They all stopped at the sight of her.

Dietrich ran up to her. "Mama, they're making fun of my na-name!"

She put her arm around him and surveyed the boys, who stood silent. Before she could decide what to do, Mr. Jakeman approached, looming over the semicircle.

"Hey, Tom, is that you?"

The biggest boy replied, "Yes, sir."

"Evening, Willie," he said to another.

The boy tugged at his hair. "Evenin', Mr. Jakeman."

"Hello, Edgar."

He went around the circle until each boy was forced to greet him. Then he said, "Have you been making Dietrich here feel welcome to our community the way Reverend Grayson asked us to?"

No one answered.

"He's come from far away and has never been to a Maine village. I hope you're making us proud by showing him the fun he can have with Down East boys."

"Yes, sir," a few of them mumbled, shifting their feet.

"His name is a little different from any you've heard, since he was born in—uh—Germany." He turned to Dietrich for corroboration. "Isn't that right, Dietrich?"

"In Austria," he answered, squaring his shoulders.

Mr. Jakeman gave a soft laugh. "See, boys, you all are

probably better'n I at geography. Have you studied about Austria in school?"

"A little," one of the boys answered.

"You know, they speak a different language in Austria." He paused. "Do any of you speak any language except for English?" He waited until they'd shaken their heads or mumbled, "No, sir." Then he turned to Dietrich. "Why don't you tell us something in one of the languages you speak?"

Mara squeezed him by his thin shoulders. "Say good evening in German, dear."

"Guten Abend."

"See there, can any of you understand that?"

Another round of denials. "Can you say that in any other language, son?"

Dietrich nodded.

"Say it in French," Mara suggested.

"Bonsoir."

"That's pretty good, don't you think, boys?" Mr. Jakeman asked, again waiting until the boys were forced to admit it. "Just think if you could say something no one around you understood. It would be sort of a code only you and another person knew. I bet Dietrich and his mother can talk about things no one else can catch."

"It's like a secret," Tommy suggested, a smile breaking out on his face as he eyed Dietrich, impressed.

"Maybe he can teach you a few of the code words, eh, Dietrich?" Mr. Jakeman smiled and winked at her son.

Dietrich looked at all the boys and then began to nod.

"Maybe you can all get together sometime. But first you have to learn to respect Dietrich's name. All right? It might be a little different than any you've heard, but if you went to some of the places he's lived in, your names would sound unusual. Would that be a reason for someone to laugh at them?"

Again there came a chorus of "No, sirs."

"Well, good then." Mr. Jakeman turned to Mara and her son. Before he could speak, she said, "I think it's time we got going home. Let me see if Mrs. Blackstone is ready to leave."

He nodded. "Very well. Come along, Lizzie, I think we'll take our leave as well."

They left the boys and trooped silently back to the house. With a quick "Excuse me" and a smile she hoped conveyed the gratitude she felt, Mara hurried off to locate Carina. Too many thoughts whirled through her head, from the memory of Mr. Jakeman's arms around her to his deft defense of her son.

"Well, it's about time! Where on earth did you go off to? I've been waiting an age to tell you it's high time to leave. I am really not feeling at all myself. I don't think Mrs. Matthews's baked beans agreed with me. She always puts too much salt pork in them."

Mara said nothing as she followed her stepmother to the hallway to retrieve their wraps, longing for the moment when she'd be alone in her room to reflect on all that had happened this evening.

When she emerged outside once more, she found their wagon waiting at the door. Mr. Jakeman held the reins.

She stopped short at the sight of him. "Oh, thank you. How thoughtful of you to bring it around."

"Good evening, Gideon." Mrs. Blackstone considered him through narrowed eyes. "Fancy seeing you here with the wagon. Are you leaving, too?"

"Yep. Got an early day ahead of me."

Lizzie stepped forward with a shy smile. "Thank you, Mrs. Keller, for teaching me to waltz."

On an impulse, Mara leaned over and gave the girl a quick embrace. "You're most welcome. Perhaps we can have another lesson soon."

"Oh!" The girl looked more pleased than ever, her cheeks turning bright pink in the lamplight.

Mara allowed Mr. Jakeman to help her into the wagon and took the reins he handed her. Before he went to the other side to assist Carina, she held out her hand. "Thank you, sir, for all you did for Dietrich."

He gave a shrug and didn't quite meet her eyes. "It was nothing. Boys'll be boys, I guess."

"Yes, but you certainly knew how to handle them."

With a quick nod, he backed away from her and went to her stepmother.

They exchanged good-evenings and then he waved to Dietrich. "Come to me if those boys bother you again, you hear, son?"

"Yes, sir."

With a wave and some final good-nights, Mara started the wagon. She gave one look back, watching father and daughter standing there.

Her heart felt warmed by the kind act of the large, silent man, so different from her temperamental, high-strung husband, who cared more about himself than he did about his son.

What kind of childhood would Dietrich have had if he'd had a father like Mr. Jakeman?

Mara sat at her old piano, the one her father had bought for her twelfth birthday. She touched the elaborate carvings on the music stand of the Brazilian rosewood cabinet before setting some sheet music upon it.

At the time, it had been a great extravagance on her father's part to buy her such an instrument. The Civil War had recently ended and the country was still in an economic decline. She doubted her father had sold many of his paintings.

But her mother passed away that year, and by the time Mara's birthday arrived, her father insisted her mother would have wanted to celebrate it in this way. In her childish inno-cence, Mara didn't think then about the economic hardships her father had doubtless undergone to provide her with the piano. He had smiled at her and said her only repayment was to learn to play pretty pieces to soothe away his sadness—a promise she gladly made.

From a heretofore enjoyable activity, music had become a consolation and gradually developed into a passion in the ensuing years until she turned eighteen. By then, her fa-ther's artistic abilities had begun being recognized and they became comfortably well-off. Her father had purchased this farmhouse on the Maine coast, wanting a place to retreat from the hustle and bustle of Boston and pursue an interest in painting the wild coastline.

She had never expected that it would be in this small vil-lage that her father would remarry. She found her new step-mother a cold and exacting woman. A few years older than her father, Carina was nothing like Mara's warm, joyful mother. But her father seemed comforted by his new com-panion, so Mara had gracefully retreated to a new life at the Boston conservatory rather than cause her father any grief.

Mara ran her fingers lightly over the ivory keys now, not pressing on them yet. She had not played her old piano since her return home. Since Carina did not encourage it in the house, Mara had felt easier in letting it go.

Thinking of the few short visits she had made to her fa-ther's home after his marriage, she wondered if perhaps the lack of welcome she had felt on her stepmother's part had been a reason Mara had decided to pursue her music studies in Vienna. She'd been barely twenty when she'd met Klaus there. Perhaps if she'd had a home and family to return to, she would not have been so quick to marry the first young man who had evinced an interest in her.

What an innocent, naive young woman she had been—

hoping for a marriage as happy as her mother and father's had been.

Mara pressed her forefinger down on middle C and the subsequent three keys with her other fingers and listened to the tones echo in the silent parlor.

Thankfully, her stepmother had taken the buggy into town today to visit some lady friends, so Mara felt safe in playing, for a few hours at any rate. She'd finished the morning's chores. Time enough in the afternoon to begin the preparations for winter. Dried beans to be shucked, the flower heads and herbs to be gathered for drying, more windfall apples to be picked up, leaves to be raked for banking the sides of the house.

But after her foray into town a few days ago, in a vain attempt to find work at the various stores and hostelries, a woman at the local dry goods store had suggested she offer music lessons. She'd been present in church, Mara had found out, so she knew of Mara's musical abilities.

When Mara had mentioned deportment lessons, she'd given Mara a good up-and-down, nodding. "Plenty of mamas would pay to have their daughters acquire a bit o' that refinement you have along with music lessons. Make'm more marriageable when they get that age."

Mara had wondered aloud if there would really be such a demand in this remote, rural area of the country.

"Oh, you'd be surprised," the woman had added, "since the railroad come to town, we've been getting more and more visitors. Rusticators in the summer months—some from as far as New York, imagine that. And, o' course, we got plenty of well-off folk of our own, the mill owners, the bankers and shopkeepers, some lawyers and doctors. Oh, I think there'd be plenty of work for you, if you're of a mind. You can put up a few advertisements around town."

She indicated a board near the counter. "Right there for starters. And I'll tell those I know with daughters o' the right age about you and your abilities. I could tell right off when I saw you in church that you had some real ladylike qualities."

So, after returning home, Mara had thought over her words and decided she had little choice. If she wanted to begin to earn her keep—and a way to leave her stepmother's residence—she had better exert herself to let people know she was available to teach music and deportment. She couldn't help a smile at that last, grandiose term.

She certainly didn't consider herself any more ladylike or refined than any other woman. When she'd first arrived in Europe she'd been intimidated by the fine ladies and gentlemen she'd met as Klaus's star had risen.

But in the latter years, as he'd squandered his money, and their lodging houses had grown meaner and meaner until the final one where he'd lived his last days, she'd seen how little all the fine manners meant. He'd received no help from the important people who'd flocked to him in years past and who'd been so eager to lead him astray to the gaming houses and other, worse places.

She shook her head. No use revisiting those memories. They were over and she had more pressing needs now— Dietrich's future. Taking a deep breath, she began to go through some scales to warm up her fingers before turning to the music on her stand.

Gideon set down the bushel basket of cranberries in front of Mrs. Blackstone's woodshed and opened the door. Paul, his cousin's oldest son, who worked as a handyman here, wasn't around, so Gideon hefted the basket up again and walked through the shed to the kitchen door. If no one was home, he'd leave the basket and go.

He knocked on the door. Hearing the muffled sound of piano music through the panels, he knocked louder. After waiting a few minutes and knocking a few more times, he hesitated then opened the door to the kitchen.

It was empty. He left the basket in the woodshed, where it would stay cool, and entered the kitchen, drawn by the music coming to him more clearly now. It was beautiful and sounded much more complicated than anything he'd ever heard since a long-ago chamber concert in town.

His thoughts going at once to Mrs. Keller, he was hardly aware of his boots on the floor as he made his way across the kitchen and into the hallway and finally to the threshold of the front parlor.

The room was dim, its windows shaded by a roofed verandah that wrapped around the house. Gideon's gaze went immediately to the piano at the end of the room.

Mrs. Keller sat straight on the wide bench, her fingers moving over the keys, her head bent slightly down and to the side as if she could hear which key was to be played next. Her fingers seemed to fly across the keyboard at times and at others linger as if caressing the keys.

She had not heard him and he dared not move, too captivated by the music created by her mere fingertips.

Then the music slowed and her fingers came to rest on the last keys. As the final notes reverberated in the room, she slowly lifted her fingertips.

Gideon made a slight sound—hardly aware that he did so and she whirled around on the piano bench, bumping her knees against the piano. She winced but recovered immediately.

He moved into the room, an apology already on his lips.

Her hand on her chest, she said, "I didn't know anyone was there."

He cleared his throat, his hat in his hands. "I'm sorry. I didn't mean to startle you. I knocked on the kitchen door but no one answered. Y-you probably didn't hear me over the sound of the piano. Mrs. Blackstone's not in?" He finally stopped to draw breath.

Mrs. Keller stood, smoothing down her skirt as she did so. "No, she's not. She drove into town this morning." She advanced toward him, her calm, dignified manner clearly restored, but a smile dissipating any notion that she might be standoffish. "I took advantage of her absence to practice a little. I'm quite rusty as you probably noticed."

"Rusty? I'd hardly say so. You play…beautifully," he said for lack of a better word to describe the sublime sounds coming from the piano.

A pretty color suffused her cheeks. "It's kind of you to say so, but I—I haven't played in some months, so my fingers needed some limbering up."

He nodded. "Yes, I know how that is." He could have bitten his tongue, at the audacity of comparing his fiddling with her virtuosity.

"Of course. The violin is even more tricky."

"Oh, no, I just fiddle a few old tunes."

Her smile deepened. "I admire anyone who can entertain people with music."

A silence fell between them. To fill it, he asked, "Reverend Grayson said your husband was a piano player?"

"Yes." She touched a wisp of hair at her nape, and he couldn't help notice its graceful curve. "We both played until, that is, until Dietrich was born, and…and then I gave it up, except for giving lessons when I was able."

"That's a shame."

She stared at him as if not understanding his simple statement.

"I mean," he hastened, "seeing as you play so well."

"Oh, I don't think anyone missed my playing." She gave a short laugh. "I made enough mistakes this morning."

"Well, I couldn't hear any. I just watched your fingers go across those keys as if the very hounds were after you."

She laughed as if she genuinely enjoyed his clumsy compliment. "Thank you. I shall remember that image the next time my fingers do not want to obey what my brain is commanding them."

Another awkward pause fell between them, and he wished he was easy at making small talk. For some reason he wanted to prolong these moments with this woman, whom he'd normally never think to approach.

She drew herself up a fraction and began to speak just as he did. "Would you care—"

"I just stopped—"

They both fell silent just as quickly, each smiling slightly. He remained silent, determined to allow her to speak first.

"I was just going to ask you if you cared for a cup of tea or some refreshment."

He could feel his color deepen. He hoped she didn't think he'd been expecting her to offer him something. "Oh, no. I—uh—just stopped by with a bushel of cranberries Lizzie and I picked."

"How lovely."

"I left them in the shed. I don't know if that's where you want them." He began backing out of the parlor.

"Oh, that's fine, I'm sure. Let me have a look." She preceded him and led him back to the kitchen. He hastened to open the kitchen door for her and she stepped into the woodshed. The morning sun streamed into the rough-hewn wood interior through the two windows facing east.

She bent over the basket which was full to the brim with the bright crimson berries. "Oh, my, I haven't enjoyed some good cranberry sauce since I left New England." She put her hand into the berries and let them fall through her fingers, smiling up at him.

He swallowed, mesmerized by her grace. There was an air of sadness about her until she smiled and then she looked so young and carefree.

Before he could think what to say, he heard running footsteps and the next second her son pulled open the door and rushed into the shed. He stopped short at the sight of Gideon. "Oh—you're here. Hello."

Mrs. Keller straightened. "Dietrich, where are your manners? Say a proper hello to Mr. Jakeman."

The boy bobbed his head. "Hello, sir."

He smiled in encouragement. "Hello, Dietrich. How are you today?"

"Fine." His gaze landed on the bushel basket. "What are those?"

"Cranberries. Haven't you ever seen cranberries?"

He shook his head then approached the basket and took one between his fingers.

"They're too sour to eat raw," Gideon warned before the boy could put it in his mouth, "but your mother can cook them up into a nice, sweet sauce. You'll probably have some with your turkey for Thanksgiving."

"Thanksgiving?" Dietrich looked from Gideon to his mother.

Gideon blinked at the boy's question. Didn't the boy have a notion about Thanksgiving?

His mother smoothed back his hair from his forehead. "Yes, dear. It's an important holiday here in America. We shall celebrate it in a few weeks. Now, where have you been? You've been gone all morning."

Dietrich tossed the berry back into the basket and scuffed his toe against the rough floor. "Oh, just around. I went to the pond and climbed one of the apple trees."

"Well, be careful climbing trees."

Gideon cleared his throat. "Have you seen any of the boys from the cider pressing?"

"Only at school."

Mrs. Keller added, "We don't know where they live. I'm

sure most live down at the harbor or on the other side of the hamlet."

There were only a few farms down on their peninsula so Gideon sympathized with the boy and found himself offering, "Would you like to help Lizzie and me pick some more berries next time we go?" He turned to his mother. "They're in a bog about a mile down the road."

"May I, Mama?"

Gideon marveled at how foreign the boy sounded to him. Even the way he said "mama" was different, with the stress on the second syllable. He pictured the lad dressed in velvet in a fancy drawing room in England like a story out of *St. Nicholas Magazine.*

"Well, I don't know..." Clearly, she was at a loss. "We don't want to impose on Mr. Jakeman's time."

"No imposition at all, ma'am. I can take him along with me now, if you'd like. We have a new litter of kittens you can see," he told Dietrich.

The boy tugged on his mother's sleeve, jumping up and down. "May I see the kittens? Please, Mama!"

She put a hand on his shoulders. "If you settle down and let me think." She turned her attention to Gideon. "Are you sure you don't mind? We can plan it for another day—"

"Not at all, ma'am." Before she could change her mind, he lifted his chin at Dietrich. "Why don't you hop into the wagon and we'll be off." As the boy ran back outside, Gideon turned to Mrs. Keller. "Don't worry about him. He'll be all right. There are plenty of things to keep him busy on the farm."

"I don't know... He can be very active, and I know you're a busy man. I don't want him to get into any mischief."

He chuckled, glad he could do something for her. "Set your mind at rest. I was his age once and know all about mischief."

She smiled back but he could tell it was with an effort.

Suddenly, his throat constricted, sensing how difficult it must be for her to be facing life alone with a boy to raise. He had faced the same situation in reverse—the prospect of raising a daughter to a fine young woman had filled him with fear and worry. And he hadn't finished the job yet, not by a long shot.

He placed his hat back on his head. "Well, I'll be off then. You can tell Mrs. Blackstone I'll bring her more berries if she needs. Just let me know."

Mrs. Keller followed him outside. The day was chilly although the morning sun against the house made it seem warmer than it was. "You'd best get indoors," he said gently before turning to his horse and buckboard.

She wrapped her arms around herself and walked instead to where her son had climbed up on the seat. "Be good now, do you hear me, Dietrich?"

"Yes, Mama, I promise."

She nodded, giving his arm a quick pat before stepping back from the wagon. "Very well, I'll see you later. I can come for him, Mr. Jakeman. You needn't make another special trip here to bring him back."

"It's no problem. We're only half a mile down the road. Lizzie would like to see you." Then he turned to the reins, thinking what a stupid thing he'd said. "I mean, if you're here, just to say hello."

"That would be lovely. I look forward to seeing your daughter again."

The words sounded so sincere and friendly that Gideon couldn't help but take another look at Mrs. Keller. He nodded his head once before releasing the brake and giving the reins a slap.

His spirit felt lighter, like the puffy white clouds floating high above him on the deep blue sky.

Chapter Five

Mara kept finding excuses to step outside and look up and down the road. It was half past five and Dietrich had not yet returned. Had Mr. Jakeman meant to bring him home himself or would he send Dietrich home by foot alone?

The sun was setting and the sea across the road in the bay was already taking a gray cast. The breeze caused Mara to shiver and wrap her wool shawl more tightly around herself. She stood a while longer at the end of their drive, looking down the road. She couldn't see the Jakeman farm from here as the dirt road dipped and climbed in a few shallow risings between the two properties.

She bit her lip, wondering what was keeping Dietrich so long. Soon, she'd have to have supper on the table. Another meal to be endured sitting across from Carina.

Mara sighed. She had half a mind to walk the distance to the Jakeman farm. She'd have to let Carina know.

Just as she was turning to go in, not yet sure if she wanted to face her stepmother's sharp questions, she thought she heard the sound of wheels against the dirt. She held her breath, praying it was Dietrich, and stood, waiting, her fingers gripping her shawl.

She let out a breath of relief at the sight of the buckboard cresting the slope and the young boy on one side of the seat. The driver wasn't Mr. Jakeman but his daughter.

As soon as Dietrich saw her, he began waving and bouncing on his seat. "Mama, Mama!"

Mara couldn't help a smile. "Sit still or you'll fall off," she said as soon as he was close enough to hear her without shouting.

She smiled at Lizzie who returned it with a wide smile of her own. "Good evening, Lizzie. Thank you for bringing home my son. I didn't want to trouble you."

Lizzie guided the wagon into the drive. "No trouble at all, ma'am."

"May I have a kitten, please? I was going to bring one back today, but Mr. Jakeman said to wait and ask you. May I, please, Mama? They're so tiny, all gray and black and fuzzy. I could put my finger up to their mouths and they'd start sucking." He laughed at the idea and Mara could only smile back, feeling a sudden surge of love for her dark-haired boy.

Lizzie drew up the wagon. Before Mara could help Dietrich down, he had jumped to the ground and went off toward the barn.

"Don't go too far. We'll be eating supper soon. You need to wash up."

"I won't," he shouted back. "I just want to find Paul and tell him about the kittens."

"Very well."

Mara made her way to Lizzie's side of the wagon. "Thank you so much."

"Don't mention it, Mrs. Keller." The young girl's cheeks turned rosy. "Truth was I wanted an excuse to come by."

"You don't need an excuse. You're welcome anytime."

The girl bobbed her head shyly. "That's nice of you, ma'am."

"Would you like to come in now?"

"Thank you, but I have to get back to Papa." There was a wistful look in her pale green eyes. "Maybe next time."

"Yes." She wished she could say or do something for the girl, but she didn't feel at liberty to offer much, since she felt as if she were a guest in her own house. "Wait a moment. I'd like to send something along home with you."

"You don't have to do that—"

"But I'd like to." Mara hurried into the house. Quickly, she took the lid off the cake pan and cut a generous portion of a coffee cake she had baked that morning and set it on a piece of parchment paper.

At that moment, Carina entered the kitchen. Mara tensed but continued what she was doing.

"I thought I heard someone—oh, it's just you."

"Yes."

Carina strode to the window, the heels of her boots clicking against the floor. Mara looked over her shoulder, following her stepmother's movements. Carina flicked back the lace curtain and peered through. "What's she doing here?"

Mara reined in her impatience. "She brought Dietrich back."

"Back? Where was he?"

"He went to visit the Jakemans."

"He did, did he? Hope he didn't make a nuisance of himself."

Mara ground her teeth to keep from saying anything and concentrated on continuing to wrap the piece of cake. She cut a length of string and tied it around the square. "Let me take this to her so she can be on her way."

She didn't breathe easier until she was back outside. "Here you go, a piece of cake for you and your father with your coffee tomorrow."

Lizzie took it from her, her face showing her gratitude. "Oh, Mrs. Keller, you shouldn't have, but if it's anything like that last one you made, I know Papa and I'll enjoy it."

"Well, it's not nearly as fancy, just coffee cake, but I hope you two like it. Please tell your father I'm more grateful than I can say for his patience with Dietrich. I know Dietrich can be quite restless at his age, but he doesn't mean any harm."

Lizzie set the wrapped cake on the seat beside her as if it was a fragile piece of glass. "Goodness, Dietrich wasn't any more restless than any boy I know."

"He didn't break anything, did he?"

Lizzie laughed. "'Course he didn't. Wherever did you get that idea?"

Mara thought of the bowl that had slipped through his fingers while helping clear the table the other night and Carina's sharp words. "Oh, I just know boys can be careless."

"You set your mind at rest. He did fine. Oh, ma'am—" the girl's light-colored eyebrows scrunched together "—would you like one of them kitties? I promised Dietrich I'd ask you."

"If it were up to me, I'd say yes." She glanced behind her toward the house and discerned Carina's shadow behind the curtain. "But let me ask my— Mrs. Blackstone first."

Lizzie only nodded. "Sure. Just let us know. In the meantime, the kitties'll be waiting."

Mara smiled. "Thank you."

"Well, I'd best be going."

After a final exchange of thanks and well-wishes, Mara stepped back and watched as the girl maneuvered the buckboard down the drive. With a wave, she headed up the road.

Mara wondered fleetingly what her reception would be. Her father would be relieved to see her home. They'd probably sit down to supper together. She envisioned a cozy tableau. Would he take a bit of her cake tonight? Or wait till tomorrow?

What was she thinking? Why did she care? With a shake of her head, she spun around. "Dietrich!" she called as she entered through the woodshed. "Dietrich!"

"Just a moment, Mama," he called back, his voice coming from the barn.

"Come in to supper."

As Mara reentered the kitchen, Dietrich's footsteps pounded on the wooden floorboards of the woodshed. A few moments later, he burst into the kitchen, stopping short at the sight of Carina.

"Mercy, child, that's no way to enter a house."

"Come and wash up," Mara told him, cutting off anything more Carina would say.

Mara hurried about, placing the food on the table. "Dietrich, don't take too long at the sink. You need to set the table."

Their suppers were simple, little more than bread and butter, fruit compote, a glass of milk for Dietrich, tea or buttermilk for Carina and herself.

Afterward, as she went up to tuck Dietrich into bed, she had a hard time getting him to settle down. After he'd knelt by his bed and said his prayers, Mara took up the book by his bedside to begin their story time, but every few minutes, he interrupted her reading.

"Mama, did you know Mr. Jakeman has a pig they call Gertrude? She's so big." Dietrich stretched both arms wide. "She has her own pen and is all black and just lies there."

Mara nodded. "Is that so?"

"Mmm-hmm." He nodded vigorously.

A few moments later, he said, "And he has some sheep in a pasture high on a hill beyond the fields. He took me up there with their dog, Samson. You know why they call him Samson?"

She set the book on her lap with a smile. "No, dear, why is that?"

"'Cause he's so strong. Do you know, he can get all the sheep to come back to the barn?"

"Yes, that's why those dogs are usually called sheepdogs."

"Yes, that's what he said. And he has some cows. They're brown-and-white. And some—" He scrunched up his nose as if trying to think of the word. "Oxen!" Dietrich sighed. "They have a nice house."

Mara waited to see if he would describe it. She wondered what it was like inside. She had only glimpsed it in passing, a small cape-style house, mostly obscured by the tall maples growing alongside the road in front of their property.

But Dietrich said no more.

"Did you go inside?" she asked.

He nodded his head. "Lizzie gave me a glass of milk and some oatmeal cookies. She baked them herself. She does all the cooking for her and her papa."

Mara thought of how it had been for her and her father so long ago. "Yes, I imagine she learned how to do that after her mother died."

Dietrich was pensive a few moments, so Mara took up the story again.

"I'm glad we came back to America to live."

Mara blinked at his words. She had been so worried that life would be difficult for him because it was so different from what he had known.

"I'm glad." Quietly, she closed their storybook. "What do you like best?"

"Going to the Jakemans," he said without hesitation.

She had not expected such an unequivocal response after only one visit. Should she caution him against becoming a pest? But she didn't want to squash his happiness. He'd had too little of it lately. He never spoke of his father—or of his death. Klaus had been like a stranger to his only child since almost the moment of Dietrich's birth.

Was he so starved for male companionship that he would latch on to the first male who showed him the least attention? Mara bit her lip, not sure what she should do.

Mara set the book down on the bedside stand and tucked

Dietrich in. "Good night, dear." She leaned forward and kissed his forehead, which smelled of soap. Tenderness welled up in her heart and she thanked God for the son He'd given her. In the midst of every trial and tribulation in her life, Dietrich had been the bright spot, making the struggle worth it.

"You want to get a good night's sleep. You have school tomorrow."

"Good night, Mama." He didn't protest having to go to sleep. His mind already seemed elsewhere, and Mara wondered if it was on the Jakeman farm. Or, had Mr. Jakeman just managed to tire her son out enough that he was already more asleep than awake?

Mara turned down the kerosene lamp and stepped out of the room.

Gideon rowed his skiff back to his beach with the incoming tide. He was satisfied with the good load of fish he'd caught on his lines. He stepped out into the shallow water and dragged the boat up on shore.

As he began hauling the fish out, he heard a shout from the ridge above. Lizzie was waving. He waved back. Then he saw a dark-haired, smaller figure beside her and he smiled. Dietrich.

The boy immediately began scrambling down the path to the beach.

"Hello, Mr. Jakeman," he said breathlessly. "What did you catch?"

"Hello, Dietrich. Let's see." He made a point of looking into the bushel basket. "Mostly haddock and cod. But I got a nice halibut and some pollock."

"What are you going to do with them?"

"Salt them in barrels, sell some of them and keep some for winter."

"May I help you?"

Gideon gave the boy his full attention. "Does your mother know you're here?"

The boy kicked at the round stones of the beach. "She's not home."

"Oh. Is anyone home?"

"Paul." The boy's mouth turned downward. "And Mrs. Blackstone."

"Do any of them know you're here?"

He shook his head, still looking downward. "I walked home from school with Lizzie."

Gideon thought a moment, unsure what to do. "Where is your mother?"

The boy looked up at him, his brown eyes puzzled. His skin was pale like his mother's, with a very light dusting of freckles across the bridge of his nose. His hair was so straight and shiny it reminded Gideon of a sable paintbrush. "She had to go to town."

"When will she be back?"

"Not for a while. She told me it wouldn't be before supper."

"Did she walk?"

The boy nodded.

Gideon had the sudden desire to be able to offer her a ride home again, but knew almost as soon as the desire was formed that that would be impractical. But what he could do was look out for her son.

He took a deep breath. "Very well. You can help me carry these baskets up to the yard and we'll put them in the salt barrels."

Dietrich broke into a grin, which filled Gideon with a pleasure that expanded through his whole chest. He couldn't help but reach out and ruffle the boy's hair. "Come along," he said in a gruff tone, to mask his deeper feelings. In that moment, he realized how much he missed not having had a son.

He would give his life for his daughter—and no one could ask for a better helper and companion.

But what if Elsie had lived and they had had more children, sons and daughters? He could picture them around the kitchen table filled with offspring.

Well, it hadn't been meant to be so he might as well erase the scene from his head. He had work to do, and was glad for the young companion he'd been sent this afternoon.

Mara thought her legs would collapse under her when she finally climbed the last hill before their house. She was thirsty and warm despite the brisk fall air, her satchel felt as if it weighed fifty pounds instead of perhaps five and the soles of her feet ached.

She transferred the bag containing her sheet music and a metronome from one hand to the other for the dozenth time. She hadn't known what to expect when she'd gone into town, but the shopkeeper, true to her word, had the names of local women lined up for Mara. She had visited each one and all had wanted piano lessons for their sons and daughters. Very few had had lessons previously, but at least all the families had pianos in their homes.

She sighed and began the trek down the last slope before the farmhouse. She'd already passed the Jakeman farmhouse. Smoke rose from its brick chimney but she had seen no one about.

Finally, she arrived at her long driveway. She didn't see Dietrich and hoped he was already inside. Entering the woodshed, she didn't hear anyone. As soon as she set down her satchel, she turned first toward the barn in search of Dietrich.

Paul was sweeping the stalls. "Hello, ma'am. I'll be going home soon."

"Yes. Is Dietrich around?"

"No, ma'am." He paused and scratched his head. "Haven't seen him all afternoon."

Her heart began to thump. "He wasn't with you?"

He shook his head. "Want me to look for him before I head home?"

She debated, but decided against it. His own family expected him and he was probably hungry. "No, I shall do so as soon as I ask Mrs. Blackstone."

When she reentered the kitchen, she found Carina at the table, slicing bread. "There you are at last. What kept you so long?"

Mara untied the ribbons of her bonnet. "I had four families to visit and then the walk home."

Carina raised an eyebrow. "Four? Indeed. Soon you'll be making more money than your father left me to fend with."

Wondering what her stepmother meant by the observation, she decided it was best to change the subject. "Has Dietrich come in yet?"

Carina made an unpleasant sound. "That boy? The way he runs wild, he could be all the way to Timbuktu."

Mara gripped her hands together to keep back a sharp retort. "Did he return from school?"

Carina pursed her lips. "I don't believe so."

Mara began retying her bonnet. "I'm going to take a turn about the yard and see if I can find him. I shall be right back to fix supper."

Carina merely sniffed.

Ignoring her tired feet, Mara began calling Dietrich's name as soon as she reached the backyard. She walked past the kitchen garden and toward the apple orchard.

She looked in all the places she knew Dietrich liked to go—up in an oak tree, down by the brook, crossing the road and clambering down the path to the beach. But there was no sign of Dietrich.

Trying to keep her alarm in check, she glanced down

the coastline, praying under her breath for direction. She thought about Dietrich's excitement over the kittens at the Jakemans'. But she had seen no sign of him there. Besides, could he have gone off without telling anyone? The sun had set and Mara's stomach was grumbling, but she hitched up her skirts and made her way up the beach path toward the road.

A quarter of an hour later, she was once more approaching the Jakemans' place.

Golden light shone from a front window. She opened the gate of the white picket fence, bringing the immediate bark of a dog.

A second later, a large, shaggy black dog came bounding over to her.

"Down, boy," she said, looking around, hoping to see someone come to her aid. "Hello!" she called out.

Both Mr. Jakeman and Dietrich emerged from the open barn door.

"Samson, down!"

At the stern command, the dog ran back to his master. Dietrich hurried to his mother. "Mama, come look at the kittens. Did you ask Mrs. Blackstone if I could bring one home?"

"I didn't have a chance yet." It had completely slipped her mind, if truth be told. She looked past her son to Mr. Jakeman, who was making his way more slowly toward her, the dog following at his heels.

Mr. Jakeman wore a vest over a collarless white shirt, its sleeves rolled up to his forearms, as if he didn't feel the cold night air. He inclined his head at her. "Good evening, ma'am. Hope Samson didn't startle you."

"Good evening, Mr. Jakeman. No, that's all right. I just came looking for Dietrich."

The dog sniffed at her hand.

Mr. Jakeman glanced at Dietrich. "See why it's important for you to let someone know where you're going?"

Dietrich hung his head.

Mara put her hand gently on his shoulder. "Didn't you tell anyone you were coming here?"

Dietrich shook his head.

"I asked him as soon as he showed up. I would have sent him home sooner, but somehow the time got away from us. I'm sorry about that, ma'am."

Her anger and worry dissipated. She was thankful that Dietrich was safe and in good company. "What have you two been up to?"

Dietrich tugged on her skirt. "Mr. Jakeman let me help him salt fish and feed the sow and the chickens and the turkeys—and pet the kittens. Come on, Mama, and see them."

Mr. Jakeman chuckled and she couldn't help but smile at him. "I guess you'd better come along." He gestured for her to go ahead of him, keeping a firm hand on his dog.

Mara crouched beside Dietrich at a box lined with an old quilt. A large, dark gray cat with thick white fur around her neck stared at her, a half dozen kittens nursing at her.

"What a fine litter you have," Mara crooned.

Dietrich touched one of the kittens, darker than the others. "This is the one I want. Please, may I have him?"

"What a fuzzy little fellow." She reached out and barely touched the silky fur. "I don't know yet, sweetheart."

Finally, she rose. "You have a fine cat there."

"It's a Maine coon. No hurry deciding about the kittens. They're too young to leave their mother yet."

"Thank you." She moved aside. "Well, we'd best be off. It's been a long day and I still need to get his supper. Thank you so much for your patience."

"Did you walk over?" Mr. Jakeman's eyes scanned her

features and she wondered how she appeared—windblown and haggard, no doubt.

"Yes, I just dashed back out as soon as I arrived home."

He frowned, bringing his reddish-brown eyebrows close together. "You just came back from town?"

She smiled ruefully. "Yes."

"I can give you a ride back home."

She waved a hand. "Oh, no! It's not a long walk—not like going to town."

He said nothing more but followed her back outside.

Dietrich continued kneeling beside the kittens. "Come along, dear. I have a busy day tomorrow. Putting up the cranberries you were so thoughtful to send us yesterday," she added with a shy smile at Mr. Jakeman.

"I didn't mean to make more work for you."

Her smile deepened at his look of contrition. "I appreciate the gift."

At that moment, Lizzie emerged from the house, wiping her hands on an apron. "Hello, Mrs. Keller!"

Mara smiled with pleasure at the girl. "Hello, Lizzie. I didn't mean to disturb you."

"I saw you through the window and wanted to say hello. I would'a brought Dietrich home if I'd a known you'd have to come for him."

"That's all right. You're probably getting supper, which is what I need to be doing right now."

Lizzie's cheeks filled with color and she shot a glance at her father. "That's what I come out for—that is, to ask if you'd like to stay for supper with us."

Dietrich pulled at his mother's skirt. "May we, Mama?"

Mara felt her own cheeks grow warm. "Oh, no, I mean, I didn't come for—" At the look of disappointment in the girl's eyes, her heart constricted. She didn't want Lizzie to feel she was rejecting her, but she knew she had to return home. Carina would expect her.

Before she could think what to say, Mr. Jakeman interjected, "Another time, perhaps."

She smiled at him gratefully. He seemed to understand. "Yes," she breathed out, "that would be lovely."

Dietrich kicked at the hay in the barnyard.

"Lizzie, maybe you could go over after school and help Mrs. Keller with those cranberries."

Lizzie's eyes lit up. "Oh, could I?" Her glance went from her father's to Mara's. "You wouldn't mind, would you?"

"Of course not, but I don't mean for you to come and just do work."

"It won't seem like work."

"Well, if you're sure…"

Lizzie nodded vigorously. "But please wait for me. I'll run over just as school lets out." She smiled. "I can bring Dietrich home for you."

"Very well. That would be kind of you."

Dietrich walked away from her. "I'm going to say goodbye to Samson."

"We have to go, Dietrich." But Dietrich bent over the dog and petted his black head.

Mr. Jakeman cleared his throat. "Thanks for the cake. It was delicious."

Mara found herself blushing, and quickly turned away, taking Dietrich's hand before he found something new to interest him. "Think nothing of it. Well, good evening. I'll see you tomorrow, Lizzie, if you are sure you can spare the time." As she spoke, she sent a questioning look to both father and daughter.

Mr. Jakeman nodded slowly, saying softly, "It'll be good for her."

She stood regarding him a moment longer, trying to decipher his expression. It seemed a mixture of gratitude, kindness and concern. She spun on her heel before she could express something foolish with her own glance.

Chapter Six

Lizzie showed up at the kitchen door promptly the next afternoon, giggling and talking with Dietrich. Mara welcomed them inside, offering them milk and molasses cookies.

"How was school?" she asked as they washed up at the sink.

"Boring!"

"Fine!" came two simultaneous answers. Lizzie punched Dietrich lightly on the arm. "It was not boring. Just because you got in trouble for fidgeting so much at your desk and then pinching Sally's arm."

Mara frowned at her son. "What's this about?"

Dietrich started scrubbing his hands hard.

Lizzie wiped her hands on the towel and smiled. "Nothing the other boys don't do. Don't worry, Miss Higgins knows how to keep them under control."

"We'll talk about this later, Dietrich."

As they sat at the table eating their cookies and milk, Mara headed to the woodshed. "Let me ask Paul if he'd care for a snack."

She came back a few moments later with the tall young man in tow. He wiped his feet on the doormat before stepping inside.

"Come, sit down with the children for a few minutes." As soon as Mara said the words, she knew she'd erred. Lizzie's face had taken on the shade of the crimson maple leaves littering the front yard.

She'd just taken a bite out of the large, soft cookie and at the sight of the young man coming up behind Mara, the girl whipped the cookie away from her mouth and scrubbed at her lips with her other hand.

To draw attention away from her, Mara ushered the boy toward the sink. "Here, wash the dirt off and then have some of my freshly baked cookies."

"Uh, thanks, ma'am." He shuffled his tall frame over to where Mara indicated.

Mara hid a smile at the awkwardness of youth as she bustled about getting a plate and napkin and pouring out a glass of milk from the pitcher, glad that Carina was out.

Paul sat at the opposite end of the table from Lizzie. Lizzie didn't look at him, her fingers crumbling an edge of the cookie on her plate.

"So, you got a whuppin' today at school, half-pint." Paul leaned toward Dietrich, ruffling his hair with his large, work-roughened hand.

Dietrich swung his head out of Paul's way. Mara hesitated, not wanting to interfere every time Dietrich needed defending. She knew it was important to let him fight his own battles. Nevertheless, her fingers curled into her palms as she forced a smile to her lips.

"Do you miss school, Paul?"

Paul blinked his hazel eyes at her. "School? Uh, no, ma'am."

A snigger issued from Lizzie's mouth but was quickly stifled by her hand.

Paul shot her a glance. "What? As if you're such a smarty-pants. You'll probably have to repeat the year."

Her color rose again, her nostrils flaring. "Will not! I'm smarter than you by a long shot."

"Yeah, teacher's pet."

To intervene without appearing to, Mara sat across from Dietrich. "Are you finishing your studies this year, Lizzie?"

Lizzie bobbed her head. "I graduate from grammar school at the end of this year."

Mara turned to Paul. "When did you finish?"

"Last year."

"Only 'cause he had to repeat the eighth grade three times."

"I'm sure that is not true."

Paul's cheeks were about as ruddy as Lizzie's had been a moment ago. "Yes, it is. I'm seventeen now, but didn't graduate till this past year. I hated school."

"So do I," put in Dietrich. "And Miss Higgins is so mean."

Mara frowned at her son. "I'm certain she's not. She probably has her hands full trying to teach so many children so many things before she launches you all into the world."

The children seemed to have nothing to say to that, concentrating instead on their cookies and milk.

"Would you like to continue your studies, Lizzie?"

"Papa wants me to." Lizzie wrinkled her freckled nose. "I would if it didn't mean having to go to the academy."

"You mean the high school in town?"

She nodded. "I'd have to board with someone during the week."

"That wouldn't be so bad."

"I don't want to leave home…and Papa."

Mara understood. Lizzie was her father's housekeeper. A pity the girl was so tied down, though she understood perfectly. "I used to take care of my father, like you."

Lizzie's grayish-green eyes rounded. "Did you really?"

"Yes. I lost my mother quite young, the way I imagine

you did. So, it was just my father and me. I enjoyed cooking and keeping house for him."

Lizzie looked as if she were hanging on to every word. "Yes," she breathed out. "Did you live in this house?"

Mara shook her head. "We lived in a town near Boston. It wasn't until I was your age, Paul—" she turned to him to include him in the conversation "—that my father decided to move up here. He wanted to live by the coast, to paint it."

"He was an artist, wasn't he?" the boy asked. "I seen his paintings on the walls."

"Yes, we still have a few of his paintings in the parlor. Most were sold, though," she added sadly.

"Was he famous?" Lizzie asked.

"He became quite popular, but that was after years of struggling. For many years no one wanted to buy his paintings. But then came the day that it seemed he sold his paintings almost as soon as he put the last brushstroke on them."

All three children were looking at her as if she were telling them a fairy story. She smiled and stood. "Well, I'll let you finish your snack. I need to get to work boiling up these cranberries before they go bad."

Lizzie stood immediately. "I'll help you, ma'am. That's why I came over."

"Well, finish your milk and cookies. I'll begin washing the berries."

Paul stood and pushed his chair in. "Thanks for the cookies, Mrs. Keller. I'll go back out and finish my work." When he was at the door, he turned back. "My mother wanted to ask you if you're coming over to our sociable on Friday evening. You're welcome, she said to tell you."

"I…I don't know. But please give her my thanks. I'll…I'll see what Mrs. Blackstone plans."

He bobbed his head and left the kitchen.

When Mara turned back to the bushel of cranberries, she

found Lizzie staring at the kitchen door. So, it was that way, was it?

"Come, help me lift these into the sink."

"Oh, yes, ma'am."

"Dietrich, why don't you help Paul with his chores?"

"All right, Mama." Wiping his mouth, he slipped from his chair and left the kitchen, slamming the door behind him.

"We'll have some quiet now," Mara said, lifting the pump handle to get the water, glad once again that Carina was out for the afternoon.

As they washed and picked over the cranberries, she ventured, "What's this sociable like?"

Lizzie shrugged. "Just the near neighbors getting together after supper at Cliff and Sarah McClellan's, Pa's cousins."

"I imagine a lot of people are related to each other around here."

Lizzie laughed. "Oh, yes. Most folks have kin in every household."

They filled a large iron pot with berries and some water and put it on the stove. Mara checked the fire and added some sticks of wood. "I'll get the sugar then we'll let that simmer a bit. I think we can fill another pot as well."

When the pots were on the cookstove, she returned to the subject. "So, what happens at the sociable?"

"Oh, people talk and maybe sing a little. Papa usually goes 'cause he plays the fiddle for dancing for the young folks."

Mara smiled at her. "Are you going to try your hand at dancing this time?"

Lizzie turned away, hiding her face. "No…I don't think so."

"You're young yet."

"I'm almost fifteen!"

Mara chuckled. "That's very young, though not too young to enjoy some jigs and reels."

Lizzie stirred the pot with vigor. "Nobody's going to want to dance with me anyway."

Mara set out the jars for the sauce. "I don't know about that. You're a pretty girl and because you're tall, you look older than fourteen."

Lizzie's wooden spoon stopped. "Do I really?"

"Yes. With your hair up, you'll look sixteen."

A look of expectancy lit her face. "Oh, Mrs. Keller, would you put my hair up for the sociable?"

Mara thought about how Paul's presence had affected her. "You know what would be much nicer?"

She shook her head, sending her two braids swinging.

Mara touched an end of one of the red braids. "If you wore it loose, brushed out, with a ribbon tying the front ends back, like so." As she spoke she illustrated with her hands. "Your hair has a natural curl to it which would look lovely."

Lizzie wrinkled her nose. "Wear it down? Wouldn't that be too childish?"

"Not at all. You are a girl, yet, so don't be in such a hurry to become a woman. The Bible says that a woman's hair is her glory. When you get older it won't be seemly to wear it loose. So, you should enjoy it now. It's a beautiful color, rich and deep."

Lizzie still looked doubtful. "But they call me carrottop at school."

Mara smiled. "They just haven't seen it all brushed out and hanging down to your waist with a pretty colored ribbon. Do you have a green gown?"

"I have a light green checked gingham."

"Why don't you wear that? And with a matching green ribbon tied at the back of your hair, you must stand straight and walk in unashamed, knowing the Lord gave you this beautiful shade of hair."

The cranberries began to pop as they heated up. Lizzie stirred the pot again. "I don't know, Mrs. Keller…"

Mara laughed. "Trust me. Now let me stir the other pot before it burns. How long should we let the berries cook?"

"A little bit longer. Once they've all popped then we'll see if they're sweet enough."

Mara laughed. "I'm glad your father suggested you come by this afternoon. You're the one who's teaching me to make cranberry sauce."

Lizzie tilted her head at her as Mara brought over the crock of sugar. "Haven't you ever made any?"

"Not since I was about your age. I never had any in Europe, so I don't know if they have cranberries over there. I never really had a kitchen of my own anyway."

Lizzie's eyes widened. "You didn't?"

"No." She poured out the sugar into a bowl and brought it to the stove. "How much shall we put in?"

"Oh, a few cups to each pot. We can taste it to make sure it's sweet enough."

Mara followed the girl's instructions then stirred her own pot.

"What kind of houses did you live in over there?" Lizzie asked a few minutes later.

Mara recalled the various ones over her years touring the Continent with Klaus. "All kinds, but in the latter years, it was mainly boardinghouses. That's what I meant by not having a kitchen of my own. We'd take our meals with the lady who ran the boardinghouse. Usually she was a widow who rented out rooms."

"Did you like that?"

Mara considered her answer. It wouldn't do to paint too dismal a portrait for this young girl. "Some were quite nice, others not so nice." She turned away from the stove. "Tell me more about your life here. I lived here only briefly when I was eighteen and my father had just purchased this house. Do you find it lonely with just you and your father?"

"Not so much now. At first it was hard, having Mama

gone, but now we're so used to it, I guess we don't think much about it."

They worked in silence a while, stirring their bubbling pots.

Lizzie gave her a sidelong look. "C-could you show me how to walk, all graceful-like? So, that, you know..." her face turned a deep shade of pink once again "...young men will take a second look at me—and not just because they think I look funny."

Mara touched her lightly on the elbow. "Of course, dear. Why don't you come over a half hour or so earlier on the night of the sociable, and I'll help you with your hair? Perhaps your father can fetch you on his way to the McClellans'?"

Lizzie's generous mouth broke into a wide smile. "That would be wonderful. Oh, thank you, Mrs. Keller! And he can take you and Dietrich, too."

Before Mara had a chance to reply, Carina came into the kitchen.

"Hello, Carina," Mara said, taking the pot off the stove and placing it on a folded towel atop the table.

Carina looked in surprise at Lizzie and surveyed everything arrayed on the table and countertop. "Hello, Lizzie. I didn't know you were coming over this afternoon."

Lizzie nodded to her. "Hello, Mrs. Blackstone. Pa offered to have me help Mrs. Keller with putting up the cranberries."

"Oh." It was hard to interpret the single syllable. "How thoughtful of him. My, you seem to have a lot going on here."

Lizzie smiled. "Yes, you'll have enough jars to last you all winter."

Carina smiled at the girl, leaving Mara amazed as always at how charming she could be with outsiders. "How nice of you to think of me." She removed her hat and gloves. "Is it chilly out there! I think I shall fix myself a cup of tea before I offer to help you."

Lizzie took her pot off the stove. "That's all right, ma'am. You go ahead and have your tea. We're almost finished here."

Mara took up the teakettle. "The water is hot."

After Carina took her teacup and left the kitchen, Mara breathed easier.

As they strained the cranberry sauce and poured it into jars, they couldn't speak much, but after sealing the jars with paraffin, Mara stood back and wiped the perspiration from her brow. "They look beautiful, don't they?" They admired the dozens of jars containing a ruby-red sauce.

"Yes, they do that."

"Why don't you and I have a cup of tea to celebrate?"

"That'd be fine, ma'am, and then I'd best get home and fix Papa's supper."

"Yes, indeed."

As they sat allowing their tea to cool, Lizzie asked, "Mrs. Blackstone's going with us to the sociable, isn't she?"

"I expect so."

"Do you think she'd mind if I came over early?"

In truth, Mara wasn't sure. But she smiled in reassurance. "I'm sure she wouldn't. As long as your father has no objection."

"He won't. He says you're a good influence for me."

Before Mara could react to that comment, Lizzie continued. "He can pick us up in the carryall like I said. He usually takes Mrs. Blackstone anyway, if she decides to go out in the evenings."

"That's very nice of him."

Lizzie looked toward the hallway, as if she wanted to say something more, but decided against it.

"The McClellans always invite Mrs. Blackstone for

Thanksgiving dinner and frequently on a Sunday after church," was what she finally said.

"How thoughtful of them, knowing Mrs. Blackstone is alone now."

"Yes, before she was widowed, we didn't see too much of her. She and your father kept to themselves a lot, or enjoyed the society of town."

Mara nodded, imagining it so. Her father had grown more and more reclusive after her mother died, and Mara had heard enough remarks from Carina to realize that she did prefer the ladies of the town.

Lizzie stood. "Let me clean up some of these things while our tea cools."

"I'll help you."

Lizzie didn't let Mara do any of the heavy washing up. Mara marveled, grateful for her help, and vowed to assist the girl for the sociable.

When they'd drunk their tea, Lizzie put on her cloak and wrapped a woolen scarf around her neck. At the door, she stood a moment before opening it. "Did you really mean that about fixing my hair and all for the sociable?"

"Of course."

She cleared her throat, fiddling with the fringes on her scarf ends. "And how to act like a lady. I mean, how to walk and move? I always feel like my hands are in the way and my feet are ready to trip over anything…" Her voice trailed away.

Mara took her hands in hers. "My dear, we all feel that way at your age."

The girl gave her another wide smile. "Thank you, oh, thank you, ma'am!"

Without another word, she turned around and opened the door.

When Lizzie had gone, Mara stood staring at the closed door a few seconds. Then, with a sigh of satisfaction for an afternoon well spent, she took her shawl off the hook, and went in search of her son.

Perhaps her life was taking a turn for the better.

Gideon scraped most of his shaving soap off his chin and washed off the remnants. Patting his face dry, he stared at himself in the square mirror. Well, at least he hadn't nicked himself.

The house was silent. Usually, about now Lizzie would be inspecting his shirt and tie and brushing off his frock coat. He smiled, remembering how Elsie had done the same. Well, hopefully, his tie wasn't crooked. He'd donned a clean shirt and collar.

He brushed his hair one last time, his thoughts going to Mrs. Keller. Silly to think of her and what she might think of his appearance. He was merely collecting them to go to the sociable. What he did for Mrs. Blackstone all the time. Nothing more. Period.

He set down the brush, a mite too hard that it clattered off the washstand and fell to the floor. He bent to pick it up then hit his head on the edge of the table as he rose. Stifling an exclamation, he willed his nerves to still, before setting the hairbrush down.

He adjusted the knot of his black four-in-hand tie then turned from the mirror with a gesture of impatience. He was going only to play the fiddle, not to catch some lady's eye.

As he rode toward the Blackstone place, his thoughts couldn't help but return to Mrs. Keller. Lizzie had seemed so excited to be going there early. He wondered what Mrs. Keller planned with her, hoping the lady wouldn't get his daughter's hopes up too high.

Lights shone from the kitchen window as he drove up. He didn't even have time to get down from the carryall when Lizzie and Dietrich came out the door. "There you are, Papa. I was on the watch for you!"

He scrutinized his daughter in the half-light. The first thing he noticed was her long mane of hair. But it didn't look wild. It was held back neatly away from her face. She wore her knee-length cloak so he couldn't see anything else. "Hop aboard. Hello, Dietrich."

"Hello, Mr. Jakeman," the boy said as he scrambled into the backseat after Lizzie.

By then the ladies emerged from the house. Mrs. Blackstone secured the door and turned to him. "Good evening, Mr. Jakeman. Do you have enough room for all of us?"

"Sure thing." He asked Lizzie to hold the reins while he hopped down and came around to help the two onto the front seat, wondering if Mrs. Keller was going to be in the middle next to him.

But Mrs. Blackstone came up to him first as he was nodding to Mrs. Keller. He took her arm and helped her up then turned to Mrs. Keller.

"Thank you," she murmured, meeting his gaze for only an instant before turning her attention to the carryall.

He held her by the elbow but she grasped the carriage with her other hand and hiked herself up to the seat, disengaging herself from his light hold almost as soon as he had touched her.

Mrs. Blackstone made conversation as they rode the short way to the McClellans'. Lizzie chattered away with Dietrich, leaning forward often to address a remark to Mrs. Keller though Gideon couldn't catch Mrs. Keller's replies.

When they arrived, he helped them down at the door to the large, sprawling farmhouse before going to the barn to see to the carryall.

When he entered the house, Sarah came up to him with a smile. "Hello, Gideon. I'm so glad you brought Mrs. Keller—and Mrs. Blackstone, of course. My, but doesn't Lizzie look pretty?" As she spoke, she took him by the arm and propelled him toward the sitting room, which was already full of people, mostly members of her own large family and the few neighbors who lived on this stretch of road. People smiled, lifting a hand and smiling at him.

Sarah stood with him near the doorway a few moments. "I haven't seen you in over a week, so you're not going to go off to the menfolk so fast. Just set your fiddle down here." She indicated a side table. "You must be proud of Lizzie. I've never seen her look so elegant. My, my, she's going to be a young lady soon." She shook her head.

Gideon scanned the room for his daughter, drawing in a breath at the sight of her. She was standing alongside Mrs. Keller, greeting those already seated in chairs ranged along the walls.

Her full, wavy hair was neatly brushed, falling to just above her waist. A green ribbon was tied at the back, with shorter strands caught up in it. He could see her profile when she smiled in greeting to an uncle. Her face looked radiant— not the beet-red that frequently filled her cheeks when she was embarrassed, but a soft pink—peaches and cream, Elsie would have said. Gone was the girlish look that her usual two braids gave her. The dress had a lacy white collar and tight sleeves that reached halfway down her forearms. A wide green sash emphasized her small waist, and because she had grown so tall in the past year, in the longer gown and slim boots, she looked quite grown-up.

He sighed, not sure if he liked it. But then she looked his way and smiled shyly, and all he could do was smile back. He wouldn't be able to hold back time, no matter how much he tried.

He hardly heard the rest of his cousin's conversation, his glance skimming the rest of the company, resting on the boys Lizzie's age and young men a few years older. Which one would win her heart and take her away from him?

Not that he wanted to keep her for himself. He and Elsie

were married when they were barely eighteen and nineteen apiece, and the following year they'd had Lizzie.

"You're not listening to a word I'm saying."

He turned to Sarah with an apologetic smile. "What's that?"

"What do you think of Mrs. Keller?" Before giving him a chance to formulate a reply, she continued. "I think she'll be good for Lizzie." She gave a nod in their direction.

Gideon focused on Mrs. Keller, who was standing talking to an elderly woman. He was surprised to see she was not wearing black but a gray gown with black trim. He was relieved to see her in something less severe. He wondered how long she'd been a widow. Her father had been gone almost six months now.

What was it like for her to come and live with Mrs. Blackstone? The older lady had taken a seat someone had vacated for her, and she spread the skirts of her gown around her, sitting like a queen.

He'd never had much to do with Mrs. Blackstone, but he knew from the little Paul let drop that she was a strict taskmaster.

His attention returned to Mrs. Keller. Regardless of what color she wore, she was the most elegant-looking woman in the parlor. She was taller than Lizzie and just as slim—except for having the contours of a woman. Gideon could feel his neck warm around his collar at the direction of his thoughts.

"Well, I'd better get my fiddle."

"There's time yet. Why don't you socialize a little? Lizzie seems quite taken with Mrs. Keller. She really has needed a feminine influence in her life. I wish I could do more, but you know with my brood…" She chuckled.

"You've done a lot for us already."

Sarah continued to observe Lizzie. "Now she needs someone to teach her ladylike manners. Maybe Mrs. Keller is the person to do so. She seems to be fond of her. Funny, she only has one child, too." Sarah gave him a sidelong smile. "He probably could use a male hand. Paul tells me he's always up to some mischief."

"Dietrich's all right. Probably just craving attention."

"Goodness, yes. Handsome little fellow. Well, perhaps you and Mrs. Keller can help each other out." With a final pat on his arm, Sarah moved away.

None too soon, in Gideon's opinion. The last thing he needed were sly looks and innuendos when all he was trying to do was be a good neighbor, just as he'd always been to Mrs. Blackstone.

Why did one feel like a chore and the other a privilege?

Chapter Seven

Mara sat on the piano bench with her newest pupil, a girl of twelve. "Let's try that again, Louisa," she said, holding on to her patience. The girl had not learned the simple piece Mara had given her last week.

Louisa's chubby fingers banged on the keys to the tune of "Mary Had a Little Lamb." A discordant note echoed in the parlor. She started again and made another mistake.

"From the beginning."

After several tries, the girl finally got through the short piece.

Footsteps clicked against the parquet floor. "How did it go?"

The girl's mother, Mrs. Ellison, entered and came up to the piano.

Mara smiled with effort. "A little more practice next time, eh, Louisa?"

The girl banged on the keys with all ten fingers, creating a din in the room.

"Louisa!"

Louisa ignored her mother's exclamation, sliding off the stool.

"May I be excused, Mama?"

"Not yet, my dear. Mrs. Keller is here to teach you deportment as well. You want to grow up to be a proper young lady, do you not?"

The girl stuck out her lower lip but said nothing more. She was a pretty child with honey-gold ringlets tied back with ribbons.

Mara stood, girding herself to proceed with the next portion of lessons.

Mrs. Ellison swept out of her way, her taffeta skirts rustling. Its high bustle at the rear, of the latest fashion, was straight enough to set a book upon.

Instead of leaving the room, she took a seat on the velvet love seat.

Hoping the woman would not make her daughter feel too awkward with her presence, Mara beckoned. "Come along, Louisa. Let me see you walk across the room."

The girl marched across, her swinging arms sending her skirt and pinafore swishing.

"Louisa! What kind of hoyden do you think you are?"

Mara ignored Mrs. Ellison's sharp tone and went to stand by the girl. "Let's walk together and see if you can match my pace."

Mara gently guided her, straightening her shoulders and setting a sedate pace. Each time Mara walked her through it, Mrs. Ellison offered a critique.

By the time she left that afternoon, Mara's temples were throbbing. She had to bite her tongue to keep from telling Mrs. Ellison that her services would no longer be available.

But she remembered her fee. No, she must stick it out.

She exited the overheated house, taking a deep breath of the bracing air. She would not be feeling so out of patience, she told herself, if Louisa had not been her fourth student.

But an afternoon of teaching children who had no real interest in learning only brought back the years of recalcitrant pupils in various European cities. Mara would return from a drafty piano studio only to find a cold flat. Once again Klaus had gone out and forgotten to put coal into the stove. Later, when he was lying in bed ill, too weak to get up and fend for himself, she'd have to set aside her own weariness and prepare him some food and keep his room warm with their meager supply of coal.

She shook aside the memories. She would not return there. Her life was different now. She would save enough to find a nice place for Dietrich and herself.

Gideon settled his bill at the grocer's and picked up his parcels. One more errand, and then home before Lizzie wondered what was keeping him. He stepped onto the sidewalk and made his way to the wagon.

He set his parcels in back, exchanged a few words with a passerby then got on his way.

The maple trees lining the street had lost most of their color, their leaves blown off by a couple of nor'easters.

Stately white homes with black shutters lined the rectangular green at the center of town. An American flag flapped in the breeze by a war memorial. Gideon noticed a woman ahead of him, bent slightly against the wind and carrying a heavy-looking satchel in one hand, the other clutching her bonnet.

Without making a conscious decision, Gideon guided his horse in her direction, recognizing Mrs. Keller. She had her back to him as she reached the end of the green.

As he drew abreast of her, she stopped, turning startled eyes to him.

He tipped his hat. "Afternoon, ma'am."

She smiled as she recognized him. "Oh, hello, Mr. Jakeman."

Clearing his throat, he decided to ask before he lost his nerve. She was just the one to help him with his last errand. "I wondered if you might advise me with something. That is—" he stopped, realizing she was probably on her way to a music lesson "—if you're not busy just now."

"No. As a matter of fact I'm on my way back home."

He breathed a sigh of relief. "Good."

She stood by the wagon, waiting until he remembered what he was going to say. "I wanted to pick up some cloth—a piece of fabric, that is, for my Lizzie. She's taken a notion of making herself a new gown for Thanksgiving. She said you and she had talked of it."

Her smile widened. "Yes." Then her expression grew serious. "I hope you don't mind. I didn't mean to have her ask you for something. I thought she might have some extra fabric on hand."

He waved aside her concern. "I appreciate your suggestion. It's not something that would have occurred to me." He smiled sheepishly then swallowed. "She looked right pretty the other night at the sociable."

Her deep blue eyes scanned his face as if to verify that he was being sincere. "Yes, she did, didn't she?" she said softly.

He nodded slowly. Then clearing his throat, he returned to his immediate concern. "It's just that I wasn't quite sure what to get her. Would…would you mind accompanying me to Pearce's—" he mentioned the dry goods store "—to see if there is anything she might like?"

She hesitated a moment.

Afraid she would refuse, he hurried on. "I can give you a lift back home, if you're running late."

A look of relief passed over her features. "That's very kind of you. I didn't want them to wonder where I was if… if I'm late." Before he could say anything more, she climbed up into the buckboard.

He rode around the green, coming to a stop before a two-story building with large windows displaying a host of goods on sale within.

He lifted his hat at those who recognized him as he made

his way around to help Mrs. Keller alight. After securing the horse at the hitching post, he turned to her. "Shall we go in?"

"Yes, of course." She walked beside him and he held open the door for her.

He removed his hat and led her across the wood-planked floor toward the area filled with bolts of fabric. A clerk, a middle-aged woman, came up to the other side of the counter. "Hello, may I help you?"

"I'm not sure—" he began, but Mrs. Keller pointed to a bolt.

"May we see that green, please?"

"Certainly, madam." She extracted it from the other dark, woolen fabrics and placed it on the counter. "It's a lovely spruce-green serge, perfect for the coming winter season. We just got it in this week from our supplier in Boston."

As the lady spoke, Mrs. Keller was feeling it between her fingertips. Without seeming to pay much attention to the woman, she turned to Gideon, a question in her eye.

He nodded. "Looks fine to me."

"Oh, it would make a lovely gown for you, madam."

A slight color rose in Mrs. Keller's cheeks. "Oh, it isn't for me. It's for a girl of fourteen. The shade of green would be just right with her coloring, don't you think, Mr. Jakeman?" She turned to him again.

"Yes, it would." His thoughts weren't on Lizzie at that second, but on what impression the saleslady had of him and Mrs. Keller together. He recognized her, of course, but didn't know if the two women had ever seen each other. The saleslady's remark about the fabric suiting Mrs. Keller was also lingering in his mind, as he envisioned the color against her pale skin and sable hair.

He gave himself a mental shake to focus on the interchange between the two women. Mrs. Keller was asking the lady how much the fabric cost per yard. At her reply, Mrs. Keller turned to him, looking doubtful.

"How much do you need?" he asked.

She pursed her fine lips then consulted with the saleslady.

"We'll take it," he told the lady. "Do you need anything else?"

Mrs. Keller considered. "Something for the collar and cuffs, perhaps in white, and some buttons…but I think I'll wait and come with Lizzie. That way she can have some say in her new gown." Amusement danced in her blue eyes.

He nodded and smiled, gratified with how sensitive she was to his daughter's feelings. He turned to the saleslady. "Very well, wrap it up."

As they exited the store a short while later, a paper-wrapped parcel in Mrs. Keller's hands, she asked him as he held the door open for her, "You don't think it was too dear, do you?"

"Not at all. Lizzie deserves a little something special. She rarely asks for anything for herself."

He helped her into the wagon. "Thank you," she murmured.

As he maneuvered the wagon down Main Street, he tried to convince himself this was no different than offering Mrs. Blackstone or any other widow from the hamlet a lift home.

Except this was no old widow. He gave Mrs. Keller a side-long glance as they crossed the bridge over the river on their way out of town.

Trying to figure out how to express his appreciation, he cleared his throat, his eyes firmly fixed on the point ahead above his mare's two ears. "Lizzie hasn't had anyone—that is, a woman—a lady—to show her what to do. That is, how to behave and such now that she's getting older—getting to be a young woman herself."

"It must be hard for you, but you've done a fine job."

"I appreciate your taking the time. I didn't realize till I saw her the other night at the McClellans' that in another year or so she'll be all grown up."

"Well, I commend you. I understand now what a tough time my father must have had when I was Lizzie's age. I lost my mother, too, when I was young."

Her words made him forget his self-consciousness. He glanced at her. She turned and smiled briefly—a smile touched with sadness—he thought, before she gazed forward again. He didn't know too much about her history, he realized. Her father had pretty much kept to himself. All he'd known was that he had a daughter living "overseas somewhere," as the locals said.

Before he could get up his nerve to ask her anything about herself, she asked instead, "How old was Lizzie when she lost her mother?"

"Elsie passed away when Lizzie was nine—too young for a girl to learn to do all she's had to do."

Mrs. Keller nodded. "I was only about a year older. After the initial shock and sadness of losing the person one is closest to at that age, I began to see it as my duty—a most pleasurable duty, I add—to take care of my father. We became very close."

"Yes…it's been like that with us."

"We lived in a coastal town, not so unlike here, north of Boston then. My father never liked the city, although he had to go there for exhibitions of his paintings." She shifted on the hard seat, adjusting the scarf around her neck.

"Are you cold?"

"No, I'm fine, though it is quite chilly, isn't it?"

"Yes. Not long before we'll see our first snow."

She shivered. "And then it won't be until April that we'll see signs of spring."

He thought of her walking from town. "If you ever need a ride into town, let me know."

"Oh, that's all right. If I dress warmly, it's not bad."

He said nothing, thinking of the snowbanks and chilly northwest winds in winter.

"My father and I lived as if we didn't need anyone else," she continued after a bit. "We had a lovely house beside the sea, and when I'd come home from school, I'd keep house for him. The rest of the time, I would practice my music and he would paint his canvasses."

Except for the last part, it sounded much like his life with Lizzie. "Lizzie keeps house for me and I farm. In winter, besides logging, I spend a lot more time indoors."

"Your own little haven." She gave a bittersweet laugh. "I didn't realize back then that that world limited to two was not enough for my father."

He raised an eyebrow at her, not sure of her meaning.

"Shortly after he moved up here, ever in search of new vistas to paint, he met Carina—Mrs. Blackstone—and married her."

He nodded in understanding. It must have been a difficult adjustment for a young girl to make. He didn't know Mrs. Blackstone too well, but she didn't strike him as someone who would be a warm, accepting stepmother to a girl. "How old were you then?"

"I was just eighteen. My father and I had talked for a long time about my attending the music conservatory in Boston, so it was not the fact that he was recently married that prompted my leaving home so quickly. But I felt at the time that it worked out well to both our benefits—mine and Carina's." She sighed. "My father and she were able to begin married life together without a child in tow."

"I'm sure you wouldn't have been in the way."

She said nothing, half turned from him as she regarded the passing fields and forest.

Despite the chilly breeze, the sun was pleasant upon his face. It seemed strange to be riding with a woman—one close in age—like this. He hadn't done so, he calculated, since riding home from town with Elsie. Not wanting to draw too close a comparison, reminding himself that Mrs.

Keller was only a neighbor, nothing more, he tried to concentrate on what she had told him of her girlhood and how it related to Lizzie. It was good for Lizzie to have a woman who'd gone through something so similar.

He gave the reins a slight flick. "I reckon it'll be Lizzie who'll soon be finding our life a bit too narrow. I hadn't noticed…perhaps hadn't wanted to notice…how quickly she's growing up."

"Oh, she's young yet. She has many years to be at home with you. She just wants to feel a little more confident of herself, I expect, when she is in mixed company."

He glanced at her, wondering if she were just comforting him or speaking from experience. "I don't know. Young people tend to marry early around here…seventeen, eighteen or thereabouts."

She shook her head with a smile. "Well, if she ever seeks my advice, you can rest easy that I shan't counsel her to tie the knot quite so young."

"I would like her to attend the academy in town next year."

She tilted her head toward him. "Yes, she told me. I think that's a wonderful idea. But she seems loath to leave you. I understand the sentiment, having gone through the same myself at that age."

"I'd hate for her to be stuck keeping house for me until she gets married."

"Perhaps between the two of us, we can convince her to spread her wings a little before she settles down." Mrs. Keller smiled.

The smile felt conspiratorial to him and he couldn't help but return it. It had been a long time since he had felt this kind of partnership with someone over his child. Sarah was the closest he had, but she was busy with her own daughters. This was different; this felt more like having Elsie to consult with.

He stopped that thought short in its tracks. He'd better not be getting presumptuous notions in his head.

To change the subject, he hunted about for a topic that wouldn't be too personal. "You come to town often?"

"I come in on Thursdays now." She indicated the satchel at her feet. "I've started giving piano lessons and—" she laughed with a self-deprecating note "—deportment. I was looking for some work, and the lady at the dry goods store was the one who helped me. She said there were several families who would be interested and helped spread the word."

He was still puzzling over the fact that Mrs. Keller was looking for work and didn't hear too much of the rest. "So, you've got some students now?"

"Yes, four, which fills up one afternoon a week very well. If I get more, I'll just have to come in twice a week, since the children can only come by after school."

Thursdays. He filed away this piece of information. Perhaps, if he arranged his own schedule, he could fix his trip to town for Thursdays. He hated to think of Mrs. Keller's having to make this walk once a week, let alone more. It was bearable now, but he didn't want to think of the long winter ahead. He wondered why Mrs. Blackstone didn't give her use of the buggy.

"Maybe you'll be able to get some students from the hamlet, closer to home," he began.

"Perhaps. Only, they'd have to have their own pianos, since it would be difficult to have them come to the house."

He remembered her playing. "Don't you have a piano there?"

"Yes. That was the piano my father gave me when I was twelve." She paused. "But I don't want to impose on Mrs. Blackstone, you know, having to hear children practicing scales and such."

"I see." Trying to draw out more information without seeming to, he said, "I imagine you must miss living in some of those European cities. You certainly had Lizzie impressed."

"I don't miss boardinghouse living, no matter how quaint the city was."

He quirked an eyebrow. "Boardinghouse?"

"Well, yes, that and hotels. My husband and I, and then Dietrich, lived a very nomadic life while Klaus—my husband—was a concert player. It would not have made sense to settle down in a house when he was traveling all the time. At first we stayed in hotels, but later, it was boardinghouses."

It didn't sound too romantic. "I guess it's nice to come back home then."

She didn't say anything but looked straight ahead. He sensed a tension in her straight back and folded hands. "Well, I guess it wasn't really your home, if you lived down in Massachusetts with your father."

"Yes." She looked down at her gloved hands. "This never really became home," she said softly. Then she took a deep breath. "But my father left me half the house when he…when he passed away. It came as a shock to me when I received news of his death. I so wished I could have been here." She fell silent and Gideon waited, hoping she would continue.

She slowly resumed her story. "But I wasn't able to. My husband was ill by then—he had been for a while, but he grew worse last year. Consumption," she added with a quick glance at him.

He wished he could say or do something to comfort her. Her slim shoulders seemed too young and fragile to carry the weight of a sick husband with a lingering disease and a young, rambunctious boy.

"I didn't expect to return home. But after Klaus passed away, and I found out the terms of my father's will, I realized I had little choice but to return home."

Little choice. That spoke of financial straits to him. "Your husband's family?" he ventured.

She shook her head. "They lived in Germany. I…I wasn't close to them."

It didn't sound as if she wanted to talk about them. It made him wonder all the more about the kind of life she'd led over in Europe. Life of a nomad…living in boarding-houses…not close to her husband's kin.

It didn't sound to him like a very enviable life. He thought of his life in the hamlet. Sunup to sundown it was hard, but satisfying work, and winters gave him ample time to rest. He'd had a good life with Elsie and they'd been blessed with a wonderful daughter. He no longer missed Elsie—not in that sharp, daily way he had in the beginning—and his daughter was a blessing in more ways than he could count. But beyond that, he felt thankful to live in a community where he had family and neighbors he could count on in a number of ways.

What must it be like for Mrs. Keller, a still young, single woman with a small child—with no relatives or ties to any place?

He felt instinctively that Mrs. Blackstone was no support. He couldn't believe Mrs. Keller was obliged to go out and earn her keep. Her father must have left a comfortable amount—he was quite renowned as a painter when he'd died, and Mrs. Blackstone certainly seemed to live well enough.

She was known to be a bit tight in the community, but she didn't seem to stint herself on her own pleasures in town, where she was a member of a few groups like the Daughters of the American Revolution and the Eastern Star.

Gideon wished there was some way he could assist Mrs. Keller, but didn't want to do anything to offend her. From the little he'd seen, she seemed an independent sort, which he admired.

But in this world, one also had to know when to accept a helping hand.

Chapter Eight

The next morning after she'd had breakfast and cleaned up the kitchen, Mara brought the kerosene lamps in from the parlor and bedrooms to clean and fill.

She heard the rhythmic thwack of an ax outside and drew back the lacy curtain to make sure Dietrich was out of harm's way if Paul was chopping firewood.

She drew in her breath, surprised at the sight of Mr. Jakeman, his back toward her, his arms raising an ax high over his head. The next instant he brought it down in a mighty arc to land atop an upraised length of wood. The piece split in two, each side falling off the stump it had stood upon and landing on the grass beside him.

Not pausing, he hefted one of these still thick pieces back on the stump and brought his ax down once more, splitting the piece in two. When he finished, he had four nice-size sticks of wood for the stove.

Reassured to find Dietrich at a safe distance, Mara debated going outside and admonishing him not to get in Mr. Jakeman's way.

She bit her lip. She didn't want Mr. Jakeman to think she didn't trust him to take care of her son. Casting about for a sight of Paul, she breathed a sigh of relief to see him emerge from the barn, another ax in his hand.

Yet, if both would be chopping wood today, they wouldn't be able to keep an eye on Dietrich. And they didn't know how easily Dietrich could get into trouble.

As she went over these things, she couldn't help but watch Mr. Jakeman. He'd shed his jacket and stood in his shirt-sleeves and vest, the way she'd seen him at his farm the other day.

The man was powerfully built. He must be at least six feet tall, she estimated, and the breadth of his shoulders was wider than most men's. But despite his large size, there was no excess fat on him. Her eyes traveled the length of his back to his trim waist.

So different from Klaus, a man of medium height and slim build. Klaus had probably done very little manual labor in his life. He'd come of a good family, aristocratic, she'd often heard when she was among them. In time, she realized that many Germans boasted of highborn lineage, when in reality it meant very little—just an excuse for doing no work, the majority of them impoverished, lamenting ancient kingdoms and principalities that had been stolen from them over generations of war.

She continued to admire the smooth rhythm of the wood chopping. In a matter of minutes, Mr. Jakeman had a pile of scattered pieces on the ground around him. He stopped for a moment and wiped his brow with his forearm. That's when she realized the work was not effortless.

"What are you so busy looking at?"

Mara whirled around at Carina's voice.

Before she could move, her stepmother came to stand beside her and pushed the curtain aside wider. "Humph! It's about time he came by."

Mara walked away from the window, but the words arrested her. "What do you mean?"

"He's been promising all fall to chop my wood."

Mara removed the glass cover from one of the kerosene lamps and took it to the dishpan. "I'm sure he's been busy."

Carina only harrumphed again and said no more as she went about preparing herself a cup of tea. She sat at the kitchen table and watched as Mara scrubbed the lamp covers and set them on the drainboard to dry. "I suppose we'll have to give him some dinner."

"I beg your pardon?"

"Gideon."

"Oh—" For some reason, the sound of his first name caused the color to rise in Mara's cheeks. It seemed intimate, putting him on too familiar a footing with her, something she was not ready for. "I suppose so."

"I don't know what you folks in Europe did, but it's the custom around here with a workman."

Mara pressed her lips together, not liking her tone and use of "workman." Mr. Jakeman was probably doing them a favor, and Carina was treating him as someone beneath her. She said nothing, proceeding with her chore of trimming the lamps' wicks.

"If you played your cards right, you could snare him, you know."

Mara's gaze flew to Carina's. She'd hoped Carina would have forgotten that notion.

"He's been widowed many years now. Most folks don't stay single so long. I guess you'd have to win over his daughter, though. She's probably the one keeping him all to herself."

Mara remembered how it had been between her and her father. She had been hurt when her father had abruptly announced he was engaged to Carina, after only a few meetings in church or so. Their marriage had taken place even quicker, and Carina had made sure Mara hadn't remained around long afterward.

Mara set down the scissors. "Since I am not looking for a husband, I don't think Lizzie need have any concerns."

Carina eyed her over the rim of her teacup. "A woman in your state, without two sticks to rub together?" She gave a harsh laugh. "I think you have little choice, my dear."

"I do have half this house." She hated herself as soon as the words were out. How she wished her father hadn't left things the way he had. But he'd probably had very little choice. Yet, why not leave her a few of his paintings? Or a legacy of money? She could hardly believe there had been no money left. Could they have spent it all? Or had Carina hoarded it away somewhere so her husband's only child and grandchild could have none of it?

Turning to check if the lamp globes were dry, she chided herself for the direction of her thoughts. She must trust these things to the Lord and not seek after earthly wealth. The Lord had taken care of her and Dietrich up to now; He would continue to do so. She would not lower herself to fighting Carina over personal property.

Just then she heard a muffled cry. Dietrich!

Dropping her dish towel, she ran to the door.

She arrived in the yard to see Mr. Jakeman bent over Dietrich, who was crying.

"What is it? What happened?" she asked breathlessly.

"Mama, I hurt my hand." He was clutching the fingers of one hand with the other.

"Let me see, son." Mr. Jakeman tried to gently pry them apart.

Dietrich only huddled over his hands, sobbing. "It h-hurts."

"What happened?" she repeated, her glance going from her son to Mr. Jakeman.

"I put him to stacking the wood inside. His fingers must have gotten in the way." There was a twinkle in his gray-blue eyes.

She couldn't see the humor. "Let me see, honey." She took her son's hand in hers.

He allowed his mother to touch him. His hand was red, but it could also have been from the cold. She felt his fingers. "Nothing seems broken."

Dietrich sniffled. "I was setting down the logs and they smashed my fingers."

"Come inside, dear, and we'll put them in some cold water. That will help the pain go away." She wrapped her arm around her son's narrow shoulders and ushered him toward the house.

"I'm sorry, Mrs. Keller."

She did not acknowledge Mr. Jakeman's sincere tone, too intent on her son's pain. She shouldn't have let him remain outside with men chopping wood.

Inside, she led Dietrich to a chair and hurried to pump some cold water into a bowl. "Hush now, dear, and set your hand in that for a few minutes. The pain will soon go away."

"What did he get into now?" Carina asked from the opposite side of the table.

Mara glared at her stepmother but kept her tone even. "He smashed his fingers between some logs, as he was helping stack wood."

Carina shook her head and tsk-tsked but thankfully said nothing more.

"Did you do as Mr. Jakeman told you?" Mara asked her son when his cries had dissolved to mere sniffles.

"Yes, Mama. He told me where to carry the wood and how to stack it."

"Were you wearing some gloves?"

He shook his head.

"That would have protected your fingers. You know that happened to me when I was your age and would help my papa stack wood."

Dietrich's eyes rounded. "Did it really?"

"Yes, and I'd go crying to him, too. But the pain didn't last. But you have to learn to be more careful. It happened to me when I was careless and hurried with the task."

Dietrich nodded. "I just wanted to stack all the wood they were chopping and show them I could stack as fast as they could chop."

She smiled. "I'm sure you needn't have rushed to prove to them you were a good helper."

Carina sniffed. "Underfoot, I'd say."

Before Mara could think of a good retort, the kitchen door opened and Mr. Jakeman appeared with Paul behind him. He wiped his feet on the doormat and entered a few feet, sufficient for Paul to do the same. "We just came to see how Dietrich was doing. How do your fingers feel now?" he asked with a smile.

"All right." Dietrich took his hand from the dish of water and went over to show them.

Mr. Jakeman took the boy's hand in his and turned it around. "Looks good to me. What do you think, Paul?"

"Looks better. How do they feel?"

"A little better. They still hurt some," he said, bending his fingers.

"Well, it's painful to get them caught between two heavy logs. We've done it a time or two ourselves, haven't we, Paul?"

Paul grinned. "Sure have." The youth extended both his hands for Dietrich to see. That made her son laugh. She looked toward Mr. Jakeman to find his glance on her, a twinkle in his eyes. She couldn't help but smile back.

Then remembering Carina's words about hooking a widower, she quickly looked away.

Carina stood. "It was so nice of you to come by to see to my wood. I hope you stay for dinner."

"Oh, that's all right, ma'am. I brought a lunch pail."

"Well, then if you're here at suppertime, you may join us then."

"I don't like to leave Lizzie by herself."

Mara spoke before thinking. "If you'd like, I could bring her."

Mr. Jakeman's expression softened as his eyes once more met hers. "That's kind of you. Well, if she'd like to come, then I'd be pleased to stay—if you'd honor us with your company some evening."

She knew her color was deepening, and she dreaded how Carina might construe the invitation. "Very well." She addressed herself to Dietrich, wanting to draw the attention away from herself. "I think you'd better stay away from the wood for now, don't you think so?"

"Oh, no, Mama. I feel better now."

"I thought I'd bring over a small ax I have and teach him to split wood. But it'll wait for another day, all right, son?"

Dietrich's eyes lit up, his injury forgotten.

"I don't know…" began Mara.

"But for today," Mr. Jakeman continued, "why don't you collect the small pieces for kindling? You can rake them up until you're sure your fingers are better."

Mara let out a breath of relief. Giving Mr. Jakeman a look of gratitude, she addressed her son. "Be careful out there and do what Mr. Jakeman tells you."

"Yes, Mama."

When the three had exited the kitchen, Mara turned back to her chores, dreading Carina's next remark.

It came soon enough. "Well, well, you've made yourself a conquest in—what?—scarcely more than the three weeks you've been home. I'd call that a record. You'll have all the local widows and spinsters green with envy."

Mara gritted her teeth, determined not to stoop to replying. *Grant me Your grace, Lord,* she prayed, going about her work. Her feelings for Mr. Jakeman were purely platonic. God knew that, so she needn't worry about what others thought.

She set a glass globe back on the kerosene lamp, willing her emotions to line up with her thoughts.

Gideon and Paul washed up at the outside pump then entered the kitchen through the woodshed. Despite telling himself it was no different than any supper he'd had in this house in the past when he'd helped Mrs. Blackstone with some chore or other, he felt a rising tide of excitement in his chest at the thought of sitting down at the table with Mrs. Keller.

She'd been out once to invite him and Paul into the kitchen to eat their noonday dinner from their lunch pails and had served them hot coffee, but she had quickly departed from the kitchen as soon as she'd poured their coffee.

He hadn't seen her all afternoon until she'd gone to fetch Lizzie.

The two had appeared up the road about an hour ago, talking and smiling, a sight which gratified him.

Dietrich had just called them in to supper. Gideon was tired, his shoulders and arms sore from all the sawing and splitting he'd done this afternoon. But he was satisfied that he and Paul had made a good dent in the logs he'd felled for Mrs. Blackstone's winter fuel.

He entered the kitchen alone, since Paul had just left for his own home. The kitchen was warm and brightly lit. Mrs. Keller stood at the cookstove, her black gown swathed in a light blue apron. Lizzie was slicing some bread on a bread-board. She smiled at the sight of him. Pleased that his daughter was making herself useful, he hung up his hat and coat.

"Mr. Jakeman, come sit by me." Dietrich jumped up from his chair at the table and pulled out the chair beside him. Gideon glanced at Mrs. Blackstone inquiringly. "Good evening, ma'am. It's obliging of you to have us for supper."

She stood at a chair at the head of the kitchen table. "That's quite all right. It isn't much. Please be seated."

"Thank you." Instead of complying, he went over to Mrs. Keller and took the soup tureen from her hands. Their hands touched briefly in the transfer. She looked downward, murmuring a brief "Thank you."

"Mmm, smells good," he said, to dispel the sensation the touch of her warm hands had caused inside him.

After carefully setting the tureen in the center of the table, afraid he'd slosh some over the side, he made sure everyone else was seated before standing behind the chair Dietrich indicated.

Mrs. Keller brought over the last dish. "Mr. Jakeman, please have a seat."

He still waited until she had taken her chair. She sat across from him, Lizzie beside her.

Mrs. Keller bowed her head, the rest following suit. "Dear Lord, thank You for the food set before us. Please bless it for our use, in your dear Son Jesus's name. Amen."

With a murmur of amens, they unfolded their napkins and Mrs. Keller began dishing out the chowder. She handed a bowl to Dietrich. "Please pass this to Mr. Jakeman."

The clam chowder was hot and delicious, the bread thick and soft. He savored every bite. There wasn't too much conversation as everyone ate. He felt too intimidated with both Mrs. Blackstone's and Mrs. Keller's presences to contribute much.

"Do you think you'll be able to come over soon to help me with my dress?" Lizzie asked Mrs. Keller.

Mrs. Blackstone lifted an eyebrow at Lizzie with a polite smile. "What dress is that?"

Lizzie smiled. "Mrs. Keller is going to help me make a dress for Thanksgiving."

"I see. How nice of you, Mara. I'm glad you have found the time with all your other endeavors."

Something in her tone sounded slightly acid to Gideon's ears. He cleared his throat, wiping his own mouth before speaking. "Lizzie is a good seamstress. She'll probably be able to finish it for herself if you can't."

After a quick look in his direction, Mrs. Keller directed her attention to Lizzie. He turned his head to catch the crest-fallen expression on his daughter's face. "B-but, Papa, I've never made a dress like this before."

He felt helpless, not wanting to disappoint his daughter nor cause Mrs. Keller more on top of all her duties. "Well, we'll see…" he mumbled. "My, this is delicious chowder," he said in a hearty voice, trying to change the subject. He eyed both widows, wondering whom the compliment should be addressed to.

"I taught Mara how to make chowder." Mrs. Blackstone gave a false-sounding laugh. "She came back to America knowing little of our ways of cooking. Only fancy European pastries, which most folks around here find too rich for their digestive systems. People around here like good, plain fare, isn't that right, Mr. Jakeman?"

His spoon halted halfway to his mouth. "Uh—yes, that's true." He observed Mrs. Keller's slim fingers curl around her napkin.

"I used to make clam chowder for…for my father, but it's been a long time," she said quietly. Not meeting his gaze, she turned to her son. "Don't slurp your soup."

"Dear me, no! It sounds disgusting," added Mrs. Blackstone.

Gideon swallowed his spoonful as silently as he dared then said, "I did enjoy that chocolate cake you took to the cider pressing. It was good, wasn't it, Lizzie?" He turned to his daughter for help, when all eyes turned on him.

She nodded, her mouth lifting in a smile. "Oh, yes, it was delicious. I even had a second helping."

Mrs. Keller smiled, but he could see it was strained. He

tried to think of another topic, hoping Lizzie would help make conversation. Usually, she was quite talkative, but she, too, seemed cowed by Mrs. Blackstone's presence. Even Dietrich was not his usual boisterous self.

He bent his head over his bowl, deciding he'd just finish up his supper as quickly as he could and get himself home with Lizzie.

The rest of the meal passed with Mrs. Blackstone asking him about a few people of the hamlet, correcting Dietrich for some perceived fault in his table manners and address-ing a thing or two to Mrs. Keller, mainly about household matters.

When Gideon finally rose, he felt relief. But he also felt he'd received a certain amount of insight into the Blackstone household.

Mrs. Keller seemed to do most of the work. He wondered how the late Mr. Blackstone had left his affairs to have his daughter under the thumb of his wife. And why Mrs. Keller would submit to it. He remembered their conversation on the ride home from town.

Gideon wondered how a famous concert pianist had not made enough to leave his son and wife provided for.

If anything happened to him, Lizzie had a house, acres of farm and woodland and a good bank account to her name.

Chapter Nine

A few afternoons later, Mara met Dietrich and Lizzie at the schoolhouse. Since the day Mr. Jakeman had bought the length of cloth for Lizzie's gown, Lizzie had been asking her to come by and help her cut it out.

She'd chosen today, because she knew Mr. Jakeman would still be chopping wood at Carina's. Since the night he'd stayed for supper, she'd hardly been able to look him in the eye. What impression had he taken away from that evening?

Had he seen the extent of her humiliating position, living off Carina's largesse, even when the house also belonged to her? She shuddered, partly in cold, partly in shame.

The door to the white, clapboard schoolhouse opened and the teacher dismissed the students. As soon as the children left the front step, they ran and scattered over the school yard despite the teacher's admonitions for decorum.

Dietrich ran over to Mara as soon as he saw his mother. "Hello, Mama, what are you doing here this afternoon?"

Mara smiled at her son. "I had a few minutes this afternoon and thought I'd come walk home with you…except we're not going home, I think."

Before Dietrich could ask her where they were going, she

spotted Lizzie emerging from the schoolhouse amidst all the boisterous children. She walked with another girl, her lunch pail swinging from her hand. When she saw Mara, her mouth broke open in a smile and she waved.

Excusing herself from her friend, she hurried over to Mara. "Hello, Mrs. Keller, how nice to see you. Are you here for Dietrich?"

She returned the girl's smile warmly. "Hello, Lizzie. Actually, I came to see you, too."

Hope rose in Lizzie. "Does this mean…?"

Mara nodded. "If you have time this afternoon, we could begin to make the pattern for your dress."

"Of course I have time! Let's go then."

Mara laughed.

Dietrich tugged on his mother's hand. "Does this mean you're going with us to the Jakemans'?"

"Yes, dear."

He began jumping up and down, still holding her hand, his own lunch pail clanging.

"Stand still, before your bucket comes off its handle. Now, if you're ready, we may be on our way." Although the day was sunny, the wind off the ocean was brisk, and Mara began to feel chilled from having stood there a few moments waiting for the school to be dismissed.

"Yes, let's," Lizzie agreed. She waved to her friends and stepped briskly along Mara's side.

The school was only about a quarter of an hour's walk from the Jakeman farm, along a dirt road skirting the curving, rocky coastline. The tide was out, leaving a wide expanse of mudflats strewn with rockweed. A few men were bent over double clamming.

Mara held the brim of her bonnet against the stiff breeze, listening to the children, both of whom addressed her without regarding the other.

As they neared the Jakemans', Mara took the time to

really look at the property. She had been in too much of a hurry the time before.

Mr. Jakeman owned some rolling fields of pastureland separated by stone walls and bordered by the dark green of spruce and balsam fir woodlots. Across the road was blueberry land, the fields reminding her of heather fields in Scotland, all fiery red now in their autumn color.

The meadows were still green although they'd had frost at night since September. But the fields had already been plowed, the dark soil lumpy and broken up. She knew from Lizzie and from his time at Carina's that Mr. Jakeman spent most of his days now sawing and chopping wood for the winter months, and that when the land was covered in snow, he'd go out into the woodlots to chop down logs for next year's firewood.

As they reached the house, the stone wall gave way to a white picket fence. Set back from the road behind three tall maple trees, their branches now bare, stood the cape-style house, its white shingles and black shutters neatly painted. Just like her own house, a woodshed was attached to the side of the house, which in turn was attached to a bright red barn, creating the impression of a much larger house than the simple cape.

Lizzie opened the white gate and ushered them through.

Everything was neat and trim. The grass short, the slate slabs set into the ground as a pathway clear of encroaching grass. Lilac bushes, also bare of their leaves, stood at the corners of the house and rugosa roses lined the spaces in between, but they were neatly pruned.

As with most families, the front door was rarely used, and Lizzie led them in through the woodshed.

"Wipe your feet off," Mara cautioned her son. A rope mat lay before the door. The woodshed was stacked floor-to-ceiling with chopped wood, the air redolent with its spicy fragrance. Despite being only a woodshed, its windows were brightly polished.

Lizzie opened the door to the kitchen. "Welcome to our house," she said with a shy smile.

"Thank you," Mara replied with a reassuring smile then she momentarily forgot the girl's presence. "Oh, what a lovely room!" She turned slowly, taking in the kitchen's details. A wide-planked floor was painted pine-green and didn't appear to have a speck of dust. An oval rag rug covered a large portion of it. Over this stood a good-size oval table of a burnished maple. A brass bowl filled with dried seed pods and branches with drying red berries graced the center.

A couple of high-backed rockers with calico cushions on their rush-bottom seats graced the space between the two front windows.

"Thank you," Lizzie said, her cheeks bright with pleasure. "I try to keep things the way…the way Mama always had them."

Mara entered farther into the room. "You've done a very good job. I commend you. I know it's not easy when you're so young and lose your mama."

Lizzie nodded, a look of gratitude in her gray-green eyes. "Well, let me get the fire going, 'cause I want to start work on the sewing."

"Oh, yes. We mustn't waste a moment. Thanksgiving is only a couple of weeks away."

Soon the kitchen was toasty-warm. They ate a quick snack of cookies and milk before Dietrich went out to see all the animals. Lizzie and Mara examined a few pictures of ladies' and young women's gowns in some magazines Mara had brought along.

They finally chose a pattern that was neither too juvenile nor too old for someone on the verge of young ladyhood.

Mara took her measurements and began to draw the pattern pieces for the gown.

"Are you sure these are going to end up looking like the gown we chose?" Lizzie looked doubtfully at the brown pieces of paper Mara had told her to cut out.

Mara laughed. "Yes, no matter how unlikely that appears now. The whole trick to patternmaking is to figure out how to transfer a three-dimensional garment into a two-dimensional pattern and then back again into a three-dimensional gown."

Mara continued jotting down measurements and using her ruler and curved instruments to draw the remaining pattern pieces.

"Mama used to make all our clothes," Lizzie said from where she stood cutting along Mara's lines. "She made the cushions on the rockers and the slipcovers on the sofa in the sitting room."

"She sounds very talented. She must have taught you a lot before she passed away."

"She tried to, but I don't think I listened very well back then. I just wanted to play with my dolls."

"That's only natural for a girl of nine."

"I wish I had paid more attention. After she was gone, I kept wishing she were here to ask her how to do something."

"Oh, course, sweetheart. I went through the same thing."

Lizzie looked at her and nodded. "I burnt so many dishes I tried to cook for Pa, yet he never complained. Whenever I'd cry, he'd just pat me on the shoulder and say, 'You did the best you could. It'll come out better next time.'" She smiled. "And, bless his heart, he ate everything I made, no matter how charred or dried out or curdled. He just sat down here at the table and ate every bite."

What a sweet man, Mara thought, imagining him coming in hungry and chilled from his work outside all day and sitting hunched over his plate, manly eating whatever was set before him.

Her own father had not been quite so understanding, though he had tried. But in the end, he had hired a cook, which had cut Mara to the quick, even though she realized her cooking was inedible for the most part. How she'd wished at the time that she'd had a woman to show her how to do for her father.

But in the end, she'd needed no one, because her father met Carina.

Lizzie continued speaking while Mara's thoughts were in the past. "Cousin Sarah came as often as she could and began teaching me how to make things better. She taught me all kinds of things Ma had begun to, like churning butter, putting up vegetables, darning socks, knitting and crocheting. Soon, I started being able to do them on my own."

"Your father must have been very proud."

Lizzie nodded. "The best times for me were when he'd clean his plate and sit back and sigh, and tell me that was as good as Mama had always made. And I knew then that he wasn't just saying those things to be nice. I could tell by the way he ate them with real gusto that they had come out good." She smiled. "Why, I could taste them myself!"

"Of course you could."

Dietrich ran into the kitchen at that moment. "May I bring Samson inside, please?"

"He usually doesn't come in till the sun goes down, but I guess he can come in. Just make sure his paws are clean."

Dietrich hardly heard the last words as he ran back out the kitchen door.

Lizzie shook her head. "Boys sure are different than girls."

Mara laughed. "That is so. You're probably not used to them, and Dietrich makes up for about three. I hope he hasn't made a nuisance of himself here."

"Aw, no. Pa dotes on him. And Pa has a way about him. He's gentle but he's firm. Dietrich obeys him."

"Yes, I've noticed that."

As they spoke, the two continued working. Mara straightened from the table. "There, that should do it for the pattern pieces. I'll help you finish cutting them and then we can lay them out on the fabric."

She glanced at her watch. "Although we shan't have time today. It's getting later than I thought."

Dietrich threw open the door again, the large black dog bounding in behind him and coming straight to his mistress.

"Settle down, you overgrown beast, before you tear my pattern piece," she said, shoving him away.

When she'd finished cutting her pattern piece, Lizzie set down her scissors. "What I meant to say before this dog interrupted me was, would you like to stay for supper?"

Mara felt torn, a part of her wanting nothing better, the other, more rational part, knowing it was wiser to go home. Carina expected her, and Mara didn't want to have to endure her insinuations afterward. "I don't think so…" she began but was interrupted immediately by wails from both children.

"But you promised us you'd come to our house for supper the next time—"

"Oh, Mama, may we, please? Please say yes!" He began tugging her skirts, continuing to clamor.

"Hush, Dietrich, you're not letting me think!"

Samson got up and started barking, circling around Dietrich. Into this din stepped Mr. Jakeman.

"Whoa, what's going on here?" He held up a hand, his glance going from Dietrich to Lizzie and coming to rest on Mara. She could feel her cheeks grow warm at the look of concern in his eyes.

The next second, he called the dog's name in a sharp tone. Samson obeyed immediately, coming over to him and offering him his nose, his shaggy tail wagging. As Mr. Jakeman stroked his head, he said, "Dietrich, why don't you simmer down and let your mother tell me what's afoot."

"Oh, nothing, really," she began, reaching up to a lock at the nape of her neck. "I was just getting ready to go home. I didn't realize it was so late. Your dinner will probably be delayed since I kept Lizzie so long."

"Papa, I just asked Mrs. Keller to stay for supper with us. Remember, she promised to come to our house when she was here last?"

"Of course, I remember." His gaze rested once more on Mara, and she wondered what was going through his mind. Did he see her as some designing female, out to win his daughter in order to connive her way to him? "You're more than welcome to stay."

"Thank you, but, I…ah…don't think so. I mean, I wasn't able to inform Mrs. Blackstone."

He waved a hand. "That shouldn't be a problem. Dietrich and I can walk over and let her know so she won't worry. That would give Lizzie time to get supper ready."

Lizzie surprised her by taking both her hands. "Oh, please say yes, Mrs. Keller. I know it's not much. I was just going to make some fish cakes. I've already got the fish flaked and the mashed potatoes cooked up. It won't take long. I know it's nothing fancy the way you're probably used to—"

She couldn't let the girl think she was used to fancy fare—nor could she bear to destroy the hopeful look in her eyes. "Not at all. I happen to love fish cakes, and I can help you if you'd like. I just didn't want us to impose on you both without any notice."

"Impose—oh, fiddle! You've helped me all afternoon with my dress."

Mr. Jakeman rubbed his hands together. "Well, it looks like it's settled then. I'll go along with Dietrich and get ourselves out of your hair, ladies." His smile took away any sting, and warmed Mara's heart in a way she considered out of proportion to his simple intention.

With a nod of his head, he took Samson by the collar and held out his other hand to Dietrich, who took it readily.

When they'd left, Lizzie turned to her. "I'm so glad you're staying. The time has just flown and I feel as if we've still loads to talk about…"

As Lizzie chattered away, and began clearing up the table, Mara paused a moment at the kitchen window. The tall, strongly built man walked briskly down the drive with the slight, slim boy swinging him by the hand, the dog running along ahead of them. Dietrich was looking upward and saying something, his face bright with enthusiasm and something more. Admiration.

He'd never looked at his own father in that way.

Fear, awe or watchfulness were the way he'd regarded Klaus, unsure what kind of mood Klaus was in.

Would he give him a careless hello or would he yell at him, or yell at her to get the child out of his way because his nerves couldn't take his noise and restlessness?

Mara clutched the curtain, her heart going out to Dietrich, yet at the same time fearful that he'd build up his expectations too high with Mr. Jakeman.

Her son didn't realize that he would probably never have a father. Mara had vowed never to give her heart to another man or to subjugate herself legally through marriage. She was finally free and she must keep her freedom at whatever costs.

She'd learned a hard lesson on the loss of her freedom the day she'd married Dietrich's father. And paid too high a price.

The only good thing to come out of that union was Dietrich. And she lived in daily dread that Dietrich would exhibit the same high-strung tendencies as his father.

She'd done everything possible to train him up in the right

way. And she'd spent hours on her knees praying that Dietrich would have a stable, steady personality.

But every time she saw him exhibit excitement and enthusiasm, she felt a spasm of fear, not wanting to quench any normal boyish high spirits, but terrified that they were the first sign of his father's instability beginning to manifest itself.

Chapter Ten

Gideon walked along with Dietrich, finding he liked the feel of the much smaller hand in his.

"Mr. Jakeman, I saw the turkeys. They're getting fatter and fatter. Do you know which one we're having for Thanksgiving dinner?"

"Not yet. Probably the biggest and fattest since I'll be giving it to Mrs. McClellan and she has quite a crowd to feed on Thanksgiving. But I'll have to butcher a few to give to some other folks who won't have one of their own turkeys."

Dietrich looked up at him, his brown eyes scrunched in puzzlement. "Why don't they have one of their own?"

"Maybe they don't have a farm. Maybe they've gotten too old to farm. Maybe a widow lives alone because her husband died, and she doesn't have a yard where she can raise a turkey. Maybe someone lives in town and doesn't have the money to buy one. Maybe the father lost his job and doesn't have the money to buy a turkey this year."

"Because they're poor?"

"Some of them, yes."

Dietrich looked down at his feet thoughtfully. After a few minutes he spoke. "Maybe if you had lived near us in Paris, you'd have had to give *us* a turkey."

Gideon chuckled. "I don't think you were poor."

Dietrich puckered his lips. "I think we were. I often heard Mama tell Papa there wasn't enough money for something he wanted her to buy. He was always in bed, sick, and he'd ask for things, and she had to tell him there wasn't any money. Some days there was hardly any food. Lots of times Mama went to bed with no supper. She always gave me what she had and had to fix special things for Papa, since he couldn't eat hardly anything."

"I see." Gideon didn't know how accurate a six-year-old's memory would be, but he did know that the boy had a keen eye for observation.

When they arrived at Mrs. Blackstone's farm, Gideon greeted Paul, who was milking the cow in the barn, before walking with Dietrich through the woodshed to the kitchen. He was going to knock but Dietrich pushed open the door.

Gideon made sure to knock loudly on the doorpost and call out, "Hallo!"

Mrs. Blackstone stepped into the kitchen from another room. "Oh—" She started at the sight of him. "I didn't expect you, Mr. Jakeman. What may I do for you?"

For some reason her simple question made him feel uncomfortable. He clutched his cap in his hands. "I just stopped by to let you know that Mrs. Keller is at my place. She—uh, is having a bite of supper with Lizzie and me. If that's all right with you. Didn't want you to worry…"

The widow arched a dark eyebrow. Even though he judged she was a woman in her mid-fifties, her hair and eyebrows were still dark. He sometimes wondered if she dyed them. None of his business, he chided himself.

"Indeed? Well, I must thank you, Mr. Jakeman, for being so thoughtful as to come all the way here to let me know. I would have waited for her for supper."

He shifted his weight from one foot to the other, wondering how soon he could excuse himself, but her words for some reason made him feel guilty, as if he were taking Mrs. Keller away from where she belonged. That was nonsense. She'd only just moved here barely a month ago. "That's all right, ma'am. We only live a stone's throw from each other." He tried to smile. "Gave me an excuse to get out of the kitchen."

Mrs. Blackstone placed her hands on the back of one of the kitchen chairs and smiled. "Is our premier widower finally going to succumb to the allure of a lady's out-of-town charm?"

Gideon felt his face grow hot. "Mrs. Keller is just helping Lizzie sew her new frock. You heard them the other night."

She wagged a finger at him. "All right, you may play the innocent and ignore the little machinations we females go to to attract an eligible bachelor. You know she's not so young anymore—thirty, I believe, if not more. You can't blame her if she sets her cap at you."

The longer he stood there, the more troubled he felt. It was as if Mrs. Blackstone were insinuating things about Mrs. Keller that he couldn't imagine. "You have it all wrong, Mrs. Blackstone. She's just helping out my Lizzie."

"Ah, well, you may believe what you want. I only warn you so you may realize what an eligible bachelor you are and be on your guard!" She ended with a titter.

"I'd better be off. Come along, Dietrich. She won't be back late," he threw over his shoulder before closing the kitchen door, feeling as if he was escaping a viper's nest.

"Was she mad?"

"What?" He was so lost in thought he was surprised at Dietrich's voice when they were back outside. "No, I don't think so."

Dietrich shrugged. "She always sounds mad to me."

Gideon chuckled.

"She's usually mad at me."

Gideon patted the boy's shoulder. "Oh, I wouldn't pay too

much attention. Some people are angry all the time and take it out on those around them. Maybe that's what's happened with Mrs. Blackstone."

He knew his words were small comfort, but he had a hard time trying to figure things out for the boy when he was having enough trouble figuring them out for himself.

It didn't sound as if Mrs. Keller had had it too easy in the past nor did she have it so well with the Widow Blackstone. Gideon shook off the woman's insinuations. He had no designs on Mrs. Keller nor did he believe she had any on him, but the widow's words made it seem as if they were doing something wrong. They were helping each other out with their only children. He was more grateful than he could express in words to Mrs. Keller for taking time from her busy schedule to help his Lizzie.

He would never believe the lady was doing it for some ulterior, selfish motive.

"You're walking awfully fast, Mr. Jakeman. I'm going to have to run to keep up with you!"

He looked down at his young companion, not having realized how his irritation had quickened his pace. It was as if he'd wanted to run away from the taint Mrs. Blackstone had put on his daughter's friendship with Mrs. Keller.

Once they reentered his own kitchen, he could dismiss the odious insinuations. Mrs. Keller and Lizzie were talking and laughing and seemed to be getting along as if they had known each other all their lives.

He smiled at the picture they made. Mrs. Keller smiled at him from the table where she was finishing with the place settings.

"Good, there you are, Papa. We're ready to eat." Lizzie waved a spatula at him from the stove.

He sniffed deeply. "My, it smells good in here."

"The sooner you two wash up, the sooner we'll eat."

He winked at Dietrich. "Hear that, young fellow?"

The boy nodded vigorously. "I'm starving!"

Gideon helped him off with his jacket and hung it on a peg with his cap and followed suit with his own things. "Come along then. Let's wash up."

When they were seated around the table, he bowed his head and led them in grace. As everyone echoed his "Amen," he looked around the table, unfolding his napkin.

Lizzie sat at her accustomed place at his right. She'd never wanted to occupy her mother's place at the end of the long oval table. Mrs. Keller had seated herself at the far left before either he or Lizzie could indicate a place for her. Dietrich sat at her side between the two of them.

If Mrs. Blackstone thought Mrs. Keller a conniving widow, she didn't know much about her. Mrs. Keller had hardly spoken to him or met his eyes, addressing most of her quiet remarks to either Lizzie or her son. He frowned, bending his head to cut a piece of his golden fish cake and spear it onto his fork. He hoped she wasn't afraid of him or put off by him. She'd seemed much more at ease when he'd entered.

He wanted to reassure her he meant her no disrespect or had no designs on her.

But he was intrigued by what Dietrich had told him and he did want to find out more about her.

"Mmm. These are delicious," he told his daughter, sitting back after easing his first hunger pangs.

"Mrs. Keller showed me how to add a little red pepper."

He glanced her way. She immediately averted her gaze and he found his face flushing, and he could have cursed Mrs. Blackstone for putting thoughts into his head that wouldn't normally have been there.

Or, would they? A little voice asked him, as he remembered holding her in his arms in that waltz in the dark. He cleared his throat and took a sip of water. "Tell me how the sewing is coming."

"Oh, Papa, Mrs. Keller is so good at making patterns. We already decided what kind of dress to make. She took all the measurements and drew the pattern and we finished cutting out all the pieces right when you came in."

"Goodness, it sounds like you're a seamstress." He deliberately looked at Mrs. Keller, resolving to find out more about her past.

She laid down her fork and patted the napkin to her lips— nicely shaped lips against smooth pale skin. "I've sewn my own garments since I was a girl. My mother taught me, and when she died, I just continued. I used to make my father's shirts." She addressed this last remark to Lizzie.

"I do, too," his daughter answered eagerly, "but maybe you can show me how I can do better."

Mrs. Keller glanced his way—or rather at his shirt, and he lifted his hand self-consciously to his collar, realizing he wasn't wearing one. Usually he only did so when he went to church on Sundays. Her husband had probably always worn one. He imagined a man dressed in starched linen and tailcoat as he walked onstage to perform before crowds.

"You seem to be doing a fine job on your own," Mrs. Keller said. "You've probably had lots of practice by now."

"Yes'm, that's so."

"Mama, Mr. Jakeman says he's going to bring the biggest turkey to their Thanksgiving dinner at the McClellans'. Are we going to go there, too?"

Seeing she was at a loss to answer, Gideon replied for her. "Mrs. Blackstone usually spends Thanksgiving there. I'm sure my cousin means to include the two of you in her invitation."

"We'll see." Mrs. Keller's slim, long-fingered hand rested on the table, clutching her napkin.

"Oh, I do hope you'll go," Lizzie said at once. "I was hoping I could stop by on our way and you can tell me how the dress looks."

"Why, of course. Please stop in." She looked at him. "Do you think if I spoke to Mrs. McClellan, she would let me know what we could contribute to the feast?"

"I'm sure Mrs. Blackstone will let you know. She usually brings something—a jar of preserves or something—but Sarah has such a tableful of food that nothing is really necessary."

"Very well."

As the dinner progressed, Lizzie drew Mrs. Keller out with questions about her life in Europe. Gideon tried not to appear to be listening as closely as he was.

Mrs. Keller obliged his daughter with a few amusing anecdotes of life as the wife of a pianist touring the famous capitals, but then added in a more serious tone, "But then he grew ill. At first we were hopeful that he would overcome it. He had some of the best doctors. But once he resumed the…the strenuous life of giving concerts, the consumption returned."

"That's too bad," Lizzie said in a quiet voice.

"He finally had to give up his playing. That was very difficult for him. The last few years were spent quietly. I was nursing him and taking care of Dietrich, of course."

Gideon got the impression that there was much more to her brief narrative. Between her words and Dietrich's earlier, Gideon began to form a picture of hardship once the late Mr. Keller had had to give up his concert playing. Was that when the financial hardships had begun?

Before he could decide whether to change the subject, Mrs. Keller looked at him with a soft smile. "But we've heard enough about Europe this evening. I would much prefer to hear about Eagle's Bay. What was it like in your childhood, Mr. Jakeman?"

He felt his face flush under her kind regard. "Well, I don't know, not much has changed in these parts since I was a boy."

"Papa, tell them about the time you fell in the ice pond."

His lips curved upward at his daughter. Thank goodness for his Lizzie, who always knew how to get things back on a more comfortable footing.

Dietrich's eyes rounded. "You fell through the ice? Did you freeze?"

"Just about. Let's see, I must have been about your age, maybe a year or two older. My older brothers and I had gone to check the ice on the pond to see if it was thick enough for skating."

"Where did you live then?" Mrs. Keller asked.

"Right here."

Her eyes widened slightly. "In this house?"

He nodded. "It's my homestead. My father's and grand-father's before me. My granddaddy built the original structure—what we're sitting in right now—with the first people who settled in this hamlet." He gestured around the low-beamed room with his hand.

Mrs. Keller and her son looked around them. "It seems very snug and cozy."

"It is. It was built from logs split right here on the property—oak, chestnut, pine. My daddy added on the shed and, along with my brothers and me, we pulled down the original barn and put up the one we have now."

"How many brothers do you have?"

"Three, and a sister," he said proudly. "We're scattered around the hamlet all the way to the next village down the coast."

"How nice to have such a large family."

He chuckled. "Besides them, there's a whole bunch of aunts and uncles and cousins."

The children began to talk more and more, Dietrich quizzing Lizzie on her large family, and she to ask him about his German relatives. Gideon felt himself grow more relaxed.

Soon he found himself talking more of his boyhood years and the hamlet, more than he had in a long time.

Mrs. Keller spoke the least, but he hoped she was feeling more comfortable as well. He found by the end of supper that he had enjoyed his meal in a way he hadn't…since Elsie had passed away.

The thought brought him up short.

He enjoyed the companionship of his daughter, but it had been a while since he'd enjoyed the company of an adult around his table—an adult who shared and seemed to understand his concerns for his daughter, and for whose son he could offer a guiding role.

When Lizzie got up to help clear the table, Mara suddenly realized how late it was. She stood immediately. "Thank you both so much. That was delicious."

Mr. Jakeman followed suit, stretching. Mara tore her gaze from his broad chest.

"I'm going out to get the animals in. I'll bring the wagon around to take you home."

"Oh, no, Dietrich and I will walk," she said. "It's a lovely evening."

"Very well, but I'll walk you home then."

Before she could protest, he left the kitchen, Dietrich following along behind him.

As Lizzie chattered about her new dress, pouring hot water into the dishpan, Mara finished clearing the table, her thoughts on the pleasant meal. How different from the meals she and Dietrich shared with Carina.

"I hope you can come by again tomorrow, Mrs. Keller." Lizzie looked at her shyly, her hands submerged in the soapy water.

"Let's see… Yes, I think I can. I'll get you started and then the following day I have to go to town to give piano lessons." She shook her head with a smile. "I must also teach my female pupils how to be young ladies."

Instead of laughing, a wistful note crept into Lizzie's voice. "I wish I knew how to become a lady."

"Being a lady is more a state of mind than any set of rules."

Lizzie swished a rag over a plate and dunked it into the rinse water. "Yes, but ladies do things and say things in a certain way. Anyone can see right away you're a lady." She shook her head with a laugh as she placed the dish on the rack. "Why, you probably talked the least of us at the table, and yet, anyone coming in would have said, 'What a lady.' They'd look at me and say, 'What an awkward teenager.'"

Mara took the dish and began to dry it. "Oh, I could easily teach you a few more tricks of the trade." She meant to be facetious but Lizzie took her seriously, sending her a look full of hope and eagerness.

"Would you really? I'd be so grateful. You were ever so helpful before that last sociable." She turned her attention back to a dish, swabbing it with new vigor. "I'd certainly show that Paul I'm no silly girl!"

Mara set down the dry plate and took another. "Is this what this is all about?" she said with a chuckle.

Lizzie glanced over her shoulder, a spark of fear in her eyes. "No. It has nothing to do with him!"

Mara was careful not to smile. "Of course not. Well, we'll fit in a few lessons on deportment when I come by to help you sew your gown."

As they finished tidying the kitchen, Gideon and Dietrich came back into the kitchen. Mara took up her hat and cloak. "We'd best be on our way. Carina will wonder what's been keeping me." She retied her bonnet ribbons with hands that began to shake at the thought of Carina's reception.

Gideon took the cloak from her and set it on her shoulders. "Oh—thank you." Her voice sounded flustered, but she attributed it to her worry over Carina, and not to the warm regard in his eyes.

When she stepped toward Lizzie to bid her good-night, the girl put out her arms and the two embraced lightly. "See you tomorrow after school then. Thank you for a lovely supper. Good night."

"Good night, Mrs. Keller. Thank you…you know…for everything."

Mara was conscious of Gideon's larger frame behind her as she walked through the dim woodshed. Dietrich ran ahead of them and waited outside.

Gideon cleared his throat. "Mrs. Keller—"

She turned and stopped short at how close he stood. "Yes, Mr. Jakeman?"

"I just wanted to say how much I appreciate your taking the time with Lizzie."

She let out a sigh of relief that it was only that. Her heart had begun to beat like a trip hammer. "You don't have to thank me for that," she said softly.

He fingered the edges of his hat, his eyes not meeting hers. "She hasn't known a mother in many years, and I realize she is turning into a woman before I can seem to teach her the things she…she's going to need to know."

Her heart went out to him. How much he cared for his daughter—his conversation mirrored Lizzie's own with her just moments before, as if he had overheard it. "I…I offered to teach her a few things about being ladylike, only because she asked me to," she hastened to add. "I wouldn't do so otherwise. But I wanted to have your permission as well."

Warm gratitude filled his eyes. "You have it."

"I don't mean to presume—"

"You're not, ma'am, not at all." He inhaled, expanding his chest. "Fact is, I'd be grateful. I could lend a hand with your Dietrich, that is, if you wouldn't take it amiss."

A relief so vast it threatened to undo her filled her so suddenly that she reached out and touched his forearm before she realized what she was doing. "Oh, no! I am thankful for all you've done already." Only then did she realize how much she'd wanted—needed—someone like this for her Dietrich. She removed her hand, curling her fingers into her palm. What would he think? "I-it's been…difficult. He has been through so much…after Klaus fell ill…and I fear I'm not doing a very good job making things right for him." Her voice thickened.

"You seem to be doing fine, Mrs. Keller." Gideon's voice was gruff. "Sometimes a boy needs a man to talk to."

She raised her eyes slowly to his. "Yes." He did understand.

The seconds lengthened. He cleared his throat again. "Yes, well, as I said, I can take him along with me sometimes after school and show him some things, how to do a few chores around the farm."

She tried to keep her thoughts on Dietrich and what Gideon was saying. "Would you? I need to leave early sometimes to go to town, and it's difficult for Mrs. Blackstone to know what to do with a young boy, and she fears he will hinder Paul in this duties."

She had the sense he understood more than she was saying. Her heart swelled, wishing for things she didn't dare articulate.

Chapter Eleven

Mara pinned the last section of the dress hem and sat back on her heels. "There, let's see if that's long enough."

Lizzie peered at herself in the full-length mirror in the upstairs sitting room. "Do you think it's all right?"

"Step back a bit and let's see." Mara stood and eyed the girl's gown. They'd been working at it diligently every spare moment for a week now. Lizzie had been sewing every evening on her own. She stood now in the sleeveless bodice and skirt. An overskirt and sleeves had yet to be added.

"Turn around slowly," Mara instructed. The gown just brushed Lizzie's ankles.

"Are you sure it's long enough? I don't want to look like a little girl."

Mara smiled. "Don't be in such a hurry to grow up, dear."

Lizzie pulled at the bodice, arching her back as if to push out her chest. "Being looked at as a pesky girl is no fun."

"Is Paul still teasing you?"

Lizzie glanced at her with something like panic in her eyes. "He and all the rest," she said, her lips turned down.

"Don't worry, they won't tease you for long. Soon they'll be tripping over each other to ask you to dance."

"Hah! That'd be the day."

"I think the length is fine. I'm glad I chose the tartan plaid for the overskirt. It will look very nice with this dark green serge."

"And I can have a bustle."

Mara met her eyes in the mirror. "A small one."

Lizzie pulled up her two braids atop her head and continued looking at herself in the glass. "I wish I had someplace else to wear it besides Thanksgiving."

"Hmm. There'll be church."

She sighed. "Yes."

Mara made an effort to think of something. "Perhaps we could plan a little social event, since you've been doing so well with your lessons at being ladylike."

Lizzie's mouth widened in a grin. "Truly? Oh, that would be wonderful. What about a tea party for us? You've been teaching me to do everything so properly. We could make little cakes."

Mara nodded, catching her enthusiasm. "We could use the best linens and nice china. I have a tea set my mother gave me. I only use it for special occasions." She smiled in reminiscence. "It's the only thing I brought home with me from my years in Europe. It's traveled everywhere with me."

Lizzie clapped her hands together. "I have a nice embroidered tablecloth that my mother made me. It's my favorite, with flowers all along the border."

"It will be like a bit of springtime in winter." Mara focused on the present. "Very well, why don't you take off the gown? We'll press the hem to mark it. In the meantime, I shall begin on the sleeves. But you'd better get home now before it gets dark."

"Mrs. Keller, why do you always talk as if growing up is so bad?"

Mara stopped in the act of unpinning the back of the girl's bodice, brought up short at the question. "Do I do that?"

"Well, you're always saying not to be too anxious to grow

up. Is it so bad being an adult?" Lizzie pulled off the bodice and faced Mara, her eyes honest.

Mara helped her take off the rest of the gown, pondering her answer. Did she appear that way? "Not at all. I just want you to enjoy your youth while you have it."

Lizzie pulled on her cotton shirt and buttoned it before donning her dark blue work skirt. "Didn't you enjoy yours?"

Mara folded the gown, careful of the pins in its hem. "I did. My father and I were quite happy together." She made an effort to smile. "Like you and your father. But suddenly it was over. He remarried…and I went away to school." She placed the gown on a chair and folded her arms, looking out the small octagonal window which faced the bay across the road. The marsh grass blew in the wind and whitecaps topped the incoming waves. The skies were gray and threatening. They would probably have a nor'easter in the night.

"Was Mrs. Blackstone a bad stepmother?"

"What?" The direct question startled her. "I— No, no, she wasn't. I mean, I never really lived with her." She turned from the window and smoothed down her skirt.

"She seems, I don't know, friendly in some ways, but sometimes I get the sense she doesn't really like you."

How discerning the young could be. Mara tried to laugh it off. "Oh, no. She's been very gracious. But it was probably a bit of an adjustment having me come to live with her. She didn't expect me to suddenly become a widow just after she had become one, too."

"Do you miss your husband?"

Her glance flew once more to the girl's. Goodness, where did all these questions come from?

Lizzie smiled, her freckled cheeks growing red. "I'm sorry. Papa says I need to bite my tongue before the words come out. I'm just curious. I missed Mama something awful when she first died. I can't imagine what it must be like when a person loses a husband or wife. I know Papa grieved a long time, though he didn't cry or anything. But I could tell he was hurting."

The girl's words disarmed Mara and she reached out a hand to her. "Of course, dear. I understand." She pictured the strong, silent Mr. Jakeman hurting for the absence of his wife. The fact that he hadn't remarried in all these years was proof that he mourned her still.

"What was it like for you? Dietrich hardly talks about his papa."

Mara looked down, pressing her lips together, thinking how to reply. She didn't want to be dishonest with the girl, yet she didn't want to tell her the truth. The truth was too sordid for a young girl's ears. "My husband was ill for a long time, so I think that helped soften the blow of his eventual departure. Dietrich was very young, and we didn't want to risk contagion, so he saw less and less of his father even though he lived under the same roof." She sighed deeply. "By the time Klaus, my husband, passed away, Dietrich hardly knew him, and I... Well, he was suffering so much, that it was more a blessed release than a tragedy."

Lizzie nodded. "It was like that with Mama, too, but only for a short while. She fell sick. Doctor said it was pneumonia. It was in the dead of winter. Pa and I nursed her, but it didn't do no good. She was dead in a week." The girl's eyes had filled with tears at the end, and she swiped at the corner of one eye with the edge of her sleeve. "But it seemed like she was there one day and gone the next. It didn't seem fair. I missed her so much. I still do."

Mara gathered her in her arms. Her thin shoulders shook in Mara's embrace.

"I know I shouldn't cry anymore. It's been five years and I know she's gone to be with Jesus. He must've had a reason to call her home so soon. Reverend Grayson says she's in a better place, but, oh, it was so hard to get used to having her gone."

"I know, dear. It must still be hard." As she spoke in soothing tones, she rubbed the girl's back as if she were a child. "I still miss my mother at times."

Lizzie sniffed and looked up at her. "Do you really?"

Mara nodded. "I'll want to ask her something. I guess you never get over things like that with people you were close to, like you with your mother, and your father with…with her."

Lizzie fished her handkerchief out of her pocket and wiped her face, stepping away from Mara. "Yeah, I know Papa still misses her something awful. He hasn't ever met anyone else even though folks like Cousin Sarah keep telling him he should marry again, that he's too young to go on pining." She sniffed one final time and smiled. "Of course, if he ever met someone like *you,* I wouldn't mind at all!"

Mara stared at the girl, who was gazing at her shyly. Then as the moment grew awkward, she gave a short, nervous laugh to dissipate the tension. "Why, thank you, Lizzie. That means a lot to me. Of course, you know I wouldn't have to marry someone like your dad to be close to you. We can be great friends. Isn't it nice that we live nearby to each other?"

Lizzie nodded, her smile appearing a bit wobbly. "Oh, sure." She tilted her head. "Would you mind marrying someone like Pa?"

"Of course not. Your father seems a very fine man." She fiddled with a strand of hair at her nape, praying for the right words. "It's just that I…I'm like your father, I guess. I decided I wasn't going to remarry."

Lizzie's eyes widened. "Ever again?"

Mara tried to smile in an effort to make light of the subject. "That's right."

"Was it because you loved your husband so much?"

Mara swallowed. How had the topic gotten so far? She usually managed to steer conversations away from anything too personal in her life. But then she'd never befriended anyone of Lizzie's age—a girl still young enough to be completely honest and expecting the same from the adults close to her. "No, that's not the reason." She looked away. "It's a—"

Before she could think of what to say that didn't sound as if she were shutting the girl out, Lizzie came up to her and put a hand on her shoulder. "It's all right, Mrs. Keller. You don't have to talk about it if it's too hurtful."

Mara nodded, finding it hard to swallow, let alone speak. "Thank you," she finally managed to whisper.

Just then they heard the door downstairs open. "Halloo, anyone home? Mara, where are you?" came Carina's sharp voice up the stairwell.

The two broke apart. "I'm up here," Mara called from the top of the stairs, to alert Carina before she said something unpleasant. "We're coming down."

Carina stood at the bottom of the stairs as Lizzie and Mara trooped down. "I was just trying on my new gown, Mrs. Blackstone," Lizzie said.

"I see." Carina touched a corner of the gown as Lizzie reached her. "How pretty."

"It should be ready for Thanksgiving. Are you going to join us at the McClellans' as usual?"

"Yes, I suppose so." Her gaze rested on Mara in a way she found speculative.

"I'd best be on my way. Papa will be coming by with Dietrich."

Mara turned to the kitchen in anticipation of seeing her son. Funny how she hadn't worried at all, knowing he was with Gideon. "He doesn't have to come by. I could go and fetch him."

"He said he had to come anyway. He wants to help Paul with something."

Mara began supper preparations, all the while unable to stifle a sense of expectancy at seeing Gideon step in at any moment with Dietrich. Lizzie's words came back to her, filling her with concern. She could dismiss Carina's insinuations with a shrug. It was much harder to do so with an innocent girl's.

If Lizzie began to read things into Mara's friendship with her father, Mara must have done something to have the girl misconstrue their relationship.

She'd tried so hard not to evince any interest in the widower. She'd only agreed to stay to dinner because she'd seen no way to refuse politely. She'd helped Gideon pick out the material for his daughter's dress because she truly wanted to help the girl.

The kitchen door banged open and she whirled around to see Dietrich run in. "I'm back, Mama. The kitties are growing so big. Mayn't I bring one home soon before they get too big?"

Gideon came into the kitchen and closed the door softly behind him. Mara found herself blushing as her eyes met his. He dipped his head, removing his battered hat. "Evenin', Mrs. Keller."

She wiped her hands dry on her apron. "Good evening, Mr. Jakeman." Before she could say more, Carina entered the kitchen.

"Goodness, boy, you mustn't bang the door like that. I could feel the house shudder all the way to the parlor. Good evening, Mr. Jakeman. We do seem to be seeing a lot of you these days."

An uncomfortable silence followed the remark. Mr. Jakeman clutched at his hat. "I've just come to fetch Lizzie."

"I'm all ready, Papa." She grasped her cloak and scarf from the peg by the door.

"I also wondered if I could come by soon to help Paul bank up the house before we get the first snow."

"That would be very kind of you. You know you're always welcome here." Carina's tone had become as sweet as molasses. Mara turned away from her, always amazed at how easily her stepmother could change her demeanor.

"Dietrich, wash up, supper's almost ready. Please thank Mr. Jakeman for bringing you home." She didn't dare meet Gideon's eyes again as she spoke his name.

Her words seemed to remind Dietrich of his original purpose. "Mama, may I bring home the kittie?"

"Kitten? What's this about a kitten?" Carina looked pointedly at her.

"Our cat had a litter, Mrs. Blackstone. Dietrich has taken a fancy to one little fellow. Pure Coon, he is. But Mrs. Keller wanted to wait to ask you."

Carina folded her hands in front of her skirt. "Well, I should think so. I have my own Miss Lettie, our barn cat. She wouldn't like any more of her kind around. But thank you for the offer."

"Oh, Mama, please—"

Mara shot him a warning glance. "Shush, Dietrich. We can talk about it later."

He tugged on her arm. "But Mama—"

"Come along, Lizzie, we'd best be going. So long, Dietrich." Gideon stepped forward and gave the boy a squeeze on the shoulder with his large hand. "Mind your mama." With those quiet words, he winked at Mara and then turned and headed to the door.

Mara watched his departing back. Lizzie gave her a quick wave and smile. "Thanks, Mrs. Keller, for your help."

Mara lifted her hand, hardly aware of her surroundings, her mind replaying Gideon's kind yet firm tone with Dietrich and his understanding look at her.

The next afternoon Gideon spent a good part of the day hauling hay and leaves to put around the foundations of his house to insulate it from any chinks where the cold could get in. He glanced at the gray skies. Any day now they'd have the first snow.

Lizzie came out to help him after their noonday dinner.

"Are you going over to Mrs. Keller's this afternoon?"

She brought a rakeful of hay to the edge of the house. "No, she's not home this afternoon. She went to town."

"That's right, to give lessons." He'd forgotten it was Thursday. He wondered if he could come up with any reason to go to town. It would be a cold, windy walk home for her. "How're your lessons with her going?" he asked.

Her face lit up. "Very well. The dress is more'n halfway finished. We decided we are going to have a tea party—a real one, where I can wear the dress and Mrs. Keller will use her best tea set—one that she's had since she was a girl," she said. "It was her mother's. You'll be invited, you and Dietrich." Her lips turned downward. "And Mrs. Blackstone, I suppose."

He leaned on his rake. "Sounds like quite a party."

She gave him a mischievous look. "You'll have to dress up just like if you're going to church."

"Hmm." After getting another load of hay, he asked, "When's this tea party going to be?"

"Probably after Thanksgiving. Mrs. Keller said I'd better not risk spilling anything on my dress."

"I'm sure you won't do any such thing."

After some moments of working together, she said, "Do you think Mrs. Blackstone likes them?"

He frowned, bringing his thoughts from Mara and the help she was with his daughter, to the older widow lady. "What's that?"

"Mrs. Blackstone. Have you noticed how she always seems to be scolding Dietrich for something, and even though she seems polite to Mrs. Keller, there's always something a little mean in her words? Do you know what I mean?"

Gideon chewed on a stalk of hay, not wanting to encourage his daughter in seeing more than there might be. "She seems pleasant enough."

Lizzie shook the hay from her skirt. "Pleasant like an adder before she bites."

He gave his daughter a sharp look, surprised at the perspicacity in her words. "Well, don't go saying anything to them about it."

She cast him an affronted look. "Of course not. I'm not that irresponsible!"

"Of course you're not. I apologize. I just think if there's anything going on there, Mrs. Keller probably has enough trouble handling it. She doesn't need any fuel added to the fire."

"Maybe we can have them over again for supper. That was fun the other night, don't you think so?"

He remembered the good feeling of having both Mara and Dietrich sitting around the supper table. He'd like nothing better than to repeat the event. But he sensed a hesitancy in Mara. She reminded him of a doe, beautiful to look at, but the moment one made a sound, she'd bolt through the woods.

Well, he shouldn't be thinking of her anyway. She was way out of his league. He wanted too much to help her without causing her to bolt from him.

Chapter Twelve

Gideon pulled the carryall up before the main doorway of his cousins' place. For this Thanksgiving, the McClellans had thrown open that little-used front door. Already the long driveway was filled with wagons and buggies of other relatives traveling from near and far for the holiday.

He threw a quick glance over his shoulder at his three passengers, in addition to Mrs. Blackstone who sat beside him. Mara sat in the middle with Dietrich on one side and Lizzie on the other. They'd already been to the special church service in the morning, so he'd gotten a glimpse of their appearances there although Mara and Mrs. Blackstone had sat on the other side of the church from Lizzie and him.

But both Lizzie and Mara sure looked pretty, even all wrapped up in their dark cloaks now and Mara with only her small black bonnet atop her dark curls, its black ribbon fluttering in the wind.

Lizzie sported her straw bonnet but he noticed a new green velvet ribbon, which matched her new gown. He'd been awestruck at how grown-up and ladylike she'd appeared at his side in church. Her bright red hair was dressed in a braided coronet atop her head. She'd told him that Mara had taught her how to arrange it.

Lizzie had spent a good portion of the past week with Mrs. Keller either in his kitchen or at Mrs. Blackstone's, baking for the big day. The carryall was loaded with pies and cakes they were contributing to the feast.

"I'll leave all of you here and see to the horse," he told them, getting down to help the ladies alight. Dietrich jumped down and ran off when he caught sight of some boys his age. Ever since that day when he'd been teased, he had steadily won those boys over.

Gideon went over to Mara, who'd already climbed down and was beginning to unload the boxes of pies, and touched her arm. "Don't you bother with those. I'll bring them." He nodded to some of the young men lounging around the driveway. "I'll get one of them to help, never you worry."

"Th-thank you," she answered in a rather breathless way before backing away from him.

He watched her a few seconds as she walked with Lizzie and Mrs. Blackstone to the opened front door. She was tall and elegant yet she never gave off any airs the way Mrs. Blackstone did.

He shook his head to banish the uncomplimentary thought of the older widow.

After unhitching Bessie and seeing her fed and watered in the barn, Gideon entered the house through the woodshed, followed by a couple of young men, Paul among them, bringing in the baked goods.

"There you are, Gid." Sarah left what she was doing at the kitchen table and came up to him. "Just set those down over here."

As soon as he'd emptied his hands, she leaned up to him and gave him a kiss on the cheek. "I'm so glad you were able to bring Mrs. Keller and her son."

He brushed aside the thanks, feeling uncomfortable with it. "Since I had to bring Mrs. Blackstone anyway..."

"My, but Lizzie looks pretty." Sarah clucked her tongue.

"My Paul and the other young men are all looking at her as if they'd never seen her before."

Instead of being gratified by the news, he frowned. "She's only a child. They'd better not be getting any ideas."

She laughed as she bustled over to the stove area. "Not for long! Now, go on in and say hello to Cliff. Dinner will be on the table soon."

He made his way toward the front parlor to obey, though his thoughts were driven like a dowsing rod toward Mara.

She was seated between Lizzie and Mrs. Blackstone on a small horsehair love seat. His lips drew down as he observed a distant cousin standing in front of Mara, and two adolescent boys around Lizzie. His gaze traveled to Mrs. Blackstone, who held herself as if she wanted nothing to do with either companion.

"See you're getting your wood in."

Gideon turned to Clifford, Sarah's husband. "Yep. I need to get a few more cords split before snowfall."

"Any day now. Thanks for the turkeys you brought." His eyes roamed over the parlor room. "With this crowd, we'll need every bit. Though the way the women have been baking and roasting all yesterday, I think we have enough food for the whole county."

Gideon chuckled, though his gaze continued on Mara, the little he could see from the fellow planting himself in front of her. He tried to stem his annoyance.

"Dinner's ready!" Betsey, Sarah's oldest daughter, poked her head in the doorway to announce, "Come along, everyone, before it gets cold."

Gideon waited with most of the men as the women and children made their way into the dining room. The two leaves of the table had been put in and still a smaller table had been set up in one corner of the room for the youngest children.

"You come sit here beside me at the head," Clifford beckoned with a slap on the back before Gideon could see where Mara was seated. "Seems we're always too busy to catch up on much until the winter holidays."

"That's right. Summer goes by so fast and there's always something to do."

He took the seat indicated, even as he glimpsed Mara standing behind Dietrich's chair, making sure he was settled at the children's table. He turned his attention back to Clifford. Shouldn't matter to him where Mara sat. She'd probably sit beside Lizzie, who was down the length of the table on the other side. Paul was just asking permission to take the seat beside her.

"Make way, here come the turkeys!"

Betsey jostled his shoulder as she brought in one of the large platters. Gideon stood immediately and took it from her to lay it before Clifford for carving. "You should have called me. Do you have another one for me to bring in?"

She shooed him back to his seat. "You just sit yourself down. Everything's taken care of."

"Sure smells good."

Clifford patted his stomach. "Hope you're hungry. This is only the beginning of the food. Ah, here come the chicken pies and the turkey for the other end of the table."

More women began setting down steaming bowls of mashed potatoes, relishes, cranberry sauce and roasted vegetables.

"Now, Mrs. Keller, you sit down right here. Place of honor for you," Sarah said with a chuckle.

Gideon turned to see his cousin practically dragging Mara by the elbow to the chair beside him.

Their eyes met briefly before she averted her gaze. He swallowed, tensing, as his body was conscious of her every move sitting down, taking up her linen napkin and spreading it on her lap. The people's voices and the clink of china around him faded away; his every sense fixed on the lady beside him. He rubbed a hand across his jaw, puzzling over why he was reacting like a schoolboy. His gaze strayed over to Paul, who had managed to sit beside Lizzie. The boy's— and his daughter's—color was high, though neither was looking at the other.

Part of him wanted to laugh—or turn to Mara—and show her the absurdity of the situation. Instead he could feel his own cheeks flush a deeper shade of crimson because he understood their position completely—was reliving it himself at the ripe old age of thirty-four.

What was he thinking? He'd been content with his life, the ache over Elsie's absence gradually easing so that he didn't find himself having those twinges of agonizing pain that would rear their head even years after her death, creating a wanting in him that only now, five years later, had abated into remembering his wife with fondness and the faith that someday he would see her again.

Clifford clinked his knife against his glass. "Let's bow our heads and thank the Lord for all this bountiful feast, and as Reverend Grayson reminded us this morning, all the blessings the Lord has given us this past year."

Gideon closed his eyes and listened as Cliff led them in the blessing. He added his own silent thanks for God's gifts. It had been a good year; he'd enjoyed a good harvest; they had plenty of stores laid up for the winter. Next month they'd slaughter some of their livestock for their winter's supply of meat. He had several cords of wood stacked in his shed and more to split. Fishing had been plentiful. Lizzie had shot up like a weed in this past year and was well on her way to young womanhood.

Clifford said a resounding "Amen!" and immediately everyone echoed him and began dishing out the food.

"Amen," Gideon said more slowly, opening his eyes, his thoughts still on the year's many blessings.

Clifford took up the large carving knife and two-pronged fork. "Pass me your plates and I'll heap on the turkey."

Gideon turned to Mara. Since she had not yet begun serving herself anything, he took her plate with a mumbled "Allow me."

"Thank you," she murmured back, her eyes downcast.

He set her plate back down as soon as Clifford had served her. The next few minutes were busy with passing plates back and forth. Finally, everyone settled down to eat.

He was one of the last to have turkey served. He unfolded his napkin.

"Would you care for some potatoes?"

"Thank you."

He started to take the warm bowl from Mara but she said, "I'll hold it while you serve yourself."

"Thank you," he repeated, feeling as awkward as he had around girls when he'd been Lizzie's age.

She inspected his plate. "What else do you need? Cranberry sauce, turnips, peas…" She ticked off the items and turned away to ask her other neighbor to pass those serving dishes.

When his plate was full, he took up his fork and knife. As he ate his first few mouthfuls, his mind was busy trying to think of conversation to engage in with Mara. He glanced across the table at Lizzie and found Paul saying something to her and she replying.

Gracious, he thought to himself, his shy fourteen-year-old seemed to be holding her own with a boy better than he was with a neighbor he'd seen pretty nearly every day for the past month.

He swallowed his food and wiped his mouth then reached for his glass. He took a sip of the cider to clear his throat. Before he could get any words out, Mara said softly, so only he could hear, "I'm glad to see Lizzie has overcome her antipathy of Paul and is able to talk in a friendly way with him."

Funny that they'd both noticed the same thing. He followed Mara's gaze back across the table. Lizzie and Paul were now smiling at each other and talking freely as if they were old friends, dividing their time between their food and conversation with each other.

"Hmm." He wasn't sure if he was pleased or not.

As if reading his thoughts, Mara said, "Are you concerned about them?"

He glanced at her, feeling unsettled at how closely she seemed to follow his thoughts. No one had been able to do that since Elsie. He'd never allowed anyone that close to him, for one thing. "No, of course not." He tried to laugh. "They've known each other all their lives. And he's too old for her anyway."

She tilted her head. "How much older is he, three years?"

"Yes."

A smile lit her eyes. "In another few years, three years won't mean much."

He found he couldn't look away from her sparkling blue eyes. "Maybe. But right now, three years is too much."

"You're right, of course, but I don't think it does Lizzie any harm to learn how to talk to boys. It's good to see her lose a bit of her shyness." When she finished speaking, her gaze strayed back to the young people across the table.

Instead of following suit, Gideon found himself caught by Mara's profile. He'd never found himself this close to her. She had flawless ivory skin and fine features. A slim nose, nicely curved lips, small earlobes, and a long neck. Her glossy sable hair was wound in a heavy coil at the base of her neck. He found himself wondering what it would feel like between his work-roughened hands. He imagined it tumbling down from its thick knot, hairpins scattering, silky locks falling over her shoulders.

His hands tightened on the cutlery. What had gotten into him? But he couldn't stop looking at her. His gaze traveled downward.

She wore a navy blue gown with a high neckline and long, tight sleeves reaching all the way to her wrists with only a narrow white frill visible beneath them. That seemed to be her only adornment, in contrast to most of the women at the table, young and old alike, for whom the holiday was a chance to dress up more than usual.

Despite the austerity of her gown, Mara appeared to him the most feminine, most ladylike of all the women present.

Something of her manners had rubbed off on Lizzie in the last few weeks the two had spent so much time together during.

He forced himself to look away from Mara. Cutting a piece of turkey with gravy, he tried to get his thoughts under control. But he hardly tasted the food as he looked at his daughter again. Although she was animated, there was nothing hoydenish about her manner with Paul. Even her table manners echoed something of Mara's, the dainty way she was holding a biscuit and dabbing at her mouth with her napkin.

He shook his head, amazed at how little things could make such a difference. Elsie would be proud of her.

He addressed Mara although he dared not look at her, afraid she would read the kinds of thoughts he was having about her. She would be horrified and probably refuse to speak to him ever again.

"I never thought of Lizzie as shy, but I guess it's because I see her at home where she doesn't have a whit of shyness. It's different when you're in a roomful of people, even when you're with folks you've grown up with, I imagine." Surprising how normal his voice came out. *Thank You, Lord.*

"Especially when you are fourteen, going on fifteen, and

the boys you knew as boys are beginning to look very much like young men." Amusement underlay her tone.

Despite his resolve to the contrary, he couldn't help but glance at Mara. Her lips curled upward at the corners.

He nodded slowly, digesting this observation. His gaze remained on her until she looked back down at her plate and he realized he was staring again. With a start, he turned to his own plate and took up a forkful of stuffing. He had to get ahold of himself.

With a determined effort, he turned to Clifford and asked him how his wood supply was going. He would do nothing to risk his daughter's friendship with this kind lady. She must never suspect the feelings she awakened in him.

Feelings he had long thought dead as driftwood.

But driftwood ignited like tinder when it was dry.

And he'd been dry a long, long time.

Mara walked into the large pantry carrying a stack of dishes she had just dried. "Where do these go?" she asked Mrs. McClellan.

"Right here, dear." Mr. Jakeman's cousin showed her an empty space between two other stacks of plates. "I so appreciate your help. You needn't, you know. There are plenty of women to help with the washing up."

"I can think of nothing better right now than moving about a bit. I've eaten much more than I should have."

Mrs. McClellan chuckled. "That's what Thanksgiving is for. I hope you have some room in a little while. We'll set out coffee and tea and the rest of the pies and cakes for refreshment."

Mara groaned. "I can't imagine eating anything more today."

"That's what everyone says until evening. After some games and singing—perhaps even a little dancing if that cousin of mine and a few others can be prevailed upon to break open their fiddles," she added with a wink, "you'd be surprised what an appetite can be worked up."

Mara found herself blushing at the mention of Gideon. She remembered their dinner conversation. It had been ordinary enough. Yet, why had she had the distinct feeling that there was something in his grayish-blue eyes she was sensing but not seeing? Even when she wasn't looking at him directly, she'd felt his gaze on her and wondered if there was something he'd wanted to speak to her about.

Dietrich perhaps?

Before Mara had a chance to go back into the kitchen to dry more dishes, Mrs. McClellan's next words stopped her. "I'm so glad your son has taken a liking to my cousin."

She nodded, glad to find the woman understood about her concern for her son.

"Your Dietrich can certainly benefit from Gideon's company."

Mara felt a flurry in her stomach at the mention of Mr. Jakeman's first name. *Gideon.* A fine, strong name, like its owner. "Yes, he has been very patient with my son."

"That's our Gideon. He has a heart of gold. You could find no better example for the boy. There's no finer man in all the county."

Her words caused Mara to stand transfixed. The older woman stood looking at her and something changed in her expression. Mara had the impression she was no longer thinking of Gideon as a man in relation to Dietrich, but as a man in relation to her.

"We were all so grieved when he lost his wife." Mrs. Mc-Clellan clucked her tongue. "Poor Elsie, such a fine woman, to be taken so young. And Gideon left with only the one child. I'm sure he's always wanted a son or two...."

Mara stood rooted, wanting and not wanting to hear more about Gideon's background. It had nothing to do with her.

And yet, she stood, every cell straining to know more about this quiet, gentle man.

"We all thought sure he'd take another wife after a couple of years. Life's hard here, and a man needs a good woman." Her look became knowing. "Just as a woman needs a strong pair of shoulders."

Mara twisted her hands together, looking away. She, too, used to believe so. "Not all marriages are made in heaven. They can be a curse as well as a blessing."

Mrs. McClellan laid a hand on her arm. "I'm sure you're right about that. Goodness, I see it in some of the women in our own little hamlet, poor, downtrodden souls." She drew in a breath, expanding her ample chest. "But not our Gid. He's a solid one. He'll make a woman a fine husband, if he ever realizes that he needn't be alone anymore. He's mourned long enough."

"Perhaps he prefers to retain the memory of his dear wife than risk something—someone—who will never replace her."

Mrs. McClellan arranged some cups and saucers another woman brought into the pantry. "Oh, it's not a matter of replacing her memory. It's a matter of giving another woman a chance to make a home for him, and realizing he doesn't have to continue his journey alone. It can be shared with a woman of good understanding. Someone who'll be a good helpmate. I don't know what I'd do without my Cliff."

"Well, I…I'd better go help the others, Mrs. McClellan, before the dishes get too stacked up. I do so appreciate your having asked us to your family meal."

Mrs. McClellan squeezed her arm and let it go. "Oh, nonsense. I love a good crowd. And please, it's Sarah. We live too close to each other to be going by Mrs. This and Mrs. That!"

"Thank you, Sarah." She tried to smile but felt it a tenuous effort at best. She wasn't used to the hand of friendship. "And, please, call me Mara."

Sarah nodded. "Mara, a pretty name despite its meaning."

Bitterness. She knew its meaning well from her study of the Bible. She'd thought it well suited indeed over the last few years.

The only difference between her and the Jewess Naomi was that Naomi's bitterness of spirit had begun after her widowhood, whereas Mara's had begun during her marriage. Widowhood had set her free.

She left the pantry and reentered the kitchen. She took up her dish towel and a plate and began drying again. Slowing her motions, she told herself to stop thinking so much about the past, and now even the present was dangerous. She mustn't let well-intentioned family and neighbors insinuate anything between her and Gideon.

He was merely a good neighbor who was giving her a helping hand with her boy. That was all, and that was all it would remain. The Lord had set her free and free she intended to remain.

She wiped at another plate with a vigor that caused the dish towel to squeak against the china, as if the energy she expended with her hands and arms would help wipe away her thoughts.

When the dishes were done, she was shooed out of the kitchen by Sarah even though her inclination was to hide there with the few women who remained. Her steps slowed the closer she got to the front parlor even as her heart sped up at the thought of seeing Gideon again. Was it because by having heard something of his past, she felt she had intruded into something not meant for her eyes? She wished Sarah had not put thoughts into her head.

Mara straightened the bodice of her gown, feeling her corset pinching at her. Part of her wished she could go home now, take off her best gown and sit down at the piano and lose herself somewhere where there was no past or future, only the music.

She peered into the sitting room. A group of young people was playing "Button, Button, Who's Got the Button?" Dietrich stood between two other children. Lizzie and Paul were also in the large circle, which filled up most of the room. Older folks were seated against the walls, chatting and resting after the large meal.

They were all family. She and Carina were the only ones who were not kin to the company. She had met some of Gideon's brothers and his sister and their children. What a blessing to have such a large family. She felt a bit sorry for herself on such occasions. Klaus had come of a big family and they had spent a few Christmases with them. Dietrich had been embraced by the large German clan and initiated into all the lovely holiday traditions, but Mara had always been made to feel the inferiority of her American birth.

She shook her head, determined to banish any self-pity.

Gideon stood at one end of the room talking with a couple of other men. She quickly looked away when his glance met hers as if he were aware the moment she entered the room. That was nonsense, she told herself firmly.

Instead of entering farther into the parlor, Mara backed out of the room before anyone else noticed her and asked her to sit by them.

Realizing she had left her shawl in the wagon, she decided to make her way there. A breath of fresh air would do her good. She knew from experience, only a few moments of God's presence was what she needed to regain her equilibrium.

Glancing out a window in passing, she saw it was already quite dark although it was barely six o'clock. The days had grown short, the sun setting around four o'clock in the afternoon now.

She walked quickly through the kitchen where some of

the women still lingered, some taking a breather around the large kitchen table, others setting out cups and saucers and small plates for the pie.

She and Lizzie had baked apple and pumpkin pies to bring, but it looked as if there were at least a dozen of each, as well as mince, lemon and cranberry ones.

"Take a lantern with you if you're going outside," one of the women suggested.

Mara smiled a thanks and picked up the lantern indicated. The women probably assumed she was going to use the convenience. She entered the fir-scented woodshed. Drying herbs hung from the rafters above barrels filled with grains, sugar and molasses. A barn cat slithered past her, rubbing against her skirt. "Where are you off to?" she asked, bending down and rubbing his fur. He purred in reply before scurrying off toward the barn door.

She opened it for him, peering into the cavernous space. The cows stood in their stanchions, the horses in their stalls. Against the flickering shadows from her lantern, she heard their soft nickering and snorting.

She reentered the shed and exited into the cold night air. She found the carryall halfway down the drive, between other vehicles.

Finding her cashmere shawl wedged between the seat cushions, she grasped it and turned to go. But before reentering the shed, she paused a few moments to breathe in the cold night air.

The sky was low with cloud cover. As the frosty air revived her, she thanked God for all He had blessed her and Dietrich with in the past year.

After the long, difficult years with Klaus, she felt as if an era of her life was over and the rest remained a blank book.

For many months afterward she had felt an unnatural wife, as she hadn't mourned her husband's death as a wife should. Her thoughts turned to Gideon. Both Lizzie and

Sarah had spoken highly of Elsie Jakeman. Clearly Gideon had loved her dearly.

It made her own feelings of relief at Klaus's death all the more shameful. She barely remembered the few good years. Klaus's rising star had quickly soured with her when she had to stand by and witness his extravagance and growing life of dissipation, spending his time at the casinos and with the wealthy young people his age who lived for nothing but amusement.

The rest of his time was dedicated to a grueling practice schedule, in which she was increasingly shut out. Her own desire to continue her music was mocked by him as his audience fawned over him. He lived for the reviews in the newspapers after a concert. Anything negative threw him into a temper where he railed against all those ignoramuses who knew nothing of music.

After Dietrich was born, things degenerated further. Any crying from the baby brought more angry shouts and Klaus banging out of the house, saying he could find no peace to practice his music. Mara saw less and less of her husband. Instead, she saw the bills that arrived. Klaus had no concerns over his creditors, stuffing the bills into a box and never looking at them again. Tailors, vintners, tobacconists, shirtmakers, shoemakers, art galleries, all the finest shops in whatever city they happened to be living in.

When she confronted him about the bills, his temper flared and he accused her of American provinciality. He shouted at her that she knew nothing of having to maintain a certain level of society if he hoped to continue playing in the premiere opera houses of Europe.

At first she accepted these rationales, but over time she began to argue that his talent alone assured his success. The arguments became louder and more acrimonious. She discovered an ability in Klaus to find her weak spots and attack her where she was most vulnerable. Her refuge had finally been silence—to avoid provoking him at all costs. And to find ways and means to pay the bills. It had eventually led to moving from lavish hotels and spacious apartments to dingier and dingier boardinghouses in less and less desirable parts of town.

But that was over now. Mara let out a shuddering breath and focused once more on her blessings. Besides the birth of Dietrich, one thing shone through of all those years she'd endured. Her faith in Christ had grown and deepened. Only by turning to the Scriptures and delving deeper than she ever had could she make any sense of her life and find the strength to endure.

And now the Lord had brought her back home. Things were not perfect with Carina, but perhaps in another year, if she added more pupils and continued saving as much of her earnings as she could, she and Dietrich could find a place of their own. It might have to be in town. She doubted the hamlet offered any small accommodations for a widow on a meager income and her son. But town offered a few boardinghouses.

So, her life would come full circle—back to a boardinghouse existence.

Sarah's words came back to her about having a spouse with whom to share the journey. No, she mustn't contemplate that option. Even though she had sensed an interest in a few of the widowers she'd met in town or the hamlet, she didn't trust herself to choose any better than she had the last time. Granted she'd been young and naive, but she'd never dreamed Klaus could be one person in public and another so different character in private. Never again would she forfeit her freedom—or Dietrich's well-being—to a man who could rule over her. Better to scrimp and save, put up with Carina's criticisms until such a time as they could afford a room of their own somewhere.

And as for those times of loneliness, when her burden

seemed heavy, she knew the Lord and His grace were sufficient for her. He'd brought her this far, He would continue to make a way for her to provide for Dietrich.

With a whispered "Thank You" skyward to the Lord for all His blessings in the past year, Mara took another deep breath of the night air and headed back to the house.

She secured the iron latch of the shed door behind her. Turning around in the dim light, she almost dropped her lantern at the sight of the shadowy form looming up behind her.

Chapter Thirteen

Mara clasped a hand over her mouth. "Gideon—"

"I'm sorry, Mara—"

He was standing so close to her, he must have heard her galloping heart. They stared at each other, as if in shock at the use of their given names. For several seconds neither of them moved. In that moment, Mara read something new in his gaze.

He was as aware as she of their position alone in the shed.

If she leaned forward only a few inches and he the same, they would be touching. For those seconds, she allowed herself to long for it. Oh, to rest her head on his broad chest!

Her eyes strayed to the lower half of his face. His lips looked firm yet soft and inviting.

No, she mustn't think such thoughts!

She lowered her hand to her heart, as if to shut off its ache to be held, to be loved…

"You startled me," she said with a nervous laugh, taking a step back but hitting the door instead.

"I'm sorry. I didn't mean to." He backed up into the darker shadows of the shed. With a gesture of his hand, he bade her precede him. "I saw you hadn't come back and…" His Adam's apple worked as he swallowed. "I guess I was a little worried."

She held up her shawl. "I just went to retrieve this."

"You could have told me. I'd have fetched it for you."

He continued to amaze her with his thoughtfulness—and threatened to breach her defenses. "But you couldn't have taken a breath of fresh air for me." To take away any sting in the remark, she smiled, adding, "There's nothing like standing under the night sky…to say one's own private thanks on this holiday."

He regarded her, nodding slowly. "That's so. I've done it on many occasions myself."

His gaze lingered. She tightened her hold on her shawl to prevent her hand from going to her hair. She had come out without even her hat. Her hair must be windblown.

She sensed rather than saw him make a move toward her.

"Well, I'd better get back inside." Like a rabbit scurrying for cover, she hastened past him toward the kitchen door.

Once inside, she carefully closed the door behind her, her eyes having to readjust to the light in the kitchen.

"Oh, there you are, Mrs. Keller. I'll take that from you!" A woman took the lantern with a chuckle. "Have to make a trip out to the barn!"

The few women there laughed.

Mara relinquished the lantern with limp fingers, her face a rigid mask, revealing nothing of the emotions waging war within her. Longing and fear. Regret and relief.

She must never find herself alone with Gideon again, she told herself sternly.

She was not strong enough to resist him if he ever displayed the slightest inclination to make an advance.

And once that happened, all her resolve would crumble like ash in the stove.

When they left the McClellans', the first snowflakes had begun to fall. Both Dietrich and Lizzie shouted and held their hands and tongues out, trying to catch the soft flakes.

"How much snow is going to fall, Mr. Jakeman?" Dietrich asked, climbing aboard the carryall.

Gideon squinted at the clouds. "Hard to say. You may wake up tomorrow and find everything white. Now, take this end of the blanket and give your mother the other half." He spread the thick woolen lap robe over the boy's knees, knowing if he had handed it to Mara first, she probably would have taken it from him without allowing him to help her. The way she had run off like a frightened doe when he'd found her in the shed told him clearly she wanted nothing to do with him.

The fact hadn't been lost on him that she'd scurried into the backseat for the return trip as if she couldn't get far enough away from him.

Squelching the sorrow this caused him, he walked around the carryall to Mrs. Keller's side. "You all tucked in there, ma'am?"

"Yes, thank you."

"Good." He leaned forward to make out Lizzie between the two. "How about you, Lizzie?"

"Snug as a bug in a rug!" Laughter gurgled out of her.

"Not too crowded back there? One of you could sit up front."

"We're fine, Papa."

With a nod, he took his position beside Mrs. Blackstone, giving the reins a slap to start their trek homeward.

"I'm relieved you didn't make us sit in the cold any longer, Mr. Jakeman."

He frowned at the older woman's oblique criticism. "Just making sure everyone was tucked in."

The flakes started falling faster and thicker by the time he guided the horse out of the drive and onto the dirt road. "Looks like everything will be all white tomorrow morning," he said over his shoulder to the children.

Dietrich bounced on his seat. "Yippee! Did you hear that, Lizzie? We can go sledding and make snowmen!"

"Settle down there, young man," Mrs. Blackstone scolded. "I hope you'll get us home in one piece," she added with a nervous laugh in Gideon's direction.

"Old Bessie knows these roads like the back of her hoof."

"I'm relieved to hear it!" With a few rustles, Mrs. Blackstone settled in her seat.

Gideon let the sounds of the children's voices wash over him as he allowed the horse her lead, his thoughts turning inward. What had occurred between him and Mrs. Keller a while earlier in the woodshed? Had he imagined it all, or had she looked at him with longing in her eyes? The same kind of longing he'd felt.

Before hers had been replaced by a look of fear.

The way she'd run told him he hadn't imagined the moment. And the fact that she hadn't spoken to him except for the absolutely necessary words since then. There had been music, and she'd been prevailed upon to sit at the spinet to play a few songs, while he and a few others had been asked to sing along. Then she'd resumed her place and he'd taken up the fiddle for some dancing.

He'd noticed Paul dancing with Lizzie during "Lady of the Lake." He'd never seen Lizzie so animated with a young man. But he reassured himself that it was the type of dance that didn't allow her to be with her partner exclusively. But each time young Paul swung her around, the two looked at each other in mutual admiration.

His glance then sought Mrs. Keller—in time to see her refuse another man with a gentle but firm smile. Her glance met his but quickly skittered away.

He'd never had his attention so distracted when playing for a dance. Keeping an eye on Lizzie and watching Mrs. Keller. At least Lizzie hadn't danced exclusively with Paul but with several boys in the reels and jigs. She seemed to be having a grand time with them all. So he shook aside any concern on that score.

But whenever he looked toward Mrs. Keller, she was not looking at him, though she seemed to be enjoying the music, her foot tapping or her chin moving in time to his playing. His thoughts wandered, wondering what it would feel like to lead her in one of the dances arm in arm, or swing her around or promenade with his arm about her waist...

He was crazy to be thinking such thoughts. A woman— *lady*—like Mrs. Keller would never consider a simple farmer like himself. Look how she turned down every man who approached her and seemed to stick by the elderly womenfolk as if she were already long past her prime. But then, she hadn't been widowed too long, only a few months according to his cousin. Clearly, she still mourned her husband.

When they'd finally collected their things to go home, Mrs. Keller had hardly met his eyes or spoken directly to him.

He longed to crane his neck around and see how she was doing back there beside Lizzie, but she sat directly behind him, so it would take more than a quick glance backward.

Mrs. Blackstone stirred at his side. "Well, I must say that was a fine evening, Mr. Jakeman. Your cousin outdid herself. Of course, I ate too much."

"I guess we all do on Thanksgiving."

"I say once a year isn't too bad. But I'll probably be up all night regretting my transgression," she added with a laugh.

He chuckled, thinking that if he was up, it would be for other reasons. Dreaming of nonsense...

When they arrived at Mrs. Blackstone's farm, he got down, hoping he'd be able to help Mrs. Keller down, but first he was obliged to go to Mrs. Blackstone. By the time he'd assisted her, Mrs. Keller was already shepherding Dietrich up the path to the doorway. He hurried up to her to relieve her of the burdens she carried. "Here, let me." Without waiting for her reply, he took the satchels she carried, with the empty pie plates they'd brought.

"That's all right, they're not heavy," she began at once, but didn't protest when he relieved her of them.

He reached the door first and opened it for them. "Thank you, Mr. Jakeman," she said. "I'll bid you good-night here. You and Lizzie need to get home before the snow gets any thicker."

His tongue felt glued to his mouth so he could only nod and make an unintelligible sound before stepping aside to allow Mrs. Blackstone in. "Good night, Gideon. You'd best get Lizzie home now."

"Good night," he finally managed.

Lizzie was already in the front seat, holding the reins when he climbed back up.

"Oh, Papa, I haven't had so much fun in an age! I wish it wasn't all over now till next year."

"Well, there'll be other sociables with winter here," he said as he maneuvered the carryall back down the long drive.

"And you'll let me attend them...I mean, to dance and behave like a young lady and not a girl?"

He turned to her in the dark. "As long as you behave like a young lady."

Her eyebrows drew together. "What do you mean, Papa? Would I ever shame you?"

He reached over to squeeze her mittened hand. "Of course not. I just know what it's like to be young and fancy somebody."

"Like Mama?"

"That's right."

"Did you fancy anyone before her, or did you know when you met her that she was the one?"

He didn't have to think on that one. "I knew she was the one."

"Since which moment?"

"Well, let's see… We knew each other, o' course, having grown up in the hamlet, but she lived on the other side of the harbor, so I didn't see her too often. Then one day, I saw her at a sociable—we'd both finished school by then. Neither of us went beyond the grammar school. So, it had been a while since I'd last seen her. There she stood, looking all of a young lady. Just like you did tonight."

"How old was she?"

He thought back. "Almost seventeen."

"So, she wasn't much older than I when she fell in love with you?"

He chuckled. "A few years older. But not everyone falls in love so young. And we didn't get married right away. I was eighteen and my folks told me I needed to wait and save up money before I was thinking of marrying. I worked at the sawmill in town for a year, coming home on the weekends to help my pa on the farm. When I'd saved up enough my folks gave their blessing and we were married. But I kept working another year before coming home and farming full-time."

"So, I may fall in love soon, just like Mama." She gave a satisfied sigh.

The mare stepped around a low spot in the road, which was already covered in snow. "I still want you to attend high school in town next fall."

"Oh, Papa, I don't need more schooling."

"Well, if I went to work in the sawmill to satisfy my parents, you can do the same for me, eh?"

Lizzie was quiet for a few minutes which told him his words had found a mark. Before she could reply, he added, "Mrs. Keller has been a help, hasn't she?"

"Oh, yes!" She turned to him on the seat as they neared their own drive. He turned into it, glad to be out of the thickening snow and cold. "I think that's why I felt so…so, I don't know—"

"Confident?" he supplied for her.

"Yes, that's the way I felt today. And it seemed to make a difference in the way the boys treated me. It was like I was a different person." She laughed. "Even when I was the same old person they've seen forever."

He stopped the horse in front of the barn door. "Except you weren't completely, were you?"

She stared at him in the dim light of the lantern as if surprised at his insight. "No, I wasn't."

He ruffled her cap and smiled. "You're growing up. Too fast for me, but I'm proud of you."

"Thank you, Papa. And I'll do as you want and go to the high school next fall."

His smile widened. "That's my girl."

He got down and Lizzie held the horse while he slid open the barn door. He sent Lizzie into the house while he looked after Bessie. "Good girl," he told her as he unhitched her from the wagon. "You brought us home like you always do."

After he'd seen to her and shut everything up for the night, he paused a moment before going inside. Once again, his thoughts went to Mrs. Keller.

How he longed to take her in his arms and kiss away the haunted look in her eyes.

Who had put it there? Her late husband? Or life's circumstances?

Mara trudged home from a full afternoon in town. Her schedule had filled up with pupils so she would soon have to add a second afternoon.

Her shoulder ached from the weight of her satchel. The walk was made more difficult now with the addition of snow on the road and the cold. She pulled the scarf up over her chin and mouth and hunched against the wind.

She'd made a few inquiries at boardinghouses in town. One seemed more promising than the others. It was run by a pleasant widow and the house and its small yard seemed neat and clean.

Yet, it was still a boardinghouse. Her shoulders slumped at the thought of leaving her home for a rented room. Dietrich wouldn't like it at all. He finally had made friends. How was he going to adjust to a new school—a larger one at that? There would be no Mr. Jakeman to smooth the way for him, explaining to the boys his foreign accent and manner.

Although he was quickly losing both in the couple of months he'd been in school—and seeing Gideon almost daily.

And what of him? How could she replace the good influence the man was in her son's life if she moved to town? They probably wouldn't see him much. Even if he made a point to visit Dietrich when he came to town, it would be brief encounters just to ask how he was doing.

And what of her? Would she miss seeing Gideon?

She fisted her hands in her woolen mittens. No, she wouldn't allow herself to think on such things.

Dear Lord, You see our circumstances. I trust You to provide us with adequate housing. I've tried to make peace with Carina but every day she becomes more critical of Dietrich. Please, help us. Grant us a place to live, a place where Dietrich can continue to flourish.

She was so engrossed in her prayer that she didn't hear the clip-clop of horse hooves or the creak of wheels until the horse and wagon were almost abreast of her.

Only at the masculine tone of "Whoa!" did she jump out of the way. She turned to find Gideon bringing the horse to a standstill before lifting the brim of his sealskin cap to her. "Afternoon, Mrs. Keller."

Her hand to her chest, she gave a nervous laugh. "Good afternoon, Mr. Jakeman."

His eyes narrowed on her face. "I didn't startle you, did I?"

"No—I mean, perhaps a bit. It wasn't your fault," she assured him quickly. "I was quite lost in thought."

"May I offer you a lift home? Was just going that way myself."

Mara almost smiled in gratitude but then remembered Thanksgiving evening. Had it only been a week ago? She hadn't seen Gideon since, but that moment had been in her thoughts almost constantly, popping up whenever her guard was down.

No, she must not encourage anything that might have transpired that evening, whether real or imagined.

She swallowed, to give herself a moment to formulate her reply. Above anything, she did not wish to hurt his feelings. "Thank you, Mr. Jakeman, but I'm quite fine walking."

He looked taken aback for an instant. Then he glanced skyward. "Are you sure? Hard to tell with this weather but the clouds sure look growly."

She followed his glance. The skies did indeed look "growly," dark gray and lowering.

"I wouldn't be surprised if it came on to snow in a bit. You've still a few miles to go."

How tempted she was to set aside her determination and climb into the wagon. And not just to get out of the cold and forbidding weather. But to be beside him for the journey home.

No, no, no! She mustn't allow this weakness for companionship.

She straightened her shoulders. "It's all right. I'm a fast walker and have gotten quite accustomed to this road."

He looked as if he would say something further, but then abruptly gave a nod. "Very well." With another touch of his hand to the brim of his cap, he turned his attention away from her and gave a flick of the reins. The wagon wheels creaked forward.

Mara stood a few seconds longer watching the wagon

slowly increase its distance from her. With a shake of her head, she hunched her shoulders against the breeze, adjusted the satchel and continued on her way.

It was impossible not to continue watching the wagon recede as it made its way down the slope and up the next then out of sight over the next rise. Mr. Jakeman didn't look back, and she wondered if he thought of her.

She certainly thought of having turned down the opportunity of arriving home a good hour earlier to a warm fire and hot cup of tea.

Gideon resisted the urge to turn and look around. He couldn't for the life of him imagine why a person would refuse a lift back to the hamlet. It was at least three more miles and if it didn't snow before she arrived home, he'd be mighty surprised. He hadn't lived in this part of the world all his life, fished its water, farmed its rocky soil without learning to read the signs of the skies and sea.

He shook his head, hating to ride away from her, but sensing as he did with his animals, that he wasn't going to be able to persuade her otherwise. She acted almost afraid of him. How could she be afraid of him?

The notion not only shocked him but hurt him to the quick. He'd never knowingly do anything to cause her harm. He'd tried since the day he'd met her and her son to let her know, if not so much by words, but by deeds, that he was there for anything they might need.

His gaze fixed somewhere between Bessie's two ears, he pondered what he might have done to cause her to fear him.

All he could think of was that moment in the woodshed on Thanksgiving Day. What he'd taken for perhaps a moment of awareness between them, had she taken as a reason to fear him?

The idea astounded him. Did she think he'd ever take advantage of her as a widow with no kin? He hardly reckoned

Mrs. Blackstone as someone who would succor her step-daughter willingly.

He'd tried never to let on what his true feelings might be. Except for that moment on Thanksgiving, he'd thought he'd kept them well-hidden.

Didn't she realize he'd never express himself improperly to her, that he'd never dare presume to offer her anything? She was above him socially, culturally, in education, in everything. She was a lady and he nothing but a farmer.

Dear Lord, help me to reassure her that I won't ever take advantage of her friendship. Help her to see it's just friendship I'm offering. She's been good to my Lizzie. I don't want to hinder that. Take these feelings I have for her away. I know they're not right. Help me forget them.

How was he to forget how she'd looked that evening…or how she'd felt in his arms when he'd held her dancing when those memories kept creeping on him unawares?

Chapter Fourteen

Mara opened the china closet in the parlor and looked at the tea service with its deep pink and pale yellow rose pattern. Dietrich stood at her elbow, Lizzie a little behind her. "We'll use this tea set for our tea party," she told them, handing a cup and saucer to Lizzie.

Lizzie took them from her carefully and examined them. "They're so pretty and delicate, like eggshells."

"They're French. You can see from the bottom."

Lizzie turned over the saucer. "I can't read it except for the word *Paris*."

"Yes, it's just the name of the French porcelain factory and its address. And a number. Each piece that was made was numbered, you see."

Lizzie's mouth rounded. "Goodness. Should we use them?"

Mara smiled. "Of course. This is a special occasion."

Dietrich tugged on her sleeve. "Let me carry some, too, Mama."

Mara hesitated, not wanting to risk breaking any. "Why don't you go into the kitchen and pump some water into the dishpan for me?" She glanced at Lizzie. "We'll wash them and have them all ready for tomorrow's tea party."

"Mama, why can't I carry any?" Dietrich's lips pouted, his arms folded tightly against his chest.

"Because they're very fragile. These were my mother's, your grandmother's." To assuage his feelings, she picked up a cake dish of a solid cream porcelain from the china cupboard, a dish she knew was easily replaceable and handed it to her son. "Here, take this with you. It's bigger than all the pieces Lizzie and I will bring in."

He grasped each edge proudly and marched away.

Lizzie met her glance and smiled. "This was your mother's?" she asked as the two carried a load of cups and saucers into the kitchen.

"Yes, it's the only thing I have left of hers." She set the cups down on the kitchen table and went for another stack. Lizzie followed her.

"My father bought it for her on their first trip to Paris."

"They went to Paris?" she asked in a tone filled with awe.

Mara paused at the china cupboard once again. "Yes. He had just sold a painting and wanted to go to the city that attracts most painters. He bought my mother that set at an antique shop as a gift of gratitude for my mother's willingness to go with him anywhere."

Lizzie looked wistful. "How romantic."

"Yes." Her father had loved her mother deeply, which was why it had always disappointed her that he had fallen so quickly for Carina's superficial charm. Of course, now as an adult, she better understood his loneliness.

"So, you've had this set all these years?"

Mara smiled. "Yes. My husband and I moved around a lot and weren't able to take a lot of furniture with us. We usually rented furnished rooms. But I always packed this set up and took it with me. It made any new place seem like home right away." She didn't add that at first she'd had a lot of her own things but as money grew tight, anything of any worth had to eventually be sold.

This was the only thing she hadn't been able to part with since it was the only thing left of her father and mother, the only reminder that true love between man and woman did exist even if she had not been privileged to experience it for herself.

"With all the moving, I never broke a piece. It's still as complete as when my father bought it for my mother."

Lizzie's red eyebrows drew together. "Maybe it's too good for our tea party. I'll be afraid to hold it."

"You needn't be. You're a careful person. Besides that, things are meant to be used and enjoyed. We can be careful, but we mustn't give things more value than people."

Lizzie nodded.

They took the rest of the set to the kitchen and began to wash the pieces. As Lizzie was drying and laying them back on the kitchen table, Carina entered the room. She raised an eyebrow at the stacks of cups and saucers and small dessert plates arrayed on the table. "What, are you planning to use the crown jewels?"

Mara restrained her annoyance. "We are having our tea party tomorrow afternoon. Remember, I told you about it, Carina?"

Carina held up a cup and eyed it critically. "Ah, yes, the tea party." She cocked an eyebrow. "Entertaining the widower."

Mara gasped. "Carina!"

Carina gave an unpleasant laugh. "Oh, you needn't act so shocked. I'm sure Lizzie doesn't mind my little jokes, do you, my dear?"

Lizzie's color was high and she looked in question from Carina to Mara. "No, of course not, ma'am."

Carina set down the cup and walked around the table toward the girl. "Besides, I'm sure you wouldn't mind if your father remarried, would you?"

Lizzie's eyes grew round, and Mara noticed Dietrich, too, had stopped playing with the dishpan water.

The moment of silence drew out. Then Lizzie abruptly shook her head, sending her two long braids swinging. "No, not if it's the right woman." Her gaze rested on Mara.

Mara felt her own color rise. With a firmness she didn't feel, she set down the dessert plate she was drying and took up a saucer. "Carina, this is merely a tea party to teach Lizzie how to hold one of her own one day. Since her father is the logical person to invite, as well as you and Dietrich, I wouldn't read anything into it beyond that."

"Whatever you say, my dear." She set down the cup and turned to leave the kitchen once more with a swish of her skirts.

When she was gone, Lizzie set down the piece she was drying but said nothing. Mara observed her a moment to see if she was going to say anything but when she didn't, Mara continued drying.

A few moments later, Dietrich began to splash too much. "All right, that's enough washing for you. Why don't you put on your coat and see if Paul needs some help outside?"

He turned away from the sink and ran to get his jacket from the peg. "May I go see Mr. Jakeman? I want to visit my kitten and see Samson."

Mara glanced at Lizzie.

"It's all right. Pa's home. He'll be chopping wood in the yard."

"Are you sure?"

"Yes."

"Very well. Put your scarf and mittens on, Dietrich. It's cold out there." She glanced out the window. The yard was white and the bay beyond deep blue. "But be home before dark."

"Don't worry. We'll be sure he gets home before then,"

Lizzie reassured her. "You don't mind if I stay here a little longer, do you?"

Mara smiled at her as Dietrich left the kitchen, slamming the door behind him. "Of course not. We'll set these dishes out of the way in the pantry and then begin baking our cake."

As they did these things, Lizzie seemed quieter than usual.

When they returned to the kitchen with butter and eggs for the cake, Mara hesitated but finally decided to say something. "Did Mrs. Blackstone's words bother you, dear?"

Lizzie glanced at her, her color once again deepening. "Oh, no, I mean, not the way you think."

"I'm glad. I'm sure she didn't mean anything by them."

Lizzie focused on the crock of butter she held in her hands. "I…I hope she's right."

Mara tried to remember Carina's exact words. "What do you mean?"

Her gaze slowly rose to Mara's. "About you and Papa. I wouldn't mind at all if…if you and Papa were to, you know, marry."

Mara stood still as stone. The only sound was the steady ticking of the clock on the mantel. "I…" What could she say, how to answer the girl without hurting her feelings, without giving herself away? She raised her hand and touched the girl's arm. "Oh, Lizzie, I think Carina's reading too much into our friendship."

Lizzie's lips pressed together, their corners downward as if she were keeping from crying. Mara's heart tore in her chest, wishing she could offer her something more but knowing it wasn't right to get her hopes up. "Your mother must have been a very special woman to win your father's heart. I don't think your father will find anyone to replace her. I hope for his sake that he does, but don't be in too much of a hurry for someone to take your mother's place."

Lizzie set down the crock and took one of her hands in

hers. "Oh, I'm not! But you're different. I think you and Papa—"

Mara had to stop the girl. She shook her head. "No, dear." But she couldn't meet the girl's eyes. "My father found someone too quickly. I know he must have been very lonely after my mother died, but it wasn't home anymore with another woman filling it."

Lizzie's hand squeezed hers before letting go. "I'm sorry," she whispered.

Mara only nodded. "It's all right. I just don't want you to be disappointed."

"I could never be disappointed in you."

Mara bit her lip, not knowing what else to say. That she could never remarry because her first marriage had been such a nightmare? Of course, she could never share that with anyone, least of all a girl who had dreams of her own still.

Gideon wiped his feet on the doormat before Mrs. Blackstone's kitchen door, feeling as nervous as a young man on his first courtship. He removed his low bowler and put a hand to his hair which had been combed back with pomade.

"Well, am I presentable?" he quipped to Lizzie. They stood in the dim woodshed, breathing in the cedar scent around them.

Lizzie gave him a shy smile "You look very handsome, Papa."

He readjusted the Windsor knot of his blue silk tie. The starched linen collar bit into his jaws but Lizzie had insisted he must wear his Sunday best, a woolen sack suit of dark charcoal-gray.

He didn't know why he felt so unsure of himself. He'd been inside this place plenty of times, but only once to dine with Mrs. Keller. That, an informal, impromptu supper, had been uncomfortable enough.

This was a handwritten invitation—written by Lizzie, but

coming from Mara. It sounded very formal—too formal for
the likes of him. Lizzie had also dressed in her best, her new
green dress. He tried to smile at her. "You look pretty, too."
The narrow brim of her hat was turned upward, and a wide
green silk ribbon was tied around the base of its low crown.

"Thank you, Papa. Now, why don't you knock so we can
get indoors? I don't want to keep Mrs. Keller waiting."

"No, of course not." He turned, his hand jerking toward
the door. He tapped on the panels.

Hardly a second passed and the door swung inward. "Mr.
Jakeman, you're here!" Dietrich met him with a wide smile.
He was dressed in a pair of navy blue knickerbockers and a
matching jacket with a lighter blue bow tie and snowy white
shirt.

"My, aren't you looking handsome this afternoon,"
Gideon responded, stretching his lips in a smile, despite
feeling the increasing rate of his heartbeat at the glimpse of
Mara standing at the far end of the kitchen.

"Tell our guests to come in, Dietrich," she said softly.

Dietrich opened the door wider and waved his hand in
a flourish. "Come in, Mr. Jakeman, Miss Jakeman." The
words sounded as if the boy had rehearsed them.

Gideon stood while Lizzie entered and then followed after
her. Dietrich closed the door behind them.

Clutching his hat in his fingertips, he braced himself to
greet Mara, as if this wasn't any unusual occasion. He hadn't
seen her since the day she'd refused his offer of a lift.

His breath hitched in his throat at the sight of her. She
stood by the woodstove in a dress he hadn't seen before. It
was a deep shade of blue, only a shade lighter than her son's
suit. She wore an ivory cameo at the high neck. The three-
quarter sleeves revealed pale, slim arms and wrists. She wore
a frilly apron, which she proceeded to untie now. Her dark
hair was swept up behind her head and tiny earrings decorated her earlobes.

"Good afternoon, Mrs. Keller."

She removed the apron and came forward. He thought for a moment that she would extend her hand, but she ended up clasping them loosely in front of her. "Good afternoon, Mr. Jakeman. I'm so glad you could come to our tea party."

He inclined his head. "Thank you for having me."

She glanced at Lizzie. "Why don't you take your father's hat and overcoat and show him into the parlor? Most everything is in there. I just need to bring the teapot and you can bring in the cake."

"All right."

Mara returned to the stove and Gideon unbuttoned his coat. "I can see to it," he told his daughter, holding out his hand for hers.

"No, Papa. You're the guest, and Mrs. Keller already showed me where I could put our coats. Come along, Dietrich."

She left the kitchen before he could say anything more, leaving him alone with Mara. He cleared his throat, wishing he still had his hat to clutch. "Did you make it home all right the other day?"

She turned from the woodstove, the teakettle in one hand, a pot holder in the other. "What? Oh, yes, yes, thank you."

Did she seem as flustered as he or was she just distracted as any hostess getting ready to serve something? Soft pink color suffused her cheeks but that was probably due to standing by the warm stove.

He stood quietly, watching as she approached the table, lifted the lid of the round china teapot and poured in the steaming water. He didn't dare saying anything—not that he could think of anything to say—lest she burn herself.

She righted the kettle and plopped the china top onto the pot. "There." She straightened, giving him a quick smile before returning to the stove.

She brought a tea cozy and placed it over the pot.

He wanted to offer to carry the tray into the parlor but was afraid she would refuse the offer. Thankfully, he was saved by Lizzie's return to the kitchen. "Come along, Papa."

He gave a last look Mara's way but she shooed him out of the kitchen with her hand. "Everything is ready."

Dietrich skipped along ahead of them. "Mama and Lizzie baked a cake with icing and cookies. I can't wait to try them. They didn't let me eat any yesterday, but Mama let me lick out the mixing bowl when I got back from your house."

Gideon chuckled. "Well, they'll taste all the sweeter today then." He entered the parlor and his laughter died. Mrs. Blackstone was seated in an armchair, looking as regal as royalty. "Good afternoon, Mrs. Blackstone."

"Hello, Gideon. Show your father to a seat, Lizzie."

"Yes, ma'am."

She led him to the long horsehair sofa. "Have a seat, Papa. Dietrich, you, too. I'll be right back." She motioned to the low table in front of the sofa. "Isn't everything pretty?"

He stood gazing down at the tea things on the fine embroidered cloth he recognized as one of Elsie's. Pretty china cups, saucers, plates, small silver spoons and forks and a silver platter of cookies were artfully arranged on it. "My, I've never seen anything so nice."

"It's Mrs. Keller's best tea set. Don't you like it?"

It was pretty—each cup painted with a large pink and yellow rose, the edges gold.

"Well, take a seat, Papa. I'll be right back with the cake."

He made his way around the table but knocked his shin against its edge, sending the china to rattling. His hand shot out and he stepped back, bumping into the sofa.

Lizzie came up to him. "Are you all right?"

"Yes, I'm fine. You go along." He sat down, not daring to move another inch. Dietrich joined him on one side, laughter lighting his brown eyes.

"That was a close call," Gideon told him with a wink.

Dietrich nodded. "A close call," he parroted with a giggle.

"That's enough, young man," Mrs. Blackstone reprimanded from her chair.

Dietrich quieted immediately.

Gideon touched the knot of his tie again. "Cold outside, isn't it?"

"Indeed." They both glanced toward the windows but they were shaded by gauzy white curtains so there was little to be seen. "I have stayed pretty much indoors today."

"That's wise." He placed his hands on his knees, trying to think of something else to say. "The grange is having a dance next Saturday."

"Is that so?" She fiddled with a jet button on her bodice. "Well, I expect you'll be there."

"Yes, I 'spect so, to play the fiddle with Joe and Henry."

"Of course." She chuckled. "I admit I wasn't thinking of your fiddle playing."

"Oh?"

She turned her head a fraction, giving him a coy look. "Very well, Gideon, if you want to pretend ignorance, we'll leave it that way."

He stared at her until her meaning began to penetrate. Did she mean he was going courting? His cheeks felt as warm as the sides of the woodstove in the corner of the parlor.

He jumped at the sound of footsteps. Lizzie entered with the cake platter held aloft, and Mara followed right behind her with the teapot on a tray.

He stood to help then thought better of it. Before he could make up his mind whether to help clear off room on the table, Lizzie set down her platter and turned to take the teapot off Mrs. Keller's tray and set it down. It also contained a small plate with lemon slices and a thick mug.

"Thank you," she told Lizzie. "That's everything, I think. Now, Lizzie, you take the place of honor behind the teapot and pour for us."

Lizzie came around and sat next to him. He couldn't help but be proud of her in her pretty green dress, her long hair falling in thick curls down her back, another green ribbon holding it in place away from her face.

Mara stood on Lizzie's other side and held a cup and saucer for her. Lizzie lifted the cozy off the pot and poured. "Cream and sugar, Mrs. Blackstone? Or lemon and sugar?"

"Just a spoonful of sugar, dear."

Dietrich's feet began to swing against the edge of the sofa. Gideon put his hand on the boy's knee, stilling him, and bent close to his ear. "That cake looks mighty good."

The boy's gaze traveled to the tall cake which dripped with white icing. He nodded. "Do you think we'll have it soon?" he whispered.

"I'm sure we will," Gideon whispered back, his eyes going to Mara who walked across the room, taking Mrs. Blackstone her teacup.

Lizzie turned to him. "Papa, do you want it the way you usually take it?"

"Sure, sweetheart."

He watched her pour, his pride growing at her steady and graceful hand. She put a scant spoonful of sugar into his cup and a splash of milk, gave it a brief stir then turned to hand it to him with a smile.

"Thank you," he said with an answering smile, taking the cup and saucer with great care and setting them on his knee.

"Dietrich, how about you?"

Mrs. Keller approached the table with a smile. "Dietrich will have some milk with his cake." She handed her son the mug she'd carried in earlier.

Dietrich took it without a word.

"What do you say, dear?"

"Thank you, Mama."

Lizzie poured tea for Mrs. Keller, and he noted she took

a slice of lemon with hers. Then she asked Dietrich to pass the plate of cookies around while she cut the cake.

Gideon took the boy's mug before he slid off the sofa.

Balancing these two items, he was content to watch Lizzie cut the cake. "Mrs. Blackstone, will you have some lemon cake?"

"Yes, I'll try a piece. It smelled so good when it was baking yesterday."

Mrs. Keller took her cake to her as Dietrich offered her the platter of cookies. Gideon leaned forward and set the boy's mug on the low table to receive the cake plate Lizzie handed to him. Dietrich came back and set the cookie plate back down on the table then sat back down beside Gideon.

Lizzie reached across Gideon to hand the boy his slice of cake.

"Thank you," the boy said without prompting this time and quickly dug into his cake. His mother brought him a napkin, tucking it into his collar, and then offered one to Gideon.

"Thank you," he said with a smile, leaning back carefully, the cake and tea balanced on each knee.

Mara took her cup of tea from Lizzie, glancing about the room, deciding where to sit. The logical place was on Lizzie's other side since it was a long sofa. But she opted for another armchair near Carina.

She set her cup and saucer on a small table at her side and smiled as first Dietrich offered her the plate of cookies and then Lizzie brought her a piece of cake.

"Thank you," she murmured, taking each, not because she had any desire to eat, but as an encouragement to the children. She noticed Gideon had not tasted any of his food or tea yet. Was his stomach experiencing as many flutters as hers was?

"How do you like the cake, Papa?" Lizzie looked at her father's plate. "Why, you haven't even tasted it yet!"

"No, I haven't had a chance. It looks mighty good, though." As he spoke, he managed to take up the small fork and spear a piece of cake from the plate on his knees, all the while holding the cup and saucer with his other hand on his other knee. Mara's hands clutched each other, wishing she could tell him to set his cup on the low table in front of him, but not wanting to distract him further.

"It's yummy!" Dietrich said around a mouthful of cake.

Gideon swallowed before speaking. "Yes, it certainly is. Did you bake it yourself?"

"Uh-huh," Lizzie answered promptly. "Mrs. Keller told me what to put in but I did it all myself."

Gideon nodded and took another forkful.

Mara followed suit, in order to be able to compliment the girl herself, since Carina remained silent, sipping her tea, her cake half-consumed.

"It's very good, Lizzie," she said when she had swallowed. "Light and moist at the same time. A nice hint of lemon in both the icing and the cake."

Carina eyed Mara steadily. "Lemons are certainly dear this time of year. It's not quite the season." She addressed Gideon. "By Christmastime they'll be coming into season."

Mara set her cake plate down and took up her teacup, squeezing the lemon slice with her fork and stirring the cup. Carina never failed to fault Mara for some household or food expense even when Mara bought them out of her own earnings.

"Well, it sure tastes good," Gideon said.

They fell silent. Mara could hear Dietrich chewing then gulping his milk, but she stopped herself from saying anything. Today was not the time or place.

"Are these your father's paintings?" Gideon asked, motioning with his fork at the seascapes adorning the walls.

Before Mara could answer, Carina spoke up. "Yes, they were my late husband's work after he moved up here."

Gideon studied them a few moments as if he'd never noticed them before. "They're real pretty," he said finally.

Carina asked him about someone from the hamlet who was sick and they began to speak of the man's condition.

Mara allowed herself to sit back a fraction and sip her tea. In truth, it had been stressful to plan this tea party, not only because she hadn't wanted it to seem as if she were singling out Gideon to entertain him, but because she had been forced to include Carina as well. She hadn't invited anyone else, because she hadn't wanted to create even more speculation among her neighbors.

She had gone through with the party, though, for Lizzie's sake. The poor girl so wanted to learn how to behave properly as a young lady in social situations.

Mara was so occupied with her thoughts that she didn't notice how restless Dietrich was growing. He was swinging his legs against the sofa, the heels of his shoes hitting its carved mahogany base.

Before Carina could reprimand him for scuffing it, Dietrich suddenly leaned forward, reaching for his mug of milk. Gideon reached out, rising a fraction from his seat, as if to grab the boy's plate from his knee. Instead, his own cup fell from its saucer and hit the edge of the table. Mara watched in horror, extending a hand as if she could stop the fall, but instead, hearing the shatter of porcelain.

She rose and rushed to the sofa, seeing the puddle of tea against the floorboards and three large pieces of porcelain scattered about.

Not hearing the sounds of voices around her—"I'm sorry," "Mama, Mr. Jakeman broke your cup—" "I'll get a rag—" Mara knelt down, crowded between Dietrich's legs and the edge of the table. She picked up the largest piece of broken cup. It was true what Lizzie had said, it was like an eggshell.

The next moment, she felt the table being moved away from the sofa and Gideon crouched down opposite her. "I'm awfully sorry, ma'am."

Before she could think what to say, Carina stood behind him, craning to see what had broken. She broke out into a cackle. "One of the crown jewels! Serves you right!" She addressed Gideon. "She was so proud of that set, carting it around everywhere, packing it up so carefully." She sniffed. "Pride goeth before a fall!"

"Carina!" She shot her stepmother a look of mortification.

"That's a shame," Gideon said softly. "I was clumsy."

"Please think nothing of it. It wasn't your fault." She focused on the pieces on the floor. Gideon's large hands began to pick up the remaining pieces, making more evident how fragile they were.

"That's all right, I can do that."

"It didn't break in too many pieces. Maybe you can glue it back together."

She met his sorrow-filled eyes, not having the heart to disagree. Instead she smiled, trying to put a good face on things. "Yes. I can do that and use it as an ornament on my shelf."

He nodded. "That's a good idea." He looked so hopeful her irritation and disappointment melted.

Lizzie returned from the kitchen with a rag. "Here, Mrs. Keller, let me get in there and wipe up the mess."

"Let me just get the smaller pieces."

"That's all right, I'll pick them up."

"I can get them," Gideon added. Without giving the others a chance, he began to collect them. Mara marveled at how he was able to pick up the tiniest shards between his blunt fingertips and place them gently into his palm. She had a sudden contrasting vision of Klaus's pale, long-fingered hands, which could slap her in a blink of an eye when he lost his temper or claw into her upper arms and shake her, leaving her skin bruised for days.

But worse than the physical marks were the verbal shafts, sharp, stinging, snide barbs perfectly aimed where he knew they'd hurt her the most.

Best leave the piano playing to me, dear. Your performance may have pleased your papa, but European audiences are more discerning than an American ear. Change that gown, it makes you look sallow. You'll be outshone by the countesses and duchesses we'll be seeing this evening…

"Mrs. Keller, are you all right?"

She started at the look of concern in Gideon's eyes. "What?"

"Here, let me take those—"

She drew her palm back, unwilling to relinquish the broken pieces she carried. "That's all right, I've got them." She rose from her knees, hardly knowing what she was doing. "I'll put them away."

In the kitchen, she stared at the broken pieces, the last thing she had of her mother's and father's, the only thing she had to call home. She sighed. Perhaps Carina was right. She had been putting too much stock in a pile of crockery. *Forgive me, Lord,* she whispered. *Forgive me for idolatry.* She drew in a shuddering breath and shoved the pieces into a cupboard drawer. Despite what she'd told Gideon, there was no point in trying to glue the pieces together.

She straightened her shoulders and turned her footsteps back to the parlor, determined not to let the incident ruin the tea party. She didn't want to spoil Lizzie's day nor did she want to make Gideon feel worse than he did. He'd been trying to help Dietrich.

She pasted a bright smile on her face as she pushed open the parlor door.

Chapter Fifteen

Gideon rode home in silence, Lizzie at his side. Despite Mara's cheerfulness the rest of the afternoon, he hadn't been fooled. He knew that cup had meant a lot to her. Lizzie told him when they'd first gotten into their wagon that it had been a gift of her father's to her mother and the only thing she'd kept of home from all her years of travel.

"She didn't bring anything back from Europe but their clothes and that tea set."

He felt awful inside, even though he, too, had done his best to act as if nothing terrible had happened. He'd even forced himself to stay a good half hour more, when all he'd wanted was to get out of his Sunday best and spend the rest of the afternoon in his barn among his cows and horse. He was more fit company for livestock than fine ladies in a parlor.

But he'd not wanted Dietrich to feel badly, nor ruin Lizzie's day—not that he hadn't already. Nor did he want Mara to think he took their words or the stricken look in her eyes to heart.

But he had.

Mrs. Blackstone might be a cruel, unfeeling woman, but

her words had probably contained a grain of truth in how valuable the tea set was to Mara.

He drew in a long breath now as they approached their house. "I was thinking maybe I could replace that cup of Mrs. Keller's."

Lizzie turned to him with a hopeful look in her eye. "That's a wonderful idea, Papa. I know how sad she must be even though she didn't let on. But she's like that. She never shows how she truly feels about something if it's something bad."

"That so? What kind of bad things are you thinking about?" He maneuvered the mare up the snowy drive toward the barn.

"Well, I think things Mrs. Blackstone says. Wasn't it awful what she said today?" Lizzie shook her head before hopping down from the wagon to open the barn door.

When they were both in the barn, unhitching the horse, he probed her further. "Does Mrs. Blackstone say those kinds of things often to Mrs. Keller?"

Lizzie stroked the mare's forehead. "Not as bad as this afternoon's, but little things, you know, when it's hard to tell if they're unpleasant or not, but they have a kind of edge to them. I look at Mrs. Keller and she gets real quiet. It's gotten so's I notice a tightness around her mouth, or her hands curl up, and I know she doesn't like what Mrs. Blackstone's saying, but she doesn't let on. It makes me think of a tightly wound spring, you know. You're afraid it might spring loose."

Gideon led Bessie to her stall and started rubbing her down with an old blanket, considering what Lizzie had told him. He hadn't seen Mara around Mrs. Blackstone as much as Lizzie had, but he'd come to suspect the same things Lizzie had.

Mara kept a lot bottled up.

Dear Lord, he prayed, his strokes rhythmic as he took up

a brush to the mare's coat, *show me how I can help Mara. Grant me the ability to replace that cup for her. I feel terrible, Lord. I suspect she's known a lot of loss in her life. I don't want to add to her loss.*

Lizzie gave the horse her oats. "But other than the cup breaking, it was a nice party, wasn't it?"

He looked over at his daughter and forced a smile to his lips. "It certainly was. You did me proud. You'll make a fine lady."

Her tentative smile widened. "Well, I'll go in and see to the fire. You won't be long, will you, Papa?"

He shook his head.

But the time alone in the barn helped sooth his troubled feelings. He always needed that time after being out in company. Time to pray, to allow the silence of the barn or the outdoors to settle him again. But an afternoon among ladies was particularly trying.

And to be the one to hurt the last person he wanted to hurt.

He stared out at the twilight sky before securing the barn door for the night. *Dear Lord, why'd it have to be me?*

Gideon entered the last shop on his list. The small bell above the door tinkled as he drew it open for Lizzie to precede him.

"Good afternoon, sir. How may I assist you?" a middle-aged clerk asked him from behind a glass counter whose case was filled with china dishes.

He approached the counter, feeling more adept at what to say now that he had visited a number of stores in the large city. "I'm wondering if you have any teacups in this pattern." As he spoke he withdrew his handkerchief from a coat pocket and placed it on the counter. Unwrapping it, he held up the large shard of porcelain from Mara's broken cup. "May I?"

Gideon handed it to him.

The man took it from him silently and held it up then turned it over before handing it back to Gideon with a shake of his head. "A beautiful piece. It has the name of a Parisian firm on the bottom. I only carry British and American. We don't have much call for anything else European. How did you happen to come by it?"

"It's from a neighbor of ours. From what I understand from my daughter here, it's an old French pattern."

"It certainly looks like a fine piece of porcelain. Have you checked any of the other stores in town?"

"Yes. This is the last one." His heart felt heavy, knowing he'd have to return home tomorrow without a replacement cup for Mara. He'd taken off a couple of days, asking Paul and his father to stop in and check on his livestock while he was away with Lizzie, and they'd taken the steamer from town to Bangor.

"I'm so sorry I can't help you."

Feeling it was his last hope, Gideon ventured, "Do you have anything similar in looks?"

The man took the piece from him again and studied what was visible of the pattern. Luckily it was large enough to show a bit of both painted roses.

Lizzie spoke up. "It only has the two roses on either side of the cup. And we wouldn't need the saucer."

The man took a pair of spectacles out of his shirt pocket and examined the design more closely. "I may just have something…" He looked at them, removing his glasses. "If you'll excuse me a moment."

"Certainly, sir." Gideon felt a spurt of hope. As they waited while the clerk went into his back room, Gideon turned to his daughter. "Well?"

"Oh, I hope he has something. Wouldn't it be awful to have come all the way here and not be able to take anything back to Mrs. Keller?"

He nodded, his spirits plummeting again.

In a short while the clerk returned, this time with a cup and saucer in his hands. "Well, this might serve the trick." He placed them on the countertop.

Gideon looked at the set without touching it. It did look similar, with a deep pink rose and a yellow one beside and slightly behind it.

Lizzie took up the cup and turned it around.

"It's English," the man told her.

"Oh, it looks just like it! It's very pretty," she added.

"That is so," the clerk agreed. "It's the closest match I have."

"And it's the closest we've been able to find," added Gideon. "What do you think, Lizzie?"

She took another moment looking at it and the saucer. Finally, she nodded. "I guess it'll have to do. We've been to every shop."

"Have you tried Boston?"

Gideon blinked. Boston was too far to consider going shopping there. "No, sir, I haven't."

"I could give you a few addresses to write to, antique shops that specialize in fine porcelain."

Gideon rubbed his chin. "I don't know. We've come from Down East, and Boston's quite a journey."

"You shouldn't have to go all the way there. If anyone had this specimen, they could ship it to you, I'm certain."

Gideon's hope lifted. "That would fine then, I'd appreciate the addresses."

"Very well, sir. Do you still wish to purchase this cup and saucer?"

"I'd better, just in case I can't get anything from the Boston shops. But I only need the cup."

The clerk pursed his lips. "We only sell the set, sir."

"Well, all right then." He reached for his wallet. "How much will it be?"

The clerk quoted a price.

It was a bit more than he'd expected to pay for a cup—and now saucer. He sighed, opening his billfold. His carelessness was proving expensive. "Very well."

"I shall wrap it up for you."

"I'd appreciate some good wrapping. We have a long journey home and I'd hate to have it break."

"Never fear, sir. We are experts in wrapping and shipping fragile objects."

When they left the shop with their parcel, Lizzie turned to him. "I'm glad we found that. I'm sure Mrs. Keller will like it. Do you think we could do a bit of Christmas shopping before we head home?"

Christmas was only a couple of weeks away. They'd come this far and it would be a shame to waste the opportunity of all the shops. He didn't look forward to traipsing through more stores, but he didn't want to disappoint his daughter. "Sure. Why don't we eat some dinner first and then go shopping?"

"Yes, all that hunting for china has made me famished. Let's go!"

Mara was ironing in the kitchen when she heard a wagon come up the drive. She set down the iron and went to the window and drew back the lace curtain a fraction. Gideon and Lizzie were heading to the house.

Her heart sped up a bit. She hadn't seen Gideon since the tea party some days ago. Lizzie had told her that she and her father had to go to Bangor on some errands so she knew they'd been away.

Dietrich had found the days long, not being able to go to Gideon's, and not having Paul around as much, since he was also looking after Gideon's livestock. The weather had been gray with a mixture of rain and snow, making everything too icy to go outside much. Mara had finally taken her son to visit a friend and spend the night, giving her a few hours of peace and quiet.

As she watched Gideon stop the wagon and get down, she admitted how much she'd missed him, even when it was only to look outside and see him chopping wood or deliver some item to Mrs. Blackstone, like a side of ham or bacon from his butchering.

Lizzie made her way to the woodshed door while her father saw to the horse.

Mara removed her apron and glanced at her hair in a small square mirror hanging near the door. She tucked a few stray locks into her chignon right before she heard the knock on the door.

She opened it at once, greeting Lizzie with a wide smile, feeling a genuine burst of gladness at the sight of the girl. The sentiment was returned if the girl's smile was any indication.

The next moment the two embraced. "It's so good to see you!"

"Oh, Mrs. Keller, I wanted to come right over, but we didn't arrive till late yesterday."

Mara ushered her farther into the kitchen. "Come in. Can you stay a while? I'm sure you have a lot to do at home."

Lizzie closed the door behind her and unwound her woolen scarf. "Oh, not so much. I left everything neat and tidy, and Paul and his father took good care of our animals. Dietrich must come over. The kittens are quite big now. It's a shame he can't have one. They've grown enough to be given away." She glanced around her. "Where is he, anyway? I didn't see him outside."

"I let him go visit young Tommy this afternoon. He's been cooped up for a few days."

Lizzie nodded.

Mara took her things. "Is your father coming in, or just

dropping you off?" She tried to keep her tone casual as she hung Lizzie's cloak on a hook.

"Oh, he's coming in, but he's probably chatting with Paul. He's very impressed with all he did. I know he wants to make up for it somehow." Lizzie's cheeks dimpled. "We bought him a little something for Christmas, though. I know he'll like it."

"Christmas shopping?" Mara had hardly given Christmas a thought although she knew it was around the corner. "Is that why you went to Bangor?"

"Oh, we had an errand, a very important errand to do, but we thought we might as well do a little shopping while we were there. Mrs. Keller, they have so many shops and an emporium and a dry goods store, where you can find ever so many things, so much larger than in town. Have you ever been to Bangor?"

"Once, passing through, but usually I've traveled direct by steamer from Boston."

"Boston must be vast," she said somewhat wistfully.

"Perhaps you'll visit some day."

"I don't know. It's pretty far from Eagle's Bay."

"Oh, nowadays it's not so far by steamer. Well, come in and have a cup of tea or coffee."

"Thank you." She sobered, looking around. "Is Mrs. Blackstone home?"

"No. She has gone to the harbor to visit the Allendales."

The girl seemed to breathe a sigh of relief. "Can I help you with the tea? Papa may want coffee."

"I have some in the pot here on the side of the stove, and the water's hot for tea, so you just sit down."

As she brewed the tea, there was another knock on the kitchen door and Lizzie rose to answer it. "There you are, Papa. I told Mrs. Keller you'd have a cup of coffee. Would you rather have a cup of tea?"

"Anything's fine," he said as he entered, his glance going

at once to Mara. Mara nodded, smiling shyly before turning back to the teapot. "As long as you don't go to any trouble."

"No trouble at all," she said as Lizzie added, "The coffee's all ready."

Mara watched out of the corner of her eye as Lizzie took her father's overcoat, gloves, scarf and sealskin cap. When he sat at the foot of the kitchen table, Mara brought him a mug of coffee and set the pitcher of cream beside it. "Sugar?"

He shook his head with a brief smile. "This'll be fine. Thank you." He wrapped his large hands around the mug. "Nice to have something hot. It sure is raw outdoors."

"How was your trip?" she asked when she took her seat at the other end of the table, making an effort to keep her hands still. Lizzie sat between them with her own teacup and saucer and was busy serving herself a spoonful of sugar. "Aren't you having any, Mrs. Keller?"

"In a bit."

"I hope we're not interrupting your work," Mr. Jakeman said with a nod toward the ironing board.

"Oh, I have the whole afternoon to work on my pile. I was looking forward to hearing about your trip to Bangor." It was amazing how good it was to see him. Just looking at his face was like nectar to her parched soul. How could she feel so needy of someone in such a short time?

His expression was open. She felt with him that the person he presented to the world was the same he was in private. There were no hidden flaws or sins. But she had been fooled before. Her glance went to Lizzie. But this man's daughter attested to his upright character. She adored her father.

"It was good. I don't go in much for shopping and such, but Lizzie had a good time."

Mara smiled. "We women usually do. I didn't realize Christmas will soon be upon us."

"Will you be doing anything special for the holidays?"

he asked before taking a sip of coffee, continuing to watch her over the rim.

She looked down at the table. "No. I don't believe Carina does much but, you know, with Dietrich, I'd like to make the holiday special."

"Of course. Children tend to get all worked up at the notion of presents." His eyes crinkled at the corners.

She nodded, warmed by the understanding in his eyes.

"I love Christmas," Lizzie said. "I usually make all my gifts, and start weeks, sometimes months, in advance, to make sure I have enough time, especially if it means knitting or embroidering something."

"Yes, indeed. I really must think about things like that. Not that I have that many people to give gifts to. I haven't been here that long."

"We don't put much stock in gifts," Gideon said right away. Was he trying to allay any worry she might have that she had to give them gifts? "Reverend Grayson has a nice service Christmas morning and then Lizzie makes a good dinner. Sarah or one of my brothers always invites us over, but I kind of like to eat Christmas dinner at home. Sometimes, if the weather's clear, we'll go and visit afterward."

Mara nodded and smiled. Whether he expected a gift or not, she certainly hoped she could give him and Lizzie some little token of her appreciation for all they'd done for her and Dietrich since she'd arrived.

Gideon drained the last of his coffee. Before Mara could offer him more, or a slice of cake or some of the oatmeal cookies she'd baked, he pushed back from his chair. "Well, I'd better tell you the reason we came by."

A reason? She watched, her curiosity growing as he went to his overcoat and drew out a parcel from its capacious pocket. He set the brown-wrapped box in front of her and cleared his throat. "This is for you."

She looked up at him, her eyes wide. "For me?"

"Yes."

"But it's not even Christmas," she attempted to joke to dispel the sense of panic welling up inside of her.

Gideon didn't smile. Instead, he averted his gaze, motioning to the parcel. "Why don't you open it?"

She looked at it, her heart thumping, then glanced at Lizzie, whose color was high and who was biting her lip as if to keep from smiling. She gestured with her chin, a gesture reminiscent of her father. "Go ahead, it's not going to bite you."

Mara gave a nervous laugh, feeling as if the description were accurate. "Very well." Gingerly, she reached out and began to untie the string at its top. Her fingers fumbled, with Gideon standing so close to her, observing every move.

"Here, let me." He reached out with a jackknife. In a second, he had sliced through the string and slid the package back to her.

"Th-thank you." The string fell away as she picked up the box and unfolded the paper from it. She saw the logo of a store name on the top of the box before slowly lifting it. Newspaper filled it within.

She dug about for the object and lifted it, the newspaper falling away. She saw immediately that it was a teacup. Her heartbeat increased. Could it be—?

Her breath caught. It was her pattern! But no—

Gideon saw the moment she realized the cup was not an exact match to her own only because he was watching her so closely. There was a split second where her fine eyebrows drew together a fraction. The next instant her brow cleared and a smile lifted the corners of her lips as she glanced first at him then at Lizzie. "You shouldn't have. How very thoughtful of you."

He cleared his throat. "I know it's not the same pattern

but it was the closest we could find." A heavy weight settled in the pit of his stomach, a sense of failure filling him.

She turned her blue eyes to him, her smile bright. "It looks so similar I can hardly tell them apart. Besides, it's the thought that counts." Her smile disappeared. "Please tell me you didn't go all the way to Bangor to replace the cup?"

Lizzie answered before he had the chance to make some offhand remark about having to do a lot of errands. "That we did. It was Papa's idea. Oh, but we had so much fun looking in all the stores that sold china. My, I never imagined there could be so many patterns."

"Yes, I know." Mara kept the cup cradled in her hands. "But this one is so pretty. I shall always treasure it, the more knowing it came from you."

Lizzie blushed. "The clerk said he didn't carry that French pattern, but he brought this one out. He said it's English."

She didn't turn it over to read the bottom. "The English are well-known for their porcelain. It's probably of finer quality than my set."

Lizzie nodded toward the box. "We also got the saucer. The clerk told us they always sell them together."

"I'm so sorry to have made you go to the expense." As she spoke, Mara set down the cup and dug around in the remaining newspaper, carefully bringing out the saucer and unwrapping it. She then placed it on the table with the cup atop it. "It's truly beautiful. I wish I could repay you somehow."

Gideon released a slow breath, afraid for a moment she'd insist on paying for it. He realized she would never be so crass. "You've done a lot for us—for Lizzie—already. So, don't go fretting about repayment."

She glanced briefly at him with a small nod then stood from the table. "I'll pour myself that cup of tea now in celebration."

"May we see one of the original cups? It was hard to re-

member the exact shape with only the small piece we had."
Lizzie looked expectantly at Mara.

"Oh, I'm sure it looks very similar."

Gideon removed the shard he had kept from his pocket.
"Here's the piece I took with me. I wanted to return it to
you."

She reached out for it, her fingers touching his palm
briefly. "I wondered where it had got to."

So, she must have tried to glue it back together. "I'm
sorry, I shouldn't have taken it without permission. But I
knew you were upset that day and I wanted to be able to
have something to help me find a replacement."

"It was so thoughtful of you," she murmured, looking
downward.

"Oh, please, Mrs. Keller, may I see one of your cups?"

Gideon could see Mara was reluctant but at Lizzie's in-
sistence, she merely gave a nod and left the kitchen with a
quiet "Excuse me."

She returned a moment later with one of the cups from the
tea party and set it on the table. Lizzie immediately reached
for it and held up both cups side by side. Her expectant face
turned into a frown. "It doesn't have the gold rim around it,
and the handle is shaped slightly differently."

"But it does look amazingly similar," Mara countered.

He knew she was only trying to ease Lizzie's disappointment. His daughter's shoulders slumped. "I thought for sure
it was the same."

Mara put a hand on her shoulder. "It doesn't matter. What
matters to me is that you took so much time and trouble over
a simple teacup. It's just an object, but your thoughtfulness
means more than I can say."

Gideon hid his own feelings. He didn't want to prolong
the interview any longer, knowing it must be a strain for
her to continue reassuring them that the cup was adequate.
"Well, we'd better be off. Give our regards to Mrs. Black-

stone. Tell Dietrich I missed seeing him. Maybe you could send him over tomorrow."

"I certainly shall. I know he's missed you."

Their eyes met briefly at her last words and the question crossed his mind. Had *she* missed him over the past few days?

He grabbed his hat and coat from the door, shoving the hat on his head as if it would help displace such a ridiculous question. Why should a fine lady like Mara have missed him? He was as clumsy as an ox and hadn't even been able to replace her treasured teacup.

Chapter Sixteen

Dietrich entered the kitchen and shut the door behind him with a click. Mara smiled at him. He'd finally learned not to slam it behind him. "Hello, there. You look good and healthy." His cheeks were rosy, his dark hair tousled as he drew off his woolen cap.

"I was outside with Mr. Jakeman. He took me in his sleigh up into one of the woodlots to show me where he'll be cutting trees soon with Paul."

Mara set down the potato and the paring knife she was holding. "I hope you didn't ask him to let you accompany him then."

Dietrich hung up his coat on the lower hook Mara had placed for him. "I did but he said not this year."

She breathed a sigh of relief, mentally thanking Gideon for his good sense. "Put your mittens by the stove."

He obeyed, spreading his cap, scarf and mittens on a rack standing near the woodstove.

"You can pour yourself a glass of milk or would you like a hot cup of tea with a cookie?"

"I'll get some milk."

A few minutes later, he came to sit beside her, a glass of

milk and a large molasses cookie before him. "What're you making?"

"Codfish cakes for supper." She'd finished peeling the cold cooked potatoes and now began flaking the dried, salted cod she'd set to soak the night before.

"Yum-yum," he said, rubbing his tummy.

After taking a bite of cookie and sip of milk, he turned to her. "Mama, when are we going to make Christmas decorations?"

Mara's hands stilled in the large bowl. "Hmm. I've been so busy with piano lessons I haven't had much time to think about Christmas."

"Lizzie already has fir boughs all over their house. They smell so good." He took a large sniff. "Better even than the ones you used to put in our house in Paris."

"I imagine it's because it's balsam fir. It has about the nicest scent of all the evergreen trees." She'd always made their sitting room, no matter how mean their boardinghouse, as festive as she could during the holidays. Perhaps because she'd married a man of German origin and had visited his family there a few times in the earlier years of their marriage, she'd grown to enjoy all the evergreen decorations for Christmas.

She'd loved the Christmas fairs in the German towns, where open-air stalls sold wooden decorations for the Christmas trees. And there was no prettier sight than the fir trees with their candles lit on Christmas Eve.

She wasn't sure how much Dietrich remembered, since he'd been so young, but clearly he retained some vivid memories.

"Do you still have my nutcracker?"

Mara thought how to answer. A child would not understand how limited she'd been in what she'd been able to bring home. "No, dear, we weren't able to bring it. I'm sorry. I only had enough space to pack your stuffed animal, your wooden train set and your clothes."

His mouth turned downward. For a moment she wondered if he would cry. But instead he took another bite of his cookie. "Maybe I can get another one for Christmas." His brown eyes twinkled over the rim of his glass.

Before she could reply, wondering if they even sold such types of nutcrackers in this part of the world, he continued. "Lizzie is making all kinds of Christmas presents. She says she has things hidden all over the house. She says she has something for me and you and says I'll never guess."

Mara focused on the codfish. She hadn't planned on any gift giving. Carina had made it plain she didn't want any evergreen boughs or a tree in the house. *We'll be picking out fir needles all year long from between the floorboards.*

Mara had only thought of making Dietrich some little token to acknowledge the day but hadn't had much time to do so yet. But now she realized Christmas was only a little over a week away.

"What do you have for Lizzie and Mr. Jakeman?"

"I don't have anything...yet," she added. Maybe she'd have enough time to embroider a set of handkerchiefs, perhaps knit a pair of socks for Gideon and buy some little thing like a pair of hair combs for Lizzie. She felt her face grow warm at the notion of these practical things for Gideon, the kinds of things a wife would make for her husband.

Perhaps a box of fudge or some cookies would be better. She looked over at her son. "What do you want to give them?"

He scrunched up his face, chewing on his cookie. "I don't know. Maybe some marbles for Mr. Jakeman? And a doll for Lizzie. Although she doesn't play with dolls. She has a collection in her room, though. I've seen it. She keeps them all lined up in a row. She said her mama made her all of them.

Every year for Christmas she'd get a new one, and a dress for the old one, she told me."

Mara pictured the scene. What lovely memories and mementoes the girl must have of the late Mrs. Jakeman.

"Well, we'd better get busy, hadn't we, thinking of something for the two of them? Maybe you can go into town with me one day this week and we can look in the shops." She had enough saved up now to use a little on some more frivolous things. Gifts for those she cared about most.

Her thoughts returned to the teacup Lizzie and Gideon had gone all the way to Bangor for. Even though it wasn't an exact match, their gesture had touched her deeply and made her realize how unused she was to having anyone do anything for her.

Had she become so bent on doing for herself that she'd forgotten how to receive?

Gideon was not content to rest on the matter of the broken teacup. As soon as he returned home that afternoon, he sat down and wrote to the address of the shop in Boston that the Bangor clerk had given him. The next morning, he posted his letter.

Waiting was never easy but Gideon prided himself on being a patient man. Planting and waiting for seeds to sprout and then tending them until harvest time developed patience in a person.

A person learned to read the signs in the sky and landscape.

Perhaps that's what made him able to read the nuances in Mara's face whenever he was in her presence. And cause him to spend an inordinate amount of time thinking about her when he wasn't.

He sighed now as he straightened from chopping wood, setting down his ax a moment and rolling his shoulders. The sky had been low and gray all morning and now just past noon the first flakes began to fall against his face.

He hadn't seen Mara in almost a week. Early winter was a time when folks tended to hunker down in their homes, getting prepared for the long months ahead as if for a siege. With Christmas in two days, people were busy with holiday preparations as well.

He'd tried to find out from Lizzie if the Kellers had any special plans. Mrs. Blackstone didn't do much of anything, except go to church on Christmas morning and to dinner at his cousin's house afterward. Cliff usually came by to take her to dinner, so Gideon didn't have to.

Lizzie planned on baking a roast beef from the cow that had been slaughtered. They had plenty of potatoes, carrots, turnips, parsnips and onions in the root cellar, and Lizzie had canned dozens of jars of greens from the summer garden.

He looked down the road toward Mrs. Blackstone's though it wasn't visible from the bends in the road and forest separating the two properties.

On the spur of the moment, he walked toward the barn to put his ax away. Dietrich was inside with Lizzie. The boy usually spent afternoons after school with them. Lizzie had invited him inside today to bake sugar cookies for Christmas.

They looked up when he entered the kitchen. "How much longer are you going to be baking?"

Lizzie gestured at the tray of cookies in front of her on the table. "This is the last one."

"I just wondered if you two wanted to go into the forest with me and cut some greens to deliver to Mrs. Blackstone and your mother, Dietrich?"

Dietrich jumped down from his chair, clapping his hands. "You mean a tree?"

He rubbed his chin, not bothering to remove his outer things. "Well, perhaps not a tree, but some branches to use as garlands and table decorations the way we have about the house here." Lizzie had done a good job in the parlor and dining room, making everything look festive. The two of them had already found a tree in the forest and he'd cut it down yesterday and stood it in a bucket of water in the woodshed. Tomorrow they'd put it up.

Dietrich's face fell and Gideon felt a spurt of compassion for the boy. "Maybe you could come over tomorrow and help us decorate our tree."

His eyes widened. "Could I?"

"We'll ask your mother. Well, what do you say? You want to come along with me in a little while and bring back some greens when you go home? It's just starting to snow, but we should be back before it gets too thick."

Dietrich nodded his head with vigor.

"Sounds perfect, Papa," Lizzie added. "We'll be along in a bit and even bring you some cookies."

He smiled and winked at his daughter. "I'll hold you to that!"

About an hour later they set out. Gideon took them up-country across the road to a place where he'd been felling trees so there would be lots of fallen branches on the snow.

Lizzie raised her face toward the sky. "I love the forest when it snows. Everything's so quiet and peaceful."

Dietrich stuck his tongue out to catch snowflakes. "Mmm. They taste good."

Lizzie and Gideon chuckled.

"I imagine all the animals tucked away in their nests or hideaways sleeping," Lizzie said, bending over and scooping up a handful of snow. "No good for snowballs. It's not wet enough."

Gideon nodded, eyeing his surroundings. "The temperature's dropping." He stopped at the clearing. "Here we are.

I brought some clippers. Let's get our greens and head back. I want to get you home, Dietrich, before it worsens."

"Are we going to have a snowstorm, Mr. Jakeman?"

Gideon loped off a thick balsam branch. "Looks that way, son."

It was midafternoon, the sky already darkening when they left the forest, carrying their bundles of evergreen boughs. "We'll go straight to your house, Dietrich. Your mother'll be expecting you home anyway."

They marched the rest of the way in silence. Even Dietrich was subdued, probably with the cold. Gideon's toes and fingers felt stiff, the only part of his face visible above his scarf and below his sealskin cap was chapped from the frigid air. As soon as they left the forest, the wind from off the coast hit them, making it seem several degrees colder.

Soon, the lights from Mrs. Blackstone's house appeared. As if by mutual accord, they picked up their pace as they headed toward the long drive. Gideon couldn't help but think that Mara might invite him and Lizzie in for something hot to drink.

It would probably be awkward with Mrs. Blackstone there. He didn't know why it should be. He'd never been on excessively friendly terms with her. She'd seemed to hold herself reserved from those of the hamlet as if she considered herself a bit better. That had never prevented her from accepting their help when she'd become a widow.

Gideon admired his cousin for faithfully inviting Mrs. Blackstone to all the major holiday dinners as well as to many a Sunday dinner after church, even though the two didn't have much to talk about. But Sarah was a good Christian and felt it part of that duty to "look after the orphans and widows." That's what kept Gideon doing any outside work for Mrs. Blackstone when there was more than Paul could manage on his own.

But since Mara and her son's arrival, Gideon sensed a deeper reserve, even a coldness, in the older lady's behavior toward her husband's only living family. Gideon shook his head, finding it hard to fathom.

He hefted the bundle of greens in his hand, glad to soon be able to set it down.

They finally reached the woodshed door. Dietrich yanked it open with his free hand. Stopping him by the shoulder, Gideon held him back from rushing inside. "Hold up there. Ladies first, remember."

Dietrich stepped away from the doorway.

Lizzie swept passed him, holding her skirts aloft like a grand lady in a hoop skirt. "Thank you, sir."

Gideon then gave Dietrich a pat on the back, sending him in next. "Get along with you before your mother gets anxious. Put your boughs near Lizzie's bundle."

His own heartbeat quickening a notch or two in anticipation of seeing Mara, Gideon came in last and closed and latched the door behind him. "Stamp your boots good before going into the kitchen."

Lizzie opened the kitchen door, sending a shaft of light into the dim shed. "Hallo!" She called out as she entered. "Mrs. Keller? Mrs. Blackstone?"

Dietrich ran ahead of her. "I'm home, Mama!"

Gideon set down his bundle atop the others then approached the step up onto the threshold to the kitchen, stopping short when Mrs. Blackstone entered the kitchen. "Good evening, ma'am," he said, lifting his cap.

"I didn't expect you. I thought it was Mara."

Gideon stared at her. "Mrs. Keller's not home?" Who would be out on an afternoon like today?

"No." Mrs. Blackstone entered farther into the kitchen, motioning with an arm. "Come in, please, before you let in all the cold air."

"Sorry about that." Gideon hurried in and shut the door

behind him. The kitchen felt like a warm bath after the frigid air. Before he could ask anything more about Mara's whereabouts, Dietrich spoke.

"Mama's not back from town yet?"

"No." The older lady's eyes met Gideon's with a small frown. His own must have shown the worry he was feeling. "She insisted on going in for her lessons even though I told her it looked like snow coming on, but she said she'd be back with plenty of time." She walked to the window and pushed back the filmy curtain, looking out at the dark night. "But she's usually back by now."

"Mama's out in the snow?" Dietrich's bottom lip began to quiver, his eyes filling with fear. Lizzie came up to him and took his hand.

Gideon frowned. "But it's not Thursday, her usual day."

"She's been going in two days a week the last two weeks," the widow replied.

Gideon didn't have to think about it anymore. He grasped the doorknob. "I'm going out and look for her. Come along, Lizzie."

"Yes, Papa." Lizzie hurried right behind him.

They stopped short at the sound of Dietrich's wail. "I want Mama!"

They both went up to him, Lizzie putting a hand around his shoulders, bending over him with comforting murmurs. Gideon put his hand on the boy's head. "I'll find her, son, and bring her back to you."

When they turned to go again, Dietrich pulled at Gideon's coat. "I want to go with you. Take me with you!" His crying grew harder. Gideon looked helplessly at Lizzie, knowing exactly how the little tyke must be feeling.

"He can stay with me," Lizzie said, "while you go out." She looked around Gideon to Mrs. Blackstone. "If you don't mind, ma'am. I can feed him and put him to bed."

Mrs. Blackstone shrugged. "Take him, by all means. He'll be fretting here, I'm sure, and I know nothing of children."

Gideon cleared his throat. "I— If Mrs. Keller should show up here, just tell her where her son is, that he's in good hands."

"I will indeed, though I don't see how she can make it home on her own," she added with another glance out the dark window.

Refraining from expressing his annoyance at her words in front of Dietrich, he ushered the boy from the room.

By the time Mara finished with her last pupil, it was almost dark. When the girl's mother opened the front door for her, bidding her goodbye, Mara stopped short on the threshold, not expecting the swirling snow around her.

The other woman peered out. "Goodness, it's getting thick out there. Are you sure you want to go out in that?"

"I'll be fine, ma'am," she said with more certainty than she felt, her thoughts on getting back to Dietrich, hoping Gideon had brought him home by now and hoping her son would do nothing to annoy Mrs. Blackstone before she managed to arrive home.

She wrapped her scarf more tightly around her neck, bringing it up to cover the bottom half of her face, hunching against the snow before setting out. *Guide me, dear Lord, please guide me safely home to Dietrich. Bring him home, too.* She didn't have too many worries on that score, trusting Gideon with her son after these past months.

Going down Main Street didn't prove too difficult. She crossed the river, hearing its raging waters below her, but didn't pause. She walked as fast as she could, despite the icy surfaces. She reached the end of town, following the street along the river. As soon as she passed the last houses, the wind seemed to pick up, buffeting her in gusts of snow.

Finally, she reached a forest which sheltered her some-

what from the wind and worst of the snow but made it harder
to see the road. It was still dusk and the road still passable
but she wondered how it would be four miles hence. As she
walked, she prayed and recited psalms she'd memorized over
the years in times of trouble.

By the time darkness had fallen, she was out where the
road crossed open fields and blueberry barrens. The wind
stung her cheeks and a new worry confronted her. What if
she lost the road and wandered onto the fields by mistake?

Visions of being found frozen to death filled her mind.
She renewed her prayers and strained her eyes to distinguish
the road from the fields. Thankfully the land rose on either
side of the road, but as snow filled the road, she wondered
how long before it was as high as the land.

Resolutely, she forced her thoughts in another direction.
Dietrich. Gideon had surely brought him home by now. She
couldn't help but think as she always did when her thoughts
veered in this direction of what a fine father he was to her
son.

Oh, that Dietrich had known such a father since birth!
But perhaps he'd gotten to know Gideon early enough that
all the painful memories of his own father would fade from
his young mind.

She felt no sense of betrayal in finding Gideon a superior
father than her child's natural father. Despite his talent,
Klaus was a selfish, egotistical man, whose pride had grown
in proportion to the adulation he'd received onstage. She
could have borne the brunt of his exacting demands at home,
but not the faultfinding he'd begun to inflict upon Dietrich
as their child grew old enough to understand.

A gust of wind nearly knocked her over. Mara blinked,
hardly able to see through the driving snow. She could no
longer fool herself that this was anything short of a blizzard.
The lights of the last houses had been left far behind. It was

no use to try and turn back. Chances were just as likely she'd lose her way going back as going forward.

All she could do was pray for a miracle. *Lord, please bring me back to my son.* Her lips were too stiff with cold to try to pray aloud. She could no longer see the road. The snow would soon reach her knees. The drag against her long skirts made the going only slower. The only way to tell she was on the road was the firmness of its frozen, rutted surface. She kept veering off to the sides and would realize it by the ditches or rise in terrain.

Her hands flew out, trying to right herself before falling into a ditch. If she twisted an ankle, she'd be done for.

Heavenly Father, please help me, in Your dear Son Jesus's name...

Chapter Seventeen

Before Gideon got more than half a mile from his driveway, the snow was blinding and full darkness had fallen. Thankful that his mare knew the way, he nevertheless prayed for guidance, knowing how easy it was to lose one's bearings in a snowstorm.

Even if his mare kept to the road, who was to say Mara would haven't wandered off it? It would be like finding a dory gone adrift at sea.

Firmly putting such thoughts out of his mind, he concentrated on navigating his sleigh through the high drifts of snow. Despite the two lanterns hanging on either side of the sleigh, it was difficult to distinguish the road from the surrounding land any longer. Only his horse's innate sense of direction and knowledge of the ground beneath her hooves could keep them on the right path.

Gideon huddled beneath the layers of heavy woolen blanket and bearskin rug covering his legs. Beside him on the narrow seat lay another folded blanket wrapped around a hot water flask and a foot warmer on the floor below for Mara *when* he found her. He would not entertain the word *if.*

Maybe she'd decided to board somewhere in town. He didn't know how many folks she knew, but he was certain someone, perhaps one of her pupil's parents, would offer her a place. People around here knew how serious a snowstorm was and wouldn't hesitate to offer lodging for a night.

But would she have stayed? He knew how careful she was of her son. Deep in his heart he doubted she'd stay away from Dietrich without sending word.

He drew in a deep breath, the icy air bringing a further chill to his body. A physical chill that added to the mental chill he was already experiencing with all the possibilities looming in his mind.

He recited a psalm, the only antidote he knew to keep terror at bay. *"The Lord is my shepherd, I shall not want..."*

Give her wisdom, Lord. Dear God, show her the way. If she's in town still, guide me safely there. But if Mara is somewhere between here and town, lead me to her. Keep her safe, keep her on the road until I can get to her.

He squinted into the small rims of light cast by the lanterns. Thick snow swirled in the haloes. The rest was darkness. The sleigh bells on the harness jingled, bringing a cheery sound to the still night.

Snow fell on his eyebrows and eyelashes and he had to keep brushing it off. They went by the few sparse lights of scattered farmhouses. He knew the road well, every rise, descent and turn, so he kept his attention fixed on these geographical signposts, his eyes scanning the terrain around him. He could tell when they passed the Winfields' pastures then entered the Bay Woods. The road turned away from the hamlet, whose small harbor lay in the opposite direction. He guided the mare onto the road to town, which lay inland along the river.

He judged he had about three miles to go. As they past the last light, which he knew was the Edgertons' farm, he knew in another quarter of a mile or so, they'd enter a stretch of blueberry land, the undulating heath where the low-bush crops grew in summer.

But first was a stretch of heavy forest, the tall firs looking only slightly blacker than the sky, hemming the sleigh in on either side like giant columns of soldiers. In the distance a wolf howled and he shivered at the sound.

What if she were somewhere in there? No, she wouldn't have wandered in between the thickly growing trees. What if she had fallen somewhere? Would he see her in this gloom? Would she hear the jingle of the sleigh bells?

Finally they left the pitch darkness of the forest. With a prayer upon his lips, Gideon scanned both sides of the road. Large boulders lay covered in snow like humps. What if she had fallen and lay covered in snow? Would he miss her, thinking her form was a smaller boulder?

He would get out and examine each hump that looked the size of a human body.

The sleigh moved along, the whoosh of the runners hardly audible below the jingle of the bells. Surely Mara would hear the sounds from a distance? He strained to distinguish the shadows in the dark. Would she have reached the halfway point between hamlet and town by now? He tried to calculate what time she would have left town.

He should have been more persistent in coming to fetch her on the days she gave her lessons in town, regardless of her polite rebuff. He'd hoped he'd conveyed by his behavior that he'd never presume to act on his feelings—not without any clear encouragement from her. But feelings had a way of growing whether one wanted them to or not. Each encounter of his with Mara Keller only deepened his respect and admiration...and the longing of a man for a woman—for that companionship, friendship—and for that union that transcended all.

The sense of urgency to find Mara grew in him. He began to call out her name. "Mrs. Keller! Mrs. Keller!" he shouted out in both directions then realized it sounded ridiculous to sound so formal. "Mara! Mara!"

Thinking he saw something move ahead of him on the side of the road, he pulled on the reins. "Whoa, Bessie." He strained to hear into the night. His mare tossed her head, sending the bells jangling again. "Shush, girl."

He stepped from the sleigh and sank into knee-high snow. "Stay put a moment, Bess," he told the mare with a pat to her neck. Her heavy puffs of breath created clouds of vapor in the chill air.

"Mara!"

Yes, there was a sound—a soft moan. Gideon took down one of the lanterns from its hook and hurried toward the sound, his progress impeded by the deep, thick snow.

A movement in a mound of snow from the side of the road. He scrambled down the ditch. An arm rose, shaking off a pile of snow. He reached for it.

Another moan. He quickly brushed the snow off the form. "Mara—thank God." He cleared the snow from her face as she made an effort to rise. He put his arm around her shoulders and helped her up.

"Wha—"

"Shush, don't try to talk. Here, put your arm around my neck." He set his lantern down in the snow then, bending over her, he brought his other arm under her knees and braced himself to lift her.

Her skirts, caked with snow, weighed her down. Her hands came around his neck. "I…I think I can walk."

"The snow's too deep. I've got the sleigh right here." As he spoke, he stood with a soft grunt then shifted her in his arms to get a better grip. Though she felt heavy, she also felt good in his arms. For a second, he could only stand, an overwhelming relief and thankfulness washing over him. He had found her and she was alive!

Dear God, thank You for keeping her and leading me to her.

She rested her head upon his chest and said nothing, appearing completely done in. He reached the sleigh and set her on the seat on the nearest side.

She was covered in snow but he thought it was best to get her tucked in. He had no idea if she was hurt. He unfolded the blanket and set the stone water bottle against her then covered her legs.

She brought a hand to her face. "I feel…so disoriented."

"You must have passed out. Can you feel your feet or hands?"

"I think so…they're too numb to tell." She laughed weakly.

He placed her feet atop the foot warmer and covered them in the blankets and fur lap robe. Then he took a hand in his and removed her mitten and began to rub her ice-cold fingers.

"That feels better." Her voice sounded stronger. "I don't think they're frozen."

He placed her hand under the cover and began with the other. Satisfied, he finished tucking her in. "Let's get you home."

Once he had retrieved the lantern and gotten in on the other side, wedged tightly beside her in the small space, he finished tucking the blankets around them both and took up the reins to turn the sleigh around.

"Any idea how long you were there?"

"No. I'm not sure what happened. I'd gotten a good way. I'd reached the barrens, but it was getting harder and harder to get through the snow. I was being so careful to keep to the road. But it was getting difficult to see." She gave a small laugh. "I was even debating turning back but I knew I'd gone too far to make that practical."

After a moment she added, "I didn't want Dietrich to worry."

He'd been right about that. "I would have come fetch you if I'd known you'd been to town this afternoon. I didn't find out till Lizzie and I brought Dietrich home. By then, it was nigh on four o'clock."

"I didn't leave town till around three."

Under normal circumstances she'd be home. "I'm amazed you made the progress you did."

"I was pretty desperate." Again, a trace of humor underscored her words.

He urged the mare forward. The snow was coming down thick and fast. But the narrow space in the sleigh felt warm and cozy under the thick cover of blankets. The ride no longer felt scary and threatening. Instead, he felt a kind of peace, as if the two of them were the only two people in the universe. He glanced at her frequently to assure himself she was all right—and that she was really there beside him. "Warm enough?"

"Mmm. Toasty. I'm glad for the foot warmer. I can feel my toes again."

"You must not have been there too long."

"I think I fell into the ditch and wrenched my ankle. It feels a bit sore."

"We can put some liniment on it when we get home. By the way, Dietrich is at my house. When we found out from Mrs. Blackstone that you were still out, we thought it best he stay with Lizzie."

"I'm sorry for all the trouble. You shouldn't have had to go out in this storm."

"I'm just glad to have found you." His voice hitched, and he wished he could express how profoundly thankful he was.

As they approached his farmhouse, Lizzie, bless her heart, had lights blazing everywhere to light the way. He cleared his throat, having thought about this for the past half hour. "If you don't mind, I'd like to propose you stay here with Dietrich tonight. There's plenty of room."

She didn't answer as he swung into the drive. He braced himself for her refusal, but truth be told, he didn't want to have to make the final leg of the journey to Mrs. Blackstone's. Bessie was about done in, and the storm showed no signs of abating.

"Thank you," she finally said.

He imagined she had probably realized the same thing, although it likely went against the grain for her to impose. All he could do was breathe a sigh of relief that she'd acquiesced.

"Let me get the barn door."

As soon as he brought the sleigh into the barn, it felt strange not to have the thick flakes pummeling his face.

Mrs. Keller turned to him, a hand touching his arm as he made to move. "Wait."

He looked into her eyes, a question in his.

"I want to thank you."

He began to shake his head that there was no need, but he could feel the pressure of her hand increase through the thick cloth of his overcoat.

"I thank God for sending you. I wouldn't have made it otherwise."

His throat worked and he wasn't sure the words would come out in a normal tone of voice. "I thank the good Lord, too, for leading me to you."

They remained looking at each other until the door to the shed opened and they heard Lizzie's cry. "Oh, Papa, you found her!"

She and Dietrich ran up on either side of the sleigh and for the next several minutes the children's voices rang out with joyful exclamations, uttering what Gideon didn't have the freedom to express.

Mara sat ensconced in quilts on a settee in front of the fireplace. As soon as she'd been ushered inside, Lizzie had whisked her off to her room, helped her shed her cold, wet garments and lent her a flannel nightgown and wool dressing gown.

Once she'd been settled in the parlor, Mara had not been allowed to move. Voices came from the kitchen as they prepared her a supper tray, Gideon's lower-pitched one, Lizzie's and Dietrich's higher, more excited tones.

Any offers Mara had made to help had fallen on deaf ears.

In truth, she'd felt too drained of any energy to move from her warm seat. After her harrowing experience, it was all too easy to allow others to cosset her. Time enough tomorrow to fend for herself and her son once again. For now, she was grateful for Gideon and his daughter.

Dear Lord, thank You for bringing him to me, for keeping him safe on the road. Tears welled up in her eyes thinking about Gideon's miraculous appearance. Just in the nick of time. Once she'd warmed up some, she'd been able to think more clearly and remember the sequence of events. She had indeed veered off the road and twisted her ankle in the snow, and then been too cold to get up again. She attempted to move her ankle now. It felt painful but she didn't think it was a serious sprain and would probably be fine by morning. Gideon had still insisted on putting some liniment on it and binding it.

His large, rough hands had handled her ankle so gently and yet so expertly. He must have been experienced at doctoring his animals.

"Here you go." With a flourish, Lizzie carried in a tray. Gideon brought over a small table and Lizzie set it down in front of her.

Mara eyed the steaming bowl of stew, the buttered biscuits and cup of tea laced with milk. "My goodness, it looks and smells delicious."

Lizzie smiled shyly. "Venison stew. I hope you like it."

Mara unfolded the calico napkin. "I have no doubt I will. I'm quite famished, I can tell you."

Gideon removed the screen and knelt by the fire, poking it until the sparks flew and flames burned bright.

Dietrich knelt beside him. Mara smiled at how closely her son's movements imitated the man's.

As she took spoonfuls she listened to their conversation, the young boy's questions, the man's patient explanations. "What's that?"

"It's a chestnut roaster."

"Are you going to roast chestnuts over the fire?"

"Yes. Here, pour some in the pot." He allowed Dietrich to scoop the brown chestnuts from a burlap sack and place them into the brass container of the long-handled contraption with its holes around the top.

"We're also going to roast some apples and pop some popcorn, eh, Lizzie?"

Lizzie smiled. "We always do on Christmas Eve and since you two are here, we figured this was close enough." She sat down on the hearth beside them and the three set to work.

Mara finished her food and sat back against the cushions. How good it felt to feel warm again.

As if reading her thoughts, Gideon glanced her way. "All right?"

She smiled. "Very."

He returned her smile, the corners of his eyes crinkling. A new warmth spread through her limbs and she shivered.

"Cold?"

A flush rose from her neck to her cheeks. "No, not at all." She hurried to ask the first thing that popped into her head. "Is Bessie all right?"

"Brushed down and fed her oats and hay, she's safe in her stall for the night."

"I'm glad she was able to navigate through the storm."

"She knows the lay of the land pretty well."

The first kernels of corn started popping. Lizzie gave an exclamation and sped up her shaking.

Dietrich turned away from the fire to Gideon. "Why aren't my chestnuts popping?"

"You've just got to keep shaking them." He gave his attention back to her son, his much larger hands covering Dietrich's on the long handle and giving it a vigorous shake.

A while later, the three sat together, Dietrich wedged closely to her on the settee, Lizzie on his other side and Gideon in an armchair drawn up on Mara's side of the settee, close to the fireplace. A bowl of popcorn, a dish of roasted chestnuts and another of roasted apples, and a bowl of shag-bark hickory nuts were set on the low table before them.

They spent a convivial evening talking about everything from Gideon's boyhood in the hamlet to Christmas customs all across Europe. Then Gideon brought out his fiddle and played some songs. They prevailed on Mara to sing a few Christmas songs in German and French.

Dietrich yawned beside her.

"If you yawn any harder, I'll be able to see clear down to your belly," Gideon told him.

Dietrich snapped his mouth shut, his eyes round.

Lizzie poked his arm. "He's just teasing you. He used to tell me that all the time when it was my bedtime."

"You mean when it was past your bedtime and you were making a good job of ignoring the fact."

Dietrich giggled.

With a yawn of his own, Gideon got up and stretched. "What'd'ya say, son, time to hit the sack? It's Christmas Eve tomorrow and you want to be well rested up for that."

Dietrich jumped up. "Can I help you decorate your tree?"

Mara winced, feeling badly for her son who wouldn't have his own tree to decorate.

"I told you you could. Otherwise, who's going to put the star on top?"

Dietrich's eyes grew large with wonder. "Me?"

Gideon nodded. "That's right. Lizzie's going to be too

busy with all the other things going on tomorrow." He winked at his daughter then took Dietrich by the hand.

As Mara made to get up, he shooed her back with a gesture. "You stay put. If you need anything, let Lizzie know. I'll see to Dietrich."

"Very well." She watched them leave.

When Mara said she was fine, Lizzie excused herself to make up her bed. "Papa said we could share his bed. He'll sleep in mine."

Mara tried to protest but Lizzie wouldn't hear of it. "It'll be fun, like two sisters sharing a bed." Her gaze grew soft. "Or like when I was real young and I'd come to Mama at night if I had a bad dream."

Mara nodded, unable to deny the girl's wish.

After Lizzie left the parlor, Mara sat content to watch the fire crackle. She yawned though she had no desire to get up anytime soon. The night had an element of something out of time, and she was in no hurry to end it. Reality could intrude tomorrow.

She glanced about the small parlor. It was a homey, inviting room with its dark, waxed, wide-planked floors and its low-beamed ceiling and plastered walls. A large rag rug covered the greater part of the floor and smaller ones the remaining areas. Two windows faced the front yard. One doorway led to the kitchen area, on the opposite side the other led to the bedroom, where she could see Lizzie making up the bed with clean sheets.

Evergreen boughs graced the mantelpiece and windowsill, thick white candles ensconced among them. Mara felt a constriction in her throat. How nice it must be to have a home of one's own, to be free to decorate it as one wished.

She started at the sound of someone entering. Gideon came down the narrow staircase and smiled at her. "Dietrich is all tucked in. Lizzie promised to read a story to him. She'll stay with him till he falls asleep so he won't feel lonely in a strange bed."

Mara clutched the quilt around her, feeling suddenly very conscious of being alone with Gideon. "That's nice of her."

He went to the fireplace. Mara couldn't help observing him. He wore a pair of heavy corduroy trousers and suspenders and a blue flannel shirt open at the collar and rolled up on his forearms, revealing the white sleeves of his union suit beneath. The garment didn't hide the strong sinews of his forearms. As he leaned forward to put the log on the fire, the shirt stretched tight against his broad shoulders, causing her breath to catch in her throat.

He replaced the fire screen and brushed off his hands and turned to her with a shy smile. "Warm enough?"

"Oh, yes, fine." She felt like a teenager at her first sociable, she who'd spoken to lords and ladies in Europe.

With a sigh, he sat back down on the armchair. She let out the breath she'd been holding from being afraid—or wishing?—he'd take the seat beside her on the settee. They sat watching the flames for a while. She stole a look toward him, wondering if he was feeling as tense as she felt. But he looked relaxed, his long legs stretched out, his arms resting on each side of the chair, his head against the lace doily at the back of the chair.

His wife had probably crocheted the antimacassar. Her glance encompassed the room again, as well as every sampler, rug and lace table covering in the room.

"Your late wife must have been a very special woman."

He glanced sidelong at her. "Why do you say that?"

She gestured around her. "The coziness of your home. I know Lizzie has become a good housekeeper, but I'm sure she didn't do all I see around me."

He nodded against the upholstered chair back. "You're right. Most of this was Elsie's doing. We—" he cleared his throat "—haven't wanted to change anything." She caught a look that seemed apologetic.

She smoothed the quilt over her knees. "That's understandable. You wanted to honor her and remember her."

He didn't answer right away but looked toward the fire, rubbing a hand across his jaw. There was a light stubble covering it, a shade lighter than his rusty-red hair.

A pocket of sap caused a pop from a log. Mara turned her eyes reluctantly from him back to the fireplace.

"Elsie was a good woman. Quiet, helpful, a fine mother. We lost a child, a baby boy. He would have been a little older than Dietrich."

"I'm sorry," she whispered.

"It was a long time ago. Time heals all wounds."

"Does it?"

Their glances met. She regretted her words. "It has mine," he said softly.

After a few moments of nothing but the sound of the ticking clock on the mantel and the crackle of the fire, he said, "I can't imagine what it must have been like to be married to someone famous, traveling all over the place."

Gideon didn't think Mara was going to reply. After that first fixed look she'd given him that made him wonder if he'd said something wrong, she'd turned away and sat staring at the burning logs. He studied her profile. Her hair, still damp at the edges, tumbled over her shoulders, her long fingers wrapped about the teacup she'd taken up earlier. Once again, he felt badly over the broken one.

He hadn't thought his remark too forward after she brought up the subject of his own wife. She hadn't seemed to mind hearing about Elsie.

But her loss was more recent. He'd probably put his foot in it.

"Klaus wasn't quiet."

Gideon started at the sound of Mara's low words. His brow furrowed until he remembered what he'd said about Elsie.

After another shorter silence, she continued. "When he was angry, he let me know it. He would start by shouting terrible things to me, even if I had nothing to do with what had angered him. It was as if the slightest thing would fill him with rage. Finally, he couldn't contain himself and he would throw something, and if that wasn't enough, he'd—" she swallowed visibly "—hit me," she ended so softly he thought at first he'd heard wrong.

But a look at her whitened knuckles around the teacup told him he'd heard correctly. Gideon's own fingers tightened on the armchairs as he drew his body forward on the seat. A lightning bolt couldn't have stunned him more.

"At first I tried so hard to please him, until finally over time I came to understand he didn't love me, or honor me the way a man should honor his wife, the way I should be honored." She turned her gaze toward him and met his gaze full-on. His own didn't waver. If she needed strength or affirmation, he was there to give it to her.

She drew in a shuddering breath as if to cleanse herself after the confession. For confession he suspected it was. He would bet she hadn't told another soul.

"That's when I realized there was nothing I could ever do."

He didn't know what to say, so he tried to tell her with his eyes that he honored her, that he would never treat her in that way.

She shook her head, as if angry with herself. "Everyone envied me, married to such a handsome, talented, famous musician. He was a rising star, rivaling the best musicians on the European stage. What they didn't see was how he squandered away every penny he'd earned, gambling it away, giving it away to those he admired, until we had nothing left and he fell ill.

"No one visited him then," she ended softly.

How he wished he could gather her in his arms. But he still felt the few feet between them like a great divide.

They sat silent for a good while. He was surprised when she spoke again, her voice low, her focus on the fire before her. "A few years ago he was diagnosed with tuberculosis. At first, we thought he would recover. He went to the finest sanatoriums in the Alps and spas in Germany and Switzerland. But, when he was better, he continued to live a life of dissipation. His body grew weaker and weaker and less able to fight the disease when it hit again, which only made him angrier at everything and everyone around him."

She stared into the fire. "When he finally died, I was glad—relieved." Bringing a fist up to her mouth, she shook her head. "What kind of horrible person wishes for the death of her own husband? What kind of Christian was I? Yet, it was my only escape. I had nursed him night and day to the end. And death, when it finally came, left me only feeling empty. There was no grief then or later, standing by his grave, a great family mausoleum in Germany."

She let out a bitter laugh. "His family which had provided no support during his life, because they were almost as impoverished as he was, gave him all the trappings and pretensions of their great aristocratic name when he departed this earth.

"There we stood, his mother and sisters sobbing, and me in my widow's weeds, feeling nothing. It was as if he'd used up my last emotion in life."

Gideon wanted to assure her she was not to blame. But she seemed far away from him, staring into the past.

Would he ever be able to comfort her? Or were the scars of the past too deep to ever allow another man's love to erase them?

Chapter Eighteen

Mara awoke to find herself alone in the large four-poster bed. She looked to the other side where the bedding had been thrown back. Lizzie must have been up awhile. She squinted toward the window, trying to determine how late it was. She had slept like a log as soon as her head hit the pillow.

She stretched now, becoming conscious as her head sank into the feather pillow that she was lying in Gideon's bed. The bed he'd shared with Elsie. She remembered the tender note in his voice when he'd spoken of her. He hadn't said much, but what he said was full of respect, admiration and love.

The kind of love she'd once yearned for from a man. Had Klaus ever loved her like that? She'd asked herself so often in the earlier years of her marriage, finally coming to the conclusion that he'd *wanted* her. And since marriage had been the only way to obtain her, he'd proposed to her.

But once he'd married her, he'd quickly lost interest. His sole focus in life had been his music. It was his first love and outside of it, there was little room for anything else. Everything else, including the people in his life, his own wife and child, were mere pastimes to be used for amusement until he turned his attention back to his music.

She put those thoughts aside, burrowing for a moment in the pillow and sheets, inhaling the clean fragrance of balsam fir sachets. She opened her eyes, looking at the pillow beside hers, picturing Gideon's head lying there, his eyes opening upon awakening, their gray-blue depths gradually coming to awareness. Awareness of her. His rusty-red hair would be tousled, his face ruddy with sleep.

She turned away. What was she thinking? Abruptly she sat up, throwing the bedding off, shame washing over her at the thought of all she had told him on the previous night. What had possessed her? She could only blame the harrowing experience she'd had in the snowstorm for weakening her reserve.

Quickly she went to the table holding ewer and bowl. Lizzie had thoughtfully filled it with warm water. How soundly Mara must have slept not to have heard her.

As she washed and dressed—finding her clothing neatly laid out, even pressed—her mind kept remembering snatches of her late-night conversation with Gideon. Her face grew warm now, as she hid it behind a towel to dry it.

She'd never spoken of these things to anyone. How could she have now, to him?

But he'd proven such an easy person to open up to. She'd sensed only compassion and understanding—and strength— coming from him.

She went to the window and pushed back the gingham curtain. After last night's storm, the sun shone brightly, stinging her eyes, against the new fallen snow. The bare trees of the elms and the heavy, dark boughs of the evergreens were bent with snow.

She had to get back. Carina would be wondering what had happened to her. Would she care?

Shaking aside her worries about her stepmother, Mara hurried out of the room, embarrassed to have slept so late when everyone else was up. She paused at the threshold to the kitchen, hearing Dietrich's voice around a mouthful of food, Lizzie's laughter and Gideon's lower tone. She clutched the doorpost, feeling terribly self-conscious. How was she to face him this morning? What would he think of her?

As if sensing her presence, they all turned to her at once, Dietrich sitting at the table with Gideon, Lizzie bringing the iron skillet from the cookstove, a spatula in her other hand.

Lizzie's mouth broke into a smile. "Good morning, Mrs. Keller. How're you feeling?"

Mara returned the smile, forcing her feet to take a few steps forward. She looked at Dietrich. "Good morning. I'm sorry, I seem to have overslept."

Gideon rose and pulled out a chair for her. "You must have been some tuckered out. Come, have a seat. Lizzie's made some pancakes and sausages."

She couldn't quite meet his eyes, though she felt their gaze on her. She took the proffered seat, aware of his large frame towering over her as he tucked her chair in. "Thank you," she murmured.

Lizzie served the pancakes on the plate before her. "Here you go. I'll bring you some sausages."

"Would you like some coffee?" Gideon asked.

"Yes, please." Then remembering herself, she began to rise. "But I can help myself. You needn't wait on me."

He laid his large hand on her arm, staying her motion. "Sit still. You're our guest this morning."

Her eyes rose up his arm to his chest and shoulders, taking in the small V where his shirt opened at the neck, the strong, slightly cleft chin and lips, tipped up at one corner, until finally meeting his eyes twinkling down into hers.

She couldn't return his smile, her inner turmoil too great.

Gradually the amusement faded from his eyes, replaced by a question, one eyebrow lifted a fraction.

She looked down at her plate, whispering, "Thank you."

He removed his hand from her arm, allowing her to breathe again and moved away from the table.

Dietrich began speaking to her and she smiled and looked at her son, making replies without even knowing what she was saying. Gideon returned and poured coffee into her cup. She heard the sound without looking, though every cell on that side of her body was aware of him, the very hairs on her arm tingling. Finally, he moved away with "There's cream and sugar on the table." She nodded, still not looking his way, her gaze determinedly on her son, thankful for his chatter.

By noon, Gideon had the horse and sleigh hitched up once more since Mara had grown anxious to return home.

"I wish we could stay here."

He glanced down at Dietrich, bundled up in coat and scarf and hat. "Yes, I do, too."

The boy smiled, reaching up to pat Bessie. "But I'm coming back today to help you decorate your tree, aren't I?"

Gideon nodded, but Mara said only, "We'll see."

Before he could say anything to persuade her, she squared her shoulders. "Shall we go?"

At his nod, she headed for her side of the sleigh. He'd felt a barrier between them this morning and helpless to do anything about it. He had an inkling of what had brought it about. Her openness from last night.

Her shocking revelations had kept him awake much of the night. But the overwhelming feeling for him was humbleness that she'd trusted him enough to share her deepest secrets with him.

He sighed, knowing well what the light of day did to a person. She probably regretted her openness of the night before. He didn't know how to put her worries to rest.

He helped Dietrich into the sleigh and draped the fur rug around their legs.

He climbed aboard himself, noting that Dietrich had squeezed himself between his mother and him. The sleigh was really only meant for two, so they felt snug against each other. "All set?"

"All set!" Dietrich called out, drowning out his mother's quieter "Yes."

Gideon flicked the reins and set the bells jingling. He turned to wave to Lizzie who stood at the window and waved back.

When they arrived at Mrs. Blackstone's, he got down, ignoring Mara's protests that he needn't alight. He wanted to escort them all the way to the door, but she held him back then, with a light touch of her hand to his forearm. "Thank you, Mr. Jakeman." Her blue eyes, more intensely blue against the white background, beseeched him. "Thank you for everything last night."

He shuffled his feet in the snow, feeling uncomfortable with the praise. "There's no need to thank me. And—" Before he lost his nerve, he said, "Please, call me Gideon."

She looked down, hiding her lovely eyes, her lashes inky black against her pale skin. A pretty color tinted her cheeks from the ride in the cold air. She made no reply, neither a denial nor agreement. Instead of pressing her, he continued. "And no more of these lone walks from town. You let me know when you need to go in for your lessons, and I'll take you there and back, you hear?"

At that, her gaze rose to his. She pressed her lips together and finally spoke. "I can't do that." The words were low, almost as if wrenched from her.

He swallowed. "Can't or *won't?*"

Saying nothing more, she turned away, calling behind her shoulder, "Come along, Dietrich."

Gideon watched them enter the woodshed, deciding to say nothing more about decorating the tree. He'd come back

this afternoon and hope to persuade her to come along with
Dietrich to celebrate Christmas Eve with Lizzie and him.

A movement at the kitchen window caught his eye. Mrs.
Blackstone stood behind the lacy curtain. With a touch of
his hand to his cap, he turned with a sigh back to his sleigh.

Mara's feet felt heavy as she neared the kitchen door,
though her ankle hardly pained her, thanks to Gideon's care.
After the concern in his eyes and tone, returning to Carina's
felt like stepping from light into darkness, she thought bit-
terly as she opened the door. Mara stopped short at the sight
of Carina, standing at the window, her arms folded across
her chest, her mouth an unsmiling line as she stared accus-
ingly at the two of them.

"Good morning, Carina."

Carina only gave a short nod but remained silent.

Mara helped Dietrich off with his things and then proceeded with her own. "Why don't you go and play in the
parlor, dear?"

With a nod he ran off.

As Mara hung up their things, she could feel Carina stare
holes into her back. Finally, smoothing her skirt down, she
braced her shoulders and stood to face her stepmother.

"Where have you been all night, or need I bother to ask?"

Every nerve bristled but Mara forced herself to answer
civilly, "Mr. Jakeman found me along the road halfway between here and town and took me to his house. He didn't
want to force his horse any farther to bring me all the way
here. Besides which, Dietrich was already at his house."

Carina's nostrils flared. "I will not have this kind of lewd
behavior under my roof."

Mara stared at her. "I beg your pardon?"

"Staying at a man's house. Brazen! I don't know what
kind of morals you've picked up in Europe, but that kind of

behavior is not tolerated here in Down East Maine, I'll have you know!"

Mara gasped. "I was half-frozen. Believe me, even if it had occurred to me to behave immorally, I doubt if I would have been capable of it!" Her voice rose, and remembering Dietrich in the next room, she reined in her temper with an effort. She clasped her hands together to keep them from trembling.

Carina's eyes narrowed to slits. "I've put up with you since you arrived with your son, only for your father's sake, but this is too much. I live hardly a quarter mile from Gideon's. You had no reason to stay there last night. Unless you are trying to catch him, shameless hussy!" She hissed the last words.

Mara's mouth opened but she couldn't get the words out, her anger was so great. She took in deep breaths to bring her anger under control. Then she stepped before Carina, jabbing her forefinger in her face, causing her to flinch backward. "You haven't wanted me here since the moment I arrived. I'll remind you, this is my house as much as it is yours." She drew back. "But I have no desire to share it with someone as poisonous as you. I shall be out of your way today."

Before Carina could say anything more, Mara left her, swishing her skirts away from her, and marched out of the kitchen. Saying nothing to her son yet, she went to her room and began packing her portmanteau. She hadn't brought much with her and would be leaving with even less. But she could not bear being under the same roof with Carina a day longer.

Forgive me, Father, she prayed, *but I spent enough years with someone who didn't want me or love me. I can't do it anymore.*

Snapping her bag shut, she headed for her son's room and packed a small bag for him. She picked up his stuffed dog and laid it atop his clothes, her eyes tearing up, remembering when she had sewed it during the last months of Klaus's life, rocking in the chair beside his bed, which she hardly left in those days.

And, now, once again, she would be a nomad. Swiping the tears away, she snapped the bag shut and took it out into the hall to join the other. She squared her shoulders to face the most difficult part. How to break the news to Dietrich?

At first he was excited. "Are we going back to the Jakemans'? Yippee!" He began to jump up and down.

She sat down on the settee, her hands hanging limply in her lap. This was going to be harder than she'd anticipated.

"No, dear, we're not going back to the Jakemans'."

That afternoon Gideon looked across his snow-covered yard and the laden tree branches of the thick maples to the sparkling blue ocean beyond. Sunlight danced on the inky blue sea. A barquetine sailed by, on its way to Eastport no doubt.

Lizzie came to stand beside him, giving him a gentle push. "You'd best get going."

He smiled down at her, knowing she was anxious for him to return home with Dietrich—and, hopefully, Mara—so they could begin decorating the tree. "All right. I'll see you in a bit."

She nodded. "I've got to start the baking and a few other things for tomorrow's dinner." A brief shadow clouded her gray eyes. "You don't think she'll say no?"

He looked down at his gloves, pulling them on. "Well, let's not borrow trouble."

Her frown cleared. "You're right."

He decided to walk the short way to the Blackstone place. He saw no signs of anyone when he arrived, a little surprised not to see Dietrich outside building a snowman the way he'd talked about at breakfast. Paul was at his own home today, it being Christmas Eve. He'd have to see if they needed any help milking the cow or hauling firewood.

He entered through the shed door, his heartbeat stepping up its rhythm at the thought of seeing Mara again so soon. He'd been calling her Mara in his head for a while now. Of course, he'd never presume to do so to her face unless she gave him permission.

He gripped the edges of his sealskin cap between his fingers, thinking again how right it had been to see her at his kitchen table this morning. It had birthed hopes and dreams in his heart that he hadn't allowed since the day he'd met her, yet they'd found a way, nevertheless, to insinuate themselves down deep in his heart where he could control them as little as he could the waves lapping against the strakes of his dory.

Taking a deep breath, he knocked on the kitchen door.

A moment later, Mrs. Blackstone answered the door. "Good afternoon, Gideon. Is something wrong?"

Hiding his astonishment at her abrupt greeting, he dipped his head. "Good afternoon, Mrs. Blackstone. I just wanted to make sure Mara and Dietrich were all right, none the worse for wear." He tried to chuckle but it came out flat in the face of Mrs. Blackstone's disapproval. "And to fetch Dietrich, who promised to help us decorate our tree."

Her lips pursed. "I'll have to be frank with you, Gideon, I was very displeased by her comportment."

He blinked. "How's that, ma'am?"

"I'll have you know I cannot countenance such behavior."

What was she talking about? "If it's about the storm, I found Mrs. Keller halfway between here and town and brought her home. We decided it best that she stay at my place with Lizzie since Dietrich was already there."

Mrs. Blackstone said nothing, her nostrils pinched as if he brought in an unpleasant odor.

He fiddled with his cap. "Is Mrs. Keller or Dietrich about?

I know they must have been exhausted from yesterday. Did she tell you how I found her?" He felt as if he were trying to fill the silence as Mrs. Blackstone continued staring at him.

"Mara is not here, nor is her son."

"Pardon me?" He smiled nervously. "I would've expected them both to be too tuckered out to go anywhere today."

The moment became more and more awkward, Gideon wishing he'd never come. But then he wouldn't have had a chance to see Mara again. He and Lizzie had decided to invite them to Christmas dinner tomorrow. It would be the first time they'd have a guest—any guest, but particularly a female guest—to such an important family dinner.

Mrs. Blackstone looked down at her folded hands. "My late husband's daughter no longer resides here. She and her son have decided to move to town."

His chest felt as if it had been crushed under a great pine log. "Move to town?"

Mrs. Blackstone took a step back into the kitchen, her thin lips straight and unyielding. "That's right. I have no other information about her. Now, if you'll excuse me, Gideon, I don't want to let the cold air in."

He reached out as she was closing the door. "Wait—do you know where she is staying?"

"I really couldn't say."

"But why would she leave here on Christmas Eve?"

She stood as if debating whether to say anything more. "She refused to live by my rules—the rules of any God-fearing woman. Now, good day, Mr. Jakeman."

The door was closed quietly but firmly in his face. He could feel his ire rising but he took a step away, struggling to make sense of things.

Finally, he stalked out of the shed and headed home. It would do no good to get upset without knowing anything. He'd hitch up the sleigh and head to town. Lizzie would understand when he told her.

* * *

By the time he got to town it was late afternoon. The streetlamps and storefronts were decorated with evergreen boughs and red ribbons, the freshly fallen snow covering rooftops and awnings, giving everything a festive cheer, but Gideon saw little of this, too anxious to find Mara.

He began at the hotel then proceeded to the most prominent boardinghouse. An hour later, he finally located her at the last rooming house on a side street at the farther end of town.

He stood outside the wooden door on the second floor, once again clutching his cap in his hands, unsure what he would say when he saw her. He'd had a lot of time to think on his way over.

He lifted his hand and knocked, the noise sounding louder than he intended in the silent hallway, his mouth feeling as dry as chalk.

Chapter Nineteen

Mara sat staring at the faded, water-stained wallpaper surrounding her. Finally, after much whining, crying and a temper tantrum, Dietrich had fallen asleep.

More than the grueling trudge through the snow-packed road to town had been the emotional struggle of trying to make Dietrich understand why they were moving to town.

Thankfully, a farmer had given them a lift halfway there. She wasn't sure if Dietrich would have made the trek otherwise. He was worn-out from his late night and now the emotional upheaval of leaving the only home he knew.

He had finally fallen asleep shouting, "I hate you! I hate you!" No matter how much she told herself he didn't realize what he was saying, the words had pierced her to the core. What damage was she inflicting on her son after his months of steady progress in the hamlet under Gideon's patient tutelage?

She hugged herself, shivering against the drafty room. She had taken the only room she could find, anxious to get Dietrich out of the cold, but this place, with its higher rates for every fire she burned, would not do. But for the next day or two, until the holiday was over, it would have to be sufficient.

She went into the bedroom where she would have to share a bed with Dietrich and put another blanket over him. Finally, she climbed in beside him. Her head hurt, her ankle was sore from walking and there was absolutely no reason to stay awake and fight off her gloomy thoughts.

Dear Lord, please grant me Your grace to endure this new episode. Please help Dietrich adjust to living here.

Mara awoke with a start, having no idea at first where she was or what time it was. A few seconds later, eyeing the brown stains on the ceiling above and shivering under the blankets, she remembered everything. But before she could process it, she realized what had awakened her. A loud knock sounded on the door in the other room.

"Wait a moment, I'm coming," she called out, struggling to rise and find her shoes.

A hand to her hair, she straightened her bodice with the other just as she reached the sitting-room door. Prepared to find her landlady, she stopped short, her mouth dropping open at the sight of Gideon standing there, looking so big and imposing.

He clutched his sealskin cap in his hand, a question in his eyes. "Mrs. Blackstone said you had moved to town."

She stepped back, distressed that he had found them here so soon. "Yes, that's right."

With a look of inquiry, he stepped across the threshold. Saying nothing, she shut the door behind him.

When she remained silent, he cleared his throat. "I came by this afternoon to fetch Dietrich to help trim the tree and to invite you and Dietrich over for Christmas dinner after church tomorrow."

His words sounded stilted, which only deepened her awareness of her sordid situation. Was he feeling as uncomfortable as she?

What had Carina told him? She clenched her hands at the

sides of her skirt, not knowing what to say. "Th-that's very kind of you."

He glanced around, and she cringed at what he saw of her surroundings. "Where's Dietrich?"

"Asleep in the other room."

"Oh." He sounded disappointed. "I could have taken him back with me if he'd been awake."

"I'm not sure if that would be a good idea. He was quite upset when we left." She looked away, unable to bear the look of pity in his eyes. "I think going back to your place will only make it more difficult for him to adjust."

Gideon stared at her, his tongue cleaving to the roof of his mouth so he could hardly formulate the words that clamored in his mind to be asked. She seemed so aloof, as if she would resent any probing on his part. Finally, he just blurted out, "What did Mrs. Blackstone do?"

"What did she tell you?" she asked in a clipped tone.

He could feel his cheeks flush, unwilling to repeat what the old busybody had insinuated. He gestured with one hand. "Not much. Just that...that she couldn't accept—"

Mara shook her head. "You needn't say more. It doesn't matter really." She folded a pleat into her skirt, not meeting his probing look. "I—I have been intending to leave there ever since I moved out to the hamlet. It hasn't been working out between my stepmother and myself. You may have noticed a bit of friction at times. But I needed to save enough money." She sighed. "It has been hard on Dietrich."

How he longed to offer succor to both her and her son.

She moistened her lips, her fingers working nervously. "I couldn't bear to have her continuously find fault with Dietrich, even though he is not always the perfect child."

He took a step closer to her. "If you had to go somewhere immediately, why didn't you come back to our place? Lizzie would have loved to have you back for as long as you'd like and I..." He stopped, his gaze locking with hers.

But he found his throat too constricted to say what he really wanted. "I…I would have loved to have you stay as well," he finally managed in a broken whisper.

Neither looked away but she didn't speak.

He moistened his lips, plunging ahead. "You needn't move away from the hamlet. Dietrich likes it there. I… That is, I…I've been thinking…and yesterday…when you were at the house, it just seemed right." He stumbled over the words, as if feeling his way blindly. "What I'm trying to say is…I'd like to ask you to marry me." There, he'd said it, though the moment the words were spoken, he sensed they'd come out all wrong. "Then you and Dietrich can come and live with us. You wouldn't have to struggle anymore."

"Mr. Jakeman—Gideon—" She shook her head. "You needn't say such things. We'll be all right."

"You'd be a good mother to Lizzie and I'd do my best by Dietrich." He felt as if he were falling down a cliff and whatever he did to stop just made him fall all the faster.

She took a step away from him, wrapping her arms about herself as if to fend him off. "That's very kind of you, but I assure you, Dietrich and I will manage. He's used to living in boardinghouses," she ended with a short, bitter laugh.

He wished he could take his proposal back. He'd meant to go slowly. Now, he'd shocked her. Why hadn't he, instead, offered to take them to his cousin's house?

He crushed his cap between his hands. "I'm sorry, Mrs. Keller, to have spoken out of turn. I should never have presumed with such a lady as yourself. I truly didn't intend to overstep my bounds."

She reached out a hand, but stopped short of touching him. "It's not that. I'm honored by your proposal, but I find…" Swallowing, as if unsure how to proceed, she finally said in a low tone he had to strain to hear, "I cannot accept a union with someone where there is no true love. I know that sounds overly romantic but I have lived too many years yoked to someone who was incapable of loving me."

He stared at her a moment, comprehension dawning. She didn't love him. Finally, he nodded once. "I understand." Slowly, he walked to the door. Wordlessly, he took the door-knob in his hand.

But instead of turning it, he stood a few seconds. He had to tell her the truth, no matter what it cost him.

He spoke in a low tone, his back to her. "I never thought I'd feel this way about another woman after Elsie passed on. I knew since I met you that my feelings for you were wrong, that you're too much a lady for someone like me, so I didn't mean to offend you. And I don't intend to insult you further by telling you that I love you. You were married to an important man, who didn't treat you right.

"I'm just a lowly farmer. So please don't take my proposal as an insult. I didn't intend it so. But I can promise you I'll never treat you roughly. I'll honor you the way the Good Book says."

Not waiting to hear any more polite refusals from her, he opened the door and left, closing it softly behind him.

By the time Gideon ended his short speech, the stony walls around Mara's heart had not only been breached but lay scattered around her, utterly demolished. Before she could say anything, he turned and walked out the door.

"Gideon—" The cry died on her lips.

When he'd first mentioned marriage, she'd felt a profound disappointment that he offered her a way out for purely practical reasons.

Even with the unromantic proposal, it had been tempting to accept his offer. To have someone to shoulder her responsibilities. But she couldn't help but remember the way he'd talked of his first wife. It was clear he'd loved her with a deep, abiding love.

Mara hadn't thought he'd ever be capable again of the kind of love he'd had for Elsie, and she would be forever wishing for it. She couldn't bear the thought of another marriage where she felt like the beggar for the crumbs of someone's affections.

But Gideon's last words had revealed what her heart had yearned to hear.

Walking to the window, Mara was in time to see him exit the building and climb onto his sleigh. She touched the grimy windowpane, as if she could halt his progress. But the sleigh was already heading down the street, its bells jingling merrily.

Her fingertips pressing against the cold pane, she watched him ride away, her heart wondering if it was too late. Had she lost the finest man she'd ever met?

Mara spent the rest of the dreary day trying to comfort a cranky Dietrich, and praying for another chance with Gideon.

When Christmas Day dawned bright and sunny, she waited until Dietrich woke up.

"How would you like to spend Christmas Day with the Jakemans?" she asked him over breakfast.

He fiddled with his food and finally shrugged. Although she'd bought him a gift, she decided not to give it to him now, but take it with her along with the small things she'd gotten or made for Gideon and Lizzie.

Realizing how badly the separation from them had hurt him, she held her peace. "First we'll go to church and then we'll hire a sleigh and go out there."

After the Christmas service at a church in town, the ride to the hamlet went swiftly in the cold, biting air. All too soon they arrived at the Jakemans'. Mara secured the reins to a hitching post at the end of the drive, her hands shaking with nerves. What if Gideon had changed his mind? What if he had spoken prematurely and now regretted his words?

She knocked on the kitchen door, Dietrich for once subdued beside her.

Lizzie opened the door, a smile breaking out at the sight of them. "Mrs. Keller! I didn't think you'd come. Papa said you wouldn't be able to. Come in, come in," she urged them, taking her by the arm. "Merry Christmas, Dietrich. What did Santa bring you?"

"Nothing."

Lizzie's eyes widened. "Nothing?" With a question then a wink toward Mara, she said, "Well, I think he got confused, thinking you were still here, 'cause he left a couple of packages under our tree for you."

Dietrich's mouth opened. "Here? Really?"

"Yep. Go on into the parlor and have a look."

At that moment, Gideon entered from there and stopped short at the sight of them. He made no further move forward. "Hello."

Mara inclined her head, feeling her heart in her throat. "Good afternoon. I…I wondered if your invitation to dinner was still open."

He nodded. "Of course." His attention focused on Dietrich who'd reached him. "Hello there, young fellow. Where are you going?"

"Lizzie said Santa left me something here by mistake."

"I believe he did, but I don't think it was a mistake, do you?" Although he addressed Dietrich, his eyes found Mara's, and she swallowed.

Instead of coming farther into the kitchen, he took Dietrich by the hand and led him off to the tree. "Come, let's have a look."

Lizzie helped her off with her wraps, taking her satchel from her, chattering all the while. The kitchen was redolent with the smells of food. "I hope you like dinner. We're having roast beef."

"Everything smells wonderful. I brought a few gifts, including Dietrich's. I thought it would be more fun for him to open it here, where it was more festive."

"What a good idea. Why don't you go on into the parlor? I'll be right there as soon as I check on the roast. I didn't see you in church."

"We went to one in town." Mara asked her about the sermon, using the pretext to linger in the kitchen, afraid now that she was here to face Gideon.

When the two of them finally entered the parlor, Dietrich's countenance was wreathed in smiles. He hurled himself toward her, showing her the wooden horse he'd received. "There are more presents, but Mr. Jakeman said we have to wait for you and Lizzie."

Mara made the appropriate praise over the horse and the Christmas tree, all the while conscious of Gideon's gaze on her. He excused himself to see to her horse as Lizzie ushered her to the settee once more.

When he returned, he distributed the gifts, placing hers beside her.

Mara was hesitant to open them, preferring to watch Dietrich open his. They'd also gotten him a little hoe and rake, to "help in the garden next spring," as Gideon told him, an orange, peppermint stick and a small wooden wagon to go with the horse. Mara had bought him a picture book.

She felt ashamed of her poor offering for the Jakemans, and thought she'd need to speak to Gideon afterward about giving Dietrich too many gifts.

She watched Lizzie open the small packet of hair combs. "Oh, thank you, Mrs. Keller, they're so pretty. You'll have to help me arrange them in this frizz of mine."

Gideon took more time with his, and she cringed. The few handkerchiefs she'd embroidered him did not merit such attention. He glanced at her and nodded. "Thank you very much. I can always use these." His thumb traced over the monogram. "You even got my initials right."

GTJ—Gideon Tyler Jakeman. "I...I asked Lizzie."

Lizzie scrunched up her face. "I remember! But I didn't know it was for this! Oh, how pretty. Your work is so much finer than mine."

Finally, they waited for her to open her gifts. First, she opened Dietrich's. It was a watercolor seascape of what she took to be the view from their house. "It's beautiful, sweetheart." She leaned over to where he stood and hugged him.

His thin arms came around her neck and she felt her throat thicken with emotion that her child was no longer angry at her.

"I painted it here and Lizzie helped me wrap it." He smiled proudly at her. "She let me keep it here till Christmas."

Mara looked over his head and met Lizzie's smiling face. She mouthed the words *thank you*.

"This one's from me." Lizzie handed her another package.

It held a scarf and pair of mittens knitted in a sapphire-blue wool. Mara drew in her breath. "They're gorgeous."

"I thought the shade would bring out your blue eyes," Lizzie said shyly, her hands folded in front of her.

Mara stood from the sofa and hugged her. "That was very thoughtful of you. I shall wear them to church on Sunday."

"But they're for every day, too."

Mara smiled. "Then I shall wear them whenever I go out into the cold."

When she sat back down, there was only one gift left. She didn't have to ask who it was from. Without looking at Gideon, she took the small, square box on her lap. It reminded her of the box which had held the replacement teacup he'd brought her from Bangor. Oh, dear, she hoped he hadn't gone to the effort and expense of another one. She must tell him that it really didn't matter anymore.

She lifted the lid of the cardboard box then peeled away the tissue paper and gasped. Lifting out the teacup, she gazed in wonder. It was an exact replica. Her eyes lifted to Gideon's. "Where on earth did you find this?"

He grinned sheepishly. "I wrote to a firm in Boston. The store clerk in Bangor had given me the address. They were able to find one. It isn't new," he hastened to add, his brow furrowing. "I guess the factory no longer exists."

"It's an antique." How much it must have cost him. Mara felt doubly ashamed. She gazed down at the cup and saucer, shaking her head. "You shouldn't have."

He shrugged. "I disagree."

"It's beautiful, but so was the other one. I'm afraid this has cost you much more than it should have."

"We'll have no talk of cost today." His gray-blue eyes smiled into hers, displaying no resentment for her coldness to him yesterday.

Suddenly, her heart overflowed with emotion. That someone cared enough about her to go to such trouble and expense. Her eyes filled with tears and she brought a finger up to the corner of one to halt them.

But she found she couldn't control them. Too long she'd held her feelings in check. A sob escaped her.

"There now, it's no cause for tears," Gideon began, showing the first signs of distress.

Mara covered her mouth, but she was unable to stop crying. Lizzie tried to comfort her, but Gideon approached the settee and told his daughter in a low voice, "Why don't you take Dietrich out to make a snowman? I'll see to Mrs. Keller."

"All right, Papa." She rose. "Come along, Dietrich."

"Is Mama all right?"

"I'll be fine," she gasped.

The settee sank as Gideon sat down beside her. The next second his arm came around her and he pulled her against his chest. "If I'd known it would set you to crying, I would have waited till after Christmas to give it to you."

A laugh erupted between sobs. "I—I'm s-sorry, I don't know why I'm crying so much."

His large hand stroked her hair. Gradually her sobs subsided and she sniffed. He handed her his handkerchief. "I should give you one of my new ones," he said with a chuckle, "but they're too dear to me."

She gave a watery laugh. Feeling she ought to move, she remained instead in the warm circle of his arm, wiping her eyes and blowing her nose. A stillness settled between them.

"You know, Mrs. Keller, as I told you yesterday, I never thought I'd ever want to marry anyone again. My Elsie, she was a special woman. But you have a way of making a man forget his resolve."

She eased away enough to be able to see his features. He looked at her calmly, speaking in a conversational tone. "I know most folks around here wonder why I haven't married before now, if only to give Lizzie a stepmother. But I haven't met anyone good enough to replace the mother she had. Not until now, that is."

He brought his other hand to her face and ran his forefinger down the length of her chin. "I've been pretty content with just keeping things the way they were. Until I met you."

He paused and she lost herself in the tenderness in his eyes. "Everything seemed brighter when you were around." His lips curled upward. "You even made food taste sharper, and my Lizzie's a pretty good cook, as you know."

Slowly her own lips curved upward.

"I know you're much too fine a lady for someone like me—"

Her fingertips went to his mouth, stilling the words. "Shush. You are a prince among men, Mr. Jakeman—

Gideon," she added, gauging his reaction to his name on her lips.

The warmth in his gaze deepened. "Mrs. Kell—"

"Mara."

"Mara," he repeated. "You're a brave, strong, beautiful woman who's put up with I don't know how much from your stepmother, and I'd like to offer you, again, a home, and a way out."

A sharp stab of disappointment sliced through her. She didn't realize how much she still wanted to hear his avowal of love. She chided herself for being greedy, telling herself he was not a man of flowery speeches. She swallowed. "Is that all you think I need?"

He didn't answer right away, his fingertip continuing to caress her cheek, his gaze roving over her features. Finally, it returned to her eyes and with a deep breath he began, "No. I think you need a man who can love you as his very self, who can shelter you, provide for you and your son, honor you, be a partner with you, and face whatever needs facing in this life…and finally, grow old together with."

For a man of few words, he had given her all she'd dreamed of and more. "Are you offering those things to me?" she whispered.

"I know I'm not worthy of you, but, yes, I am." His forthright gaze never left hers. Before she could accept him, he took her chin between his fingertips and tilted it upward.

She held her breath as he leaned closer until the tip of his nose grazed her. Then he shifted, his lips meeting hers. Mara sighed, leaning toward him, her arms coming up to grasp the wide breadth of his shoulders.

It was as if all constraints between them fell away. His brawny arms wrapped around her, drawing her closer. This shy, gentle man revealed a depth of emotion she'd hardly imagined him capable of, yet it was a controlled power. He

showed a restraint that proved she could trust him never to
hurt her or abuse her.

"I'd never dared hope," he murmured against her lips,
"that you could feel anything for me."

She brought her fingers up to his face, feeling the dear,
rough skin of his jaw. "I'm sorry I kept you at arm's length.
I was so afraid of trusting a man ever again. And I didn't
want you to think I was 'setting my cap' for you as Carina
accused."

A look of annoyance crossed his features. "Carina's just
a bitter old woman." Then he touched a finger to her cheek,
saying soberly, "I'll never do anything to hurt you, Mara."

She looked into his eyes. "I know you won't. And I promise to be a good mother to Lizzie."

"Do you?" He kissed the palm of her hand, his eyes
watching her. "Does that mean you'll marry me?" The corners of his eyes crinkled, their gray-blue depths twinkling.
At her nod, he drew her once more into his embrace.

"When will we tell the children?" she asked when they
drew apart again.

"I guess Lizzie has a good notion already. We can tell
Dietrich whenever you'd like." He frowned. "I hope you
don't plan on going back to that rooming house this afternoon."

She swallowed, dreading returning to town. "I did."

He shook his head. "I think you should go back to Mrs.
Blackstone's. After all, you own half that house. It was your
father's. If you are afraid to stand up to her, I'll do it with
you."

She felt a thrill go through her at the thought of having
someone to defend her. "Thank you."

He tilted his chin in acknowledgment then smiled. "In any
case, you shouldn't have to stay there long. It's your son's
heritage, but there's no reason to live under the same roof
with her if she treats you so disagreeably." He brought his

thumb up to her eye and wiped away the last hint of tears. "I won't have anyone making you cry. The sooner we're married, the sooner you can move in here."

Her gaze roamed over the cozy room, a room that had known three generations, a room that already felt like home. She squeezed Gideon's hand, smiling, then reached up and kissed him softly on the lips. "Thank you for the honor of being your wife."

His heart swelled with emotion. *Dear Lord, thank You for this lady's love. I will cherish her as long as I have breath in this body.*

Without saying anything more, he joined his lips with hers once more.

Epilogue

June 1885

Gideon drew the carryall up to the front of the large brick high school building.

"Where is Lizzie?" Dietrich asked from the backseat.

"Oh, I expect she'll be along as soon as we hear the school bell ring." Gideon turned to Mara and smiled.

She reached over and squeezed his hand. "I'm sure she's looking forward to coming back to the hamlet for the summer. She'll probably be one of the first ones to race out of the building."

Gideon returned the pressure on her hand. "She wouldn't have attended the academy if you hadn't encouraged her."

"I'm glad she has made new friends in town. But it will be nice to have her back home full-time and not just on the weekends."

Gideon stroked his thumb over the top of her hand. "When shall we tell her?"

"Tell her what?" Dietrich piped up from the back.

Mara blushed, not needing her husband to explain what he meant. Her glance couldn't help going to her waistline.

Only Gideon knew her news. She'd just broken it to him a few days ago, when she had been sure herself.

She'd never thought she would be blessed with a second child. In the past year, the Lord had not only blessed her with a prince among men, as she'd told Gideon on more than one occasion, but with a ready-made family of his child and hers.

Now, they could look forward to a child of their union.

Thankfully, Gideon spoke to Dietrich, saving her from having to think of how to answer. Her son's new father distracted him by offering to take him for a walk around the school building while they were waiting for Lizzie.

She watched her two men, the seven-year-old boy with his hand in the large man's. As always, she admired her husband, his tall, broad form, his sure stride. But most of all she admired the patient, kind way he had with Dietrich and with her.

At that moment the school bell rang. Young men and women rushed out the double front doors. She scanned each face until, at last, she saw the bright red hair of a tall girl on the threshold of womanhood.

Instead of racing out, she walked sedately, carrying herself straight. But then, seeing her father and Dietrich, her mouth broke into a wide smile and she waved.

Looking toward the street, she spotted Mara and waved some more. Mara smiled and returned the gesture.

As the three dearest people in the world to her walked back to the carryall, she whispered, "Dear Jesus, thank You for Your unaccountable grace and blessings."

* * * * *

Dear Reader,

I often hear veteran Love Inspired Books authors talk about the "pioneer days" in the late '90s, when the line first started. There were some growing pains and struggles to be accepted as Christian fiction in the mainstream market, but no one envisioned the amazing popularity of this type of book with the general public.

But readers were hungry for a story of love in a faith-filled setting, where the romance was not watered down, but still left plenty to the imagination in a time when most mass-market romances pushed the limits of propriety further and further.

I was honored when my editor asked me to be part of the debut of the Love Inspired Historical line. Even though I had published some longer novels under Steeple Hill Books, with my first Love Inspired title, *Hearts in the Highlands,* I was able to join the ranks of Love Inspired Books authors, a great bunch of talented and resourceful women from all parts of the U.S. and Canada, whose Christian faith is evident in their stories *and* lives.

I'm just as honored today to be publishing *Hometown Cinderella,* my fifth Love Inspired Historical title, during their special month celebrating the line's fifteen-year anniversary. With this book, I'm returning to one of my favorite settings, Down East Maine, the location of some of my earlier books (*Wild Rose, Lilac Spring*).

Down East Maine is the last stretch of coastline, beyond scenic, touristy southern and mid-coast Maine. Once you leave Bar Harbor behind, you enter a place of wild, rugged, breathtakingly beautiful rocky coast few tourists discover. It's a place where living is tough. Lobster fishing, clamming, logging and seasonal harvesting of blueberries, cranberries and apples offer some of the few ways to earn a living.

What fascinated me in my reading of nineteenth century coastal Maine was how it was the end of the era of the small, self-sustaining farm. These farmers worked hard, but lived well. They were people of independent spirit, self-reliance and thrift.

Gideon Jakeman is such a person. I hope you enjoy his and Mara's journey as much as I enjoyed writing it!

Be blessed in the reading,

Ruth Axtell Morren
General Delivery
Cutler, ME 04626
Cutler207@hotmail.com

Questions for Discussion

1. When Mara and Gideon first meet in church, they each have misconceptions about the other. How are first impressions often misperceptions?

2. Normally, Gideon and Mara would move in different circles. What brings them together at this point in their lives?

3. Mara quickly sees and understands Lizzie's yearnings, just as Gideon steps in to offer Dietrich the gentle yet firm guidance the boy needs. How does this help reveal each one's true character to the other?

4. Outwardly, Mara is reserved, elegant and ladylike. What does Gideon see that others don't see?

5. Even though Gideon appears to be a rough, uneducated farmer, what gestures show Mara that he is a true gentleman?

6. Mara has learned the hard way not to trust surface charm. How does Gideon counter this distrust?

7. Gideon has never expected to meet anyone to make him consider remarrying. Mara seems so different from his first wife. Yet what things about her cause him to reconsider his widowhood?

8. Mara was married to a talented and famous man who left her and their son penniless. Gideon can't under-

stand how a man would not provide for his spouse and child. How does this reflect Gideon's faith and moral code?

9. How does Gideon's quiet strength balance Mara's worries over Dietrich's rambunctious behavior and help put her fears into perspective?

10. Lizzie's stories of her father when he was first widowed reveal to Mara the kind of man he was, caring and sensitive, and endear him further to her even when she refuses to allow herself to trust again. Why is it hard to refute Lizzie's testimonials about her father?

11. Christians usually have to deal with someone unpleasant in their lives. How does both Mara's and Gideon's behavior toward Carina show their spiritual maturity?

12. When Mara sees Gideon in the woodshed at Thanksgiving, she can no longer deny that there is something between them. What is her immediate reaction?

13. Gideon is able to read Mara's reactions even when she doesn't express herself openly. What does this tell her of his sensitivity and perception, despite his having less formal education and polish than she does?

14. Even though Mara expresses her sincere gratitude to Gideon for rescuing her during the snowstorm, further breaking down the barriers between them, why does Gideon still fear he'll never be able to help her overcome the scars of the past?

15. Why does Mara feel ashamed after confessing her past
to Gideon? Have you ever regretted opening up to someone for the first time? Why?

Emma Wadler has made a good life for herself, running the Wadler Inn in the town of Hope Springs, Ohio. She has accepted her life as an "old maid," and is content catering to the tourists who come to view her Amish community. She had once hoped to marry and raise a family of her own, but her fiancé died tragically when they were both only seventeen, and Emma has guarded her heart ever since.

Adam Troyer fixes things. Having just returned to the faith after years in the English world, Adam is hoping to prove to his father that he is committed to a simple life. So he's happy to be hired by Emma's mother to make repairs to the inn during the winter off-season. The old Swiss-style chalet has its share of problems, but nothing he can't fix. Nothing except perhaps the broken heart of the owner....

THE INN AT HOPE SPRINGS
Patricia Davids

Chapter One

"Stop right there. What do you think you're doing?"

Inside the front door of the Wadler Inn, Adam Troyer froze, his ladder balanced precariously on his shoulder. He didn't dare swing around to see who was scolding him. If he tried, he'd break a window or take out a row of Grandma Yoder's jams and jellies lining the display shelves beside the door. A window could be replaced, but good gooseberry jam was a work of art. Grandma Yoder's was the best.

"What is the meaning of this?" A woman moved into his line of sight from behind the jam display. Planting herself in front of him, she prevented him from advancing into the lobby. Arms akimbo in her brown Amish dress, a scowl on her face beneath the white prayer cap on her auburn hair, the little woman reminded him of a hen with her feathers ruffled in annoyance. An angry Rhode Island Red with spectacles.

He struggled to keep from laughing. "You are Emma Wadler, *jah?*"

"I am. Who are you, and why are you bringing that ladder in here?" Her tone was cold as the February temperature outside.

He swallowed his grin. He needed this job. "I'm Adam

Troyer. I'm here to fix the loose stones in the fireplace and some of the shutters outside."

He'd only seen her a few times before this. Although they belonged to different Amish church districts, he'd spent time in Hope Springs when he'd visited his cousins. His cousin David called her a plain-faced *alt maedel*.

She didn't look that old, maybe thirty at the most. Not all that plain, either, with her peaches-and-cream complexion and full red lips. At the moment those lips were pressed into a hard line, but he figured a smile would make her almost pretty.

Behind wire-rimmed glasses, her hazel eyes narrowed. No smile appeared. "There's nothing wrong with our shutters. Who hired you?"

"The owner did."

She folded her arms. "I'm the owner."

"You are?" That surprised him. Very few Amish women owned businesses outright, although many owned them jointly with their husbands.

"I asked Mr. Parker to hire the lad, Emma. Now let him get to work. I don't want another quilt smoked up." A tall, gray-haired woman in a royal-blue dress crossed the room. Bright-eyed and smiling, tall and big-boned, Naomi Wadler was the opposite of her daughter in every respect.

Stopping in front of him, she pointed to one end of the lobby. "We have several stones loose in the fireplace. Can you fix them?"

The impressive stone structure soared two stories high and was at least eight feet wide. Made in the old-world fashion using rounded river stones in mortar with a massive timber for a mantel. Someone had added a quilt hanger near the top. It made a fine place to display a handmade quilt.

Emma spoke up. "Don't start work just yet, Mr. Troyer.

Mudder, I need a word with you," she stated, a hint of steel in her tone.

As Adam watched the women leave the room, he had the sinking feeling he was about to lose this much-needed job.

Chapter Two

Emma led the way to the small office behind the front desk and closed the door after her mother. "I wish you had discussed this with me. We can't afford to have a lot of work done. I can take care of most things myself."

"Nonsense. We can't afford *not* to get the work done. And now is the best time—it's the middle of winter and we have so few guests. Mr. Parker mentioned to me his growing list of things that need repairs. Didn't he mention them to you?"

"He did. I will get to them."

Emma had hired Mr. Parker to take over the day-to-day contact with guests and to handle the phone and computerized reservations that her religion didn't allow her to do. He had been an invaluable employee for five years. If he felt the need to go over her head, she shouldn't have brushed aside his concerns.

"I discussed it with Dr. White when I ran into him at the grocery store yesterday," Naomi said. "He does own half this inn. I felt he needed to know."

He owned fifty-one percent to be exact. Dr. Harold White was the town's only physician. He and her father had been great friends. She could not own such a business by herself outright because of her religious restrictions so she had asked Dr. White for his help. Her bishop found it acceptable because she was unmarried and because she was working for a non-Amish partner. Dr. White left her completely in charge of running the place and that suited them both.

Her mother pressed her point. "Adam Troyer's rates are reasonable. Do you want a stone or a shutter to drop on some poor *Englischer*'s head? Besides, Dr. White's not happy the place is getting run-down."

"It is not getting run-down. A little shabby maybe."

Her mother merely raised one eyebrow.

Emma relented and admitted her mother was right. "Very well, there are some things that need fixing."

Naomi smiled brightly. "*Jah,* there are. You don't have to be the one doing all the work at this inn. You work too hard as it is."

Emma held her tongue. Her mother didn't understand that hard work was the only thing that kept the loneliness at bay.

Moving forward, Naomi reached out to straighten Emma's prayer *kapp*. "Did you notice what a nice smile the young man has?"

"I noticed he almost knocked down our jam display." Emma submitted to her mother's attention although she suspected her *kapp* was already perfectly straight.

"It wouldn't hurt you to smile back at a young man once in a while." Suddenly, Naomi sneezed, then sneezed again.

Emma took two quick steps away. The last thing she wanted was to cause her mother discomfort. What had she been thinking?

Rubbing her nose, Naomi said, "Sorry, I don't know what started that. You look tired, Emma. Is everything okay?"

She should look tired. She'd been up every two hours through the night for the past two nights. She wasn't about to explain why. How could she expect her mother to understand when she didn't know herself why she'd taken on a task doomed to failure? "I'm fine. I must get to work."

"And Adam Troyer stays, *jah?*" her mother asked.

Emma wasn't about to make a promise she might regret. "We shall see."

Chapter Three

Emma opened her office door and walked out into the lobby. Adam had set his ladder on the floor. Her jams and jellies were no longer in danger.

He stood by the fireplace carefully examining the stonework. He had taken off his hat and coat, giving her a view of his tall, lean frame. His hair, sandy brown and curly, was trimmed in the same bowl cut all Amish men wore. Since he didn't have a beard she knew he was unmarried.

Why was he still single at his age? He had to be in his late twenties or early thirties.

His plain clothes fit him well. His suspenders drew attention from where his broad shoulders filled out his white shirt down to where his dark trousers accentuated his narrow waist and lean hips.

And what was she doing thinking about such things when she had an inn to run?

Naomi pointed to the top of the fireplace. "Our innkeeper noticed at least two stones loose near the ceiling when he was taking down the last quilt I sold. I'll show you which ones, but there may be others."

Emma clasped her hands in front of her. "Exactly how many fireplaces such as this have you repaired, Mr. Troyer?"

Adam looked at her. "Like this one? None."

She blinked. "None? And you expect me to hire you?"

Adam didn't appear the least put out by her remark. His eyes twinkled as he said, "This will be the largest fireplace I've worked on but the repair principle is the same. I can do the job."

She would have to trust him. The smoke leaking out around the loose stones had left soot marks on the quilt and ceiling. "It appears you have a job. If your work is satisfactory we will discuss additional projects tomorrow morning."

Beaming a bright grin at her, he crossed the room and held out his hand. "That's a deal then, Emma."

Hesitating only a fraction of the second, she took his hand. "*Jah,* we have a deal."

His large fingers engulfed her small ones as he pumped her arm with vigor. The warmth of his touch took her by surprise. The calloused strength of his hand gripping hers did funny things to her insides. Looking up into his smiling face, she was tempted to smile back, but she didn't. Instead she pulled her hand away and folded her arms tightly across her middle.

He might be a handsome man with his curly hair and bright blue eyes, but that shouldn't matter. If he did a good job, then she would be pleased.

She didn't want to admit the warmth of his hand and the friendliness of his smile caused butterflies in the pit of her stomach. She had put such foolishness behind her after the death of her fiancé ten years ago. Her heart lay in pieces in the cold ground with William, her one true love.

The grandfather clock in the corner began to chime the hour. Emma realized with a start that she was late. "Continue with your work, Mr. Troyer. I will be back to check on you."

She rushed through the kitchen, grabbing her coat from

the hook on her way out. Pulling on her coat in the cold air, she prayed she would still find all was well, but she knew not to expect too much.

Chapter Four

Adam was finishing the fireplace when Emma showed up again. He'd found several others stones that needed repair and noticed a half dozen tiles on the large hearth with cracked grout. No one had asked him to repair those, but he couldn't leave a job half-done. Emma had purchased the mortar. The least he could do was get her money's worth out of it.

He remained on his knees by the hearth as he waited for her assessment of his work. She stepped up to run her hand along the repaired tiles. It was then he noticed bits of straw clinging to the back of her skirt and her dark socks.

Frowning, she gestured toward the top of the fireplace. "The repairs don't match the rest."

"The mortar is still damp. When it dries it will be hard to tell the old from the new. Hand me that rag and I'll finish evening out these grout lines."

Picking up a red cloth in a small basin behind her, she held it out. "This one?"

"Jah." He gestured toward her skirt. "You have some straw stuck on you."

To his surprise, her cheeks turned bright red. She brushed at it quickly. "I was seeing to our horse."

Like many Amish who no longer found employment on the farm, she still maintained a small stable and a buggy horse to carry her and her mother to church meetings and other gatherings. He had seen their neat white house and little stable on the street behind the inn. Why was she embarrassed about a little straw on her skirt? Taking the rag from her, he began to wipe the tiles free of the excess mortar.

"You missed a spot."

He leaned back and looked over his work. "Where?"

Taking up a second rag, she knelt beside him and began wiping at a spot he had already done. Finishing, she leaned back to study her work, then began wiping again. As she concentrated, her tongue peeked out from between her lips. How kissable she looked.

He pulled his gaze away from her face as his neck grew hot. Why on earth was he thinking about kissing her? That kind of loose thinking belonged to his past. She was a respectable Amish woman. Maybe his father was right and he couldn't give up his English ways after so many years.

Nee, *I refuse to accept that.*

Returning to his Amish family was the best decision he'd ever made. It wouldn't be easy, but it was what he believed God wanted him to do.

He concentrated on his work. When Emma followed behind him going over the same places he did, he finally stopped and sat back on his heels. "You don't get a discount for helping me."

She gave her spot a final swipe. "Perhaps I should."

"If the work isn't to your satisfaction, you may say so." He held his breath. He really needed this job. He was determined to prove to his father that he could live Amish again. Earning a living was a first step.

"The work looks good enough," she admitted slowly.

His hopes rose. "I can start with the shutters now, if you like."

"Come back in the morning. And be careful taking that ladder out of here."

"I will. I don't want to break any of Grandma Yoder's delicious jams," he teased.

Folding her rag, she casually began wiping the tiles again. "You like Grandma Yoder's products?"

"They're the best. Especially the gooseberry jam."

A tiny smile flashed across her face. It disappeared quickly, but not so quickly that he missed it. He had been right. It made her plain face almost pretty.

Chapter Five

The following morning, Adam was waiting in the lobby when Emma came in to start her day. She glanced at the tall grandfather clock in the corner. It was three minutes until six.

Adam shot to his feet, a bright grin on his face. "*Guder mariye*, Emma. Have you a list of jobs for me?"

Her mother was right. He did have a nice smile. And he was eager to get to work. She liked that. She tipped her head toward him. "Good morning to you, too. Yes, I have a list of things that need doing."

Behind the front desk, Mr. Parker leaned his elbows on the polished oak countertop. "Make sure he gets the ice off those gutters before they tear loose."

"It's on my list, Henry," she replied.

To her surprise, some of the color left Adam's face. "I won't be able to do that for you," he said.

Henry blew out a huff of exasperation. "Too bad, because they're calling for more snow this weekend. Are those the breakfast rolls, Emma?"

Henry came around the counter to take the basket of muffins and rolls Emma carried. Their four guests would be down soon for their continental-style breakfast. When Henry lifted the heavy towel to peek inside, the aroma of the hot cinnamon rolls filled the air.

She glanced at Adam. His eyes brightened. "Those smell *wunderbaar*. Makes me wish I was a guest here."

How could she resist such a blatant appeal? "Help yourself, Mr. Troyer."

"*Danki,* but call me Adam." He selected one. When he bit into it, his eyes closed and he made a small sound of satisfaction that did her heart good. He liked her baked goods.

She might be a plain old maid but she could cook. The prideful thought brought her back to earth with a thud. Every gift was God-given and not of her making. Humility was one of the cornerstones of her faith. Pride was a sin.

Heading to the sideboard in the dining room, she began setting out plates, cups and juice glasses. With everything arranged to her satisfaction, she spun around and almost collided with Adam. She couldn't back up with the sideboard behind her. Those crazy butterflies took flight again in her midsection.

After licking the last bit of icing from his finger, he said, "Are you the *goot* cook or is it your mother?"

"I'm sure my mother is the better cook, but I made the rolls this morning."

"It would be hard to make a better cinnamon roll than that." Reaching out, he brushed at her temple. Shocked, she pulled back and saw he held a long piece of straw between his fingers.

He smiled softly. Her heart faltered. "Wouldn't want the guests to think you've been rolling in the hay."

"*Danki.*" She sidled past him and hurried toward her office. Inside, she shut the door and leaned against it as she worked to calm her racing pulse. "How am I going to work with that man around?"

Chapter Six

What was it about Adam Troyer? Why did he have such an unsettling effect on her nerves? He was a simple handyman. He wasn't even that handsome.

Okay, he was, she admitted, but she'd never been susceptible to such shallow things before.

It wasn't even that he looked like William. Will had been only a few inches taller than she was. He hadn't towered over her making her feel small. His white-blond hair had looked like a sleek halo in the sunlight, not like the curly mess that topped Adam's head. Where Adam was always smiling, Will had been serious and earnest. As she always tried to be.

No, she was not attracted to Adam Troyer. There was nothing about him that reminded her of William. Perhaps that was the problem.

A knock on the door made her jump. This would never do. She had to regain control. Marshaling a frown, she yanked open the door. "What is it?"

Adam stood with his thumbs hooked casually in his suspenders. His bright blue eyes sparkled with humor. "The list?"

"What list?" Her traitorous heart jumped into her throat, making her sound breathless.

Chuckling, he said, "The list of things I am to fix."

"Oh, of course." Feeling the fool, she pulled the paper from her pocket and handed it over.

He read it and nodded. "I'll give you an estimate once I've looked at the projects. If we can agree on a price, I'll do the work for you."

"Fine." Anything to put some distance between them. As soon as he turned away, she closed the door, determined to concentrate on her own work.

She had less than half an hour to compose herself before Adam reappeared with an estimate. By keeping the wide front-desk counter between them, she was able to remain composed as they settled on a price. Hopefully it wouldn't take long for him to complete the repairs. Then she'd never have to deal with him again.

Adam went to work fixing the loose railing and broken spindles on the narrow staircase that led to the second-floor landing and the guest rooms. Emma had to pass close beside him several times during the day. Each time, she prayed he wouldn't speak because she didn't trust her voice. He didn't. He merely nodded and flashed her a grin that sent her pulse skipping like a schoolgirl's.

Late in the afternoon, she rounded a corner to find him working on a lamp fixture for a pair of her guests. It wasn't on her list. Her mother and Henry stood beside them. They were all laughing at something Adam had said.

The oddest sensation of being left out settled over her. Normally, she avoided social situations. Staying in the background, making sure everything ran smoothly, that was what she did well. She didn't belong in the group laughing at her handyman's jokes, so why did she wish to be included?

Hearing the clock chime downstairs, she put away her stack of clean linens and quickly made her way to the back door. She slipped into her coat and hurried outside into the cold where four tiny lives were depending on her.

Chapter Seven

Over the next two days, Adam worked on the various projects Emma had given him. He repaired three leaky faucets and a toilet in the guest rooms, mended the dining room pocket doors, tacked down the loose runner on the stairs and replaced a broken windowpane in the pantry. Twice Emma's mother came to him and added a few more tasks to the list. He didn't mind. He needed the money. Besides, he found that he enjoyed watching Emma at work.

Quiet, efficient, always in charge of whatever situation arose, the woman was an excellent innkeeper and an outstanding cook if he could judge by the scones, shoofly pie and breakfast rolls she brought in fresh each morning. Her shoofly pie was the best he'd ever tasted.

At the moment, he was supposed to be fixing a loose shelf on the jam display, but in truth, he was admiring the way Emma was handling an upset customer. Suddenly, her mother stopped beside him. "She is a treasure, my Emma."

He agreed. "She seems to know the business."

"If only there was more business. The inn hasn't been full in weeks."

"Surely the summer months are when you have the most visitors?"

"*Jah,* that is true, but sometimes, without a steady income, it is hard for Emma to make the mortgage payments in the winter."

What was she angling for? He braced himself and said, "I can wait for my pay if that would help."

"Bless you, Adam, that won't be necessary, but it was a generous thought. Are you going to the Yoder auction on Monday?"

"I've been thinking about it."

"The Yoder family needs to raise money for their son's medical bills."

"I heard that. I did want to check out some of the tools they're selling."

"I don't want to impose, but could you drive Emma there? Our horse is old and doesn't like the snowy roads and neither do I. I want to send one of my new quilts for them to sell."

Adam glanced toward Emma. A social outing would be fun. Perhaps he'd even see her smile. "I would be pleased to drive her. I will be at your house bright and early Monday."

"*Danki,* Adam." Naomi grinned happily, then walked away.

After the upset guest checked out, Adam finished his task and took a jar of gooseberry jam from the display. He laid it on the counter in front of Emma. "That fellow wasn't very nice, was he?"

"A slight misunderstanding, that's all." She rang up his purchase.

Impressed that she hadn't taken the chance to complain, he thought more highly of her for her restraint.

"You are spending all your pay on jam. At this rate we will be out by the end of the month," she said.

"When a man finds the best, he won't settle for less."

Placing the jar in a paper bag, she handed it to him. Her eyes sparkled as if he'd done something amusing. Suddenly, he couldn't wait for Monday to roll around.

Chapter Eight

The front door of the inn opened and two young English women entered. Adam was forced to step aside as they approached the counter to speak to Emma. One of the women gave him the once-over and a sly smile. Not so long ago he would have angled for a date with her, but not now. That kind of life was behind him. He had come back to the faith, as was God's will.

Walking back to the shelves, he picked up his tools. If he wanted to date someone he'd look for a good solid Amish woman. Someone like Emma.

The thought brought him up short. When had he started thinking of her as a woman he'd like to go out with? Would she even consider it? The more he thought about it the more he liked the idea.

He looked toward her, but she was nowhere in sight. Her mother was checking in the women. Naomi chatted happily with the *Englischers,* answering their questions with ease.

That was one thing about Emma that troubled Adam. She never seemed to visit or joke with her guests or the other staff. In a business that had people around her all the time, she seemed to hold herself apart.

She seemed lonely.

And where did she go when she rushed out every two or three hours during the day? It was none of his business, but he couldn't help being curious.

Late in the afternoon, he was clearing the snow from the back steps of the inn and studying the second-story guttering along the roof. The icicles hanging from the gutters were several feet long. It was a sure sign that the downspout was frozen shut. Someone needed to do more than knock them down. He'd need to go up a ladder and rake what snow he could reach off the roof. Then he would have to put socks full of ice melt in the gutters. If the downspouts weren't opened, the meltwater could back up under the shingles and damage the walls inside.

The problem was, he couldn't do it. Climbing a ladder inside the building hadn't bothered him, but outside was a different story. No, he couldn't go up there. Not yet.

Turning away, he saw Emma come through the garden gate at the back of the property. He leaned on the shovel handle and waited for her to approach. Once again, she had hay sticking to her coat.

His curiosity got the better of him. He arched one eyebrow. "What have you been up to, Miss Emma?"

Chapter Nine

Adam watched the color bloom in Emma's cheeks. She stuttered, "I—I was seeing to the horse, that's all. You don't have to clear our walks. I was getting to that."

"I don't mind. Your mother asked me to fix the boot scraper, but the metal is old and rusty. You would be better off buying a new one from the hardware store."

"You astonish me. There is actually something you can't fix?"

He laughed. "*Jah,* so I am clearing the walkway instead before I go home for the weekend. If you need help with your stable work I'll be glad to lend a hand."

"No. I can manage. Cream doesn't need much care."

He chuckled. "Your horse's name is Cream? Is she white?"

The glimmer of humor filled her eyes. "No. Her previous owner's little girl named her Marshmallow Cream because of the spot of white on her black nose. That's a mouthful so I just call her Cream."

"Kids have such wonderful imaginations. Not like the old folks that only think of work, work, work."

The sparkle in her eyes died. "I trust you've been busy?"

Had he just implied she was old? He wanted to kick himself. "I did fix the two broken shutters on the lower-floor windows."

Walking in that direction, he indicated his work. "When the spring comes you should have them painted again. They're getting pretty weathered."

"I was thinking of taking them off. They are too fancy for my liking."

"But they are quaint and that is what the tourists like. It must be a hard line for you to walk. Running a business for the English and an Amish home."

"The tourists say they want an 'Amish experience,' but they also want electric lights, central heat and internet access."

"And for you, is it hard to go home to your gas lamps and no central heat?"

"Some cold mornings make me wish I could sleep in one of the inn's empty beds."

"Why don't you?"

Her gaze snapped up to his. "I take the vows of my faith seriously. It would be easy to stay at the inn. My cold feet would feel better but what good would it do my soul if I let temptation bend me hither and yon like the wind does a reed? *Nee,* I will not go against the teaching of our faith."

"You are a wise woman. I lived a long time in the English world. It didn't do my soul any good."

Chapter Ten

Adam didn't know why he felt the need to share his past with this woman. She would likely think the same thing his father did. That he would run back to the worldly ways of the English when things got tough.

"What made you leave the Amish?" Emma asked quietly.

He wanted her to think well of him, but he knew she would hear the story someday. It would be best if it came from him. He gathered his courage. Laying his foolishness bare for her to see was harder than climbing to any height.

He took a deep breath. "When I was young, the outside world seemed glamorous. Full of forbidden fun and over-flowing with things like cars and televisions and video games. I wanted to be a part of it. I felt smothered in my life on the farm. Did you ever feel that way?"

Emma shook her head. "*Nee,* I have not. I believed our Plain lives bring us closer to God. I find much comfort in our ways."

"I had a brother, Jason, who felt the same as I did. We went to work for an English construction company because my family needed the money after a poor summer crop. The pay was good. I even learned to drive a car and I bought one. *Dat* hated it and soon stopped taking the money we brought home. When I wouldn't give up my car, he made me move out. My brother came with me."

"How sad that must have been for all of you."

Adam swallowed the lump in his throat and nodded. "It was hardest on my mother."

"Is that why you came back?"

"*Nee,* I was too stubborn for that. My boss liked me. He taught me all about building things, fixing things, even how to work on a car, but during those years I missed the rest of my family. My mother wrote asking us to return, but we never did. Then, a year ago she died suddenly. My brother and I came home for the funeral, but *Dat* would not speak to us. So we went back to the city."

"That doesn't explain how you came to be in Hope Springs."

"Two months ago, Jason and I were working on a scaffold when it collapsed. He fell three stories. I managed to hold on to a cable until I was rescued. As I was swinging there, my fingers growing numb and slipping, I heard my mother whisper in my ear. She said, 'Hang on, Adam, God has other plans for you.' I'm not making it up, I heard her voice."

"I believe you. What happened to your brother?"

"He was killed instantly. After that, I came back to my *dat*'s farm." To another funeral and an empty ache that never went away.

The accident and the loss of his brother had forced Adam to reevaluate his own life. His Amish roots had been strangled by his sense of self-importance and the money his high-paying job brought in. He had left God behind for a fat paycheck and a used car.

"I'm so sorry." Emma's breath rose in frosty puffs. Her cheeks glowed rosy pink from the cold, but she made no move to go inside. Sympathy filled her eyes as tears gathered in the corners. He sensed she understood the terrible price he'd paid for his folly.

Suddenly, he became aware of a connection between them, something he'd never felt before with any woman. How could he have thought she was plain? There was so much beauty and peace in her eyes.

"Your *dat* must have been happy to have you home."

Sadly, Adam shook his head. "*Nee.* He's not convinced that I've changed. He thinks I will run back to my good job and easy life if I can't earn a decent living here."

"Will you?" she asked, an odd quality in her tone.

"I will not go back to my English ways. I won't lie, I miss some things about that life, but now God is with me every day."

"Your *dat* will see that in time."

"I'm not sure. He forgave me for the pain I brought on our family, but he no longer trusts me. I would do almost *anything* to be worthy of his respect again."

Chapter Eleven

The winter sky held only a hint of pink in the east as Emma pulled open the barn door on Monday morning. Under her arm, she carried a rubber hot-water bottle. Even through her coat she could feel its warmth. It reminded her of the warmth that had enveloped her when Adam shared so much about his life.

She stood there thinking about him, about his struggle with his faith, and the way he'd chosen to share it with her touched her deeply. She couldn't *stop* thinking about him.

Inside the dark stable, she paused to light a lantern on the workbench beside the door. She held it high to light her way past the black buggy to the single stall beyond it. A soft whinny from Cream welcomed her as the mare did every morning.

Hanging the lamp from the hook, Emma checked the water tank, happy to see only a skim of ice on the surface. The temperature was still below freezing, but not by much. After doling out the mare's grain and cleaning the stall, Emma quickly climbed the ladder into the hayloft. It was warmer up where the hay trapped the heat from the horse's body below. A sudden chorus of mewing erupted from a wooden box covered with a scrap of blanket in the corner.

"I'm here, little ones, don't cry." Emma sat cross-legged on the floor and raised the edge of the blanket. The mewing cries rose in volume.

She pulled out the cool water bottle and unwrapped it from a length of gray flannel. Laying it aside, she wrapped the warm bottle she carried and tucked it in the box for the four tiny kittens crawling around in search of her and their breakfast.

"You are so impatient," Emma crooned as she picked them up, one by one, and settled them in the well of her skirt between her knees. The biggest one, a yellow fellow with long fur, began climbing her coat with his needle-sharp claws.

Emma swaddled him in another length of flannel and pulled a doll bottle full of the special formula the vet had given her from her pocket. It took several tries before he got hold of the nipple.

"Look at you. You've got more milk on your face than in your tummy." The others had settled back to sleep in a multicolored ball in her lap.

To her complete surprise, the kittens seemed to be thriving. Each time she made her way to the loft she expected to discover the worst. The two-hour feedings had stretched to three hours now that they had put on some weight.

They had been only a day or two old when she found them. The local vet discouraged her from trying to hand-raise a litter of barn cats, but when she insisted he gave her the supplies she needed. Along with instructions, he gave her one piece of advice. He said, "Don't get attached to them because it will only bring you grief when they die."

Grief was nothing new to her. She took the supplies and followed his instructions to the letter. Now the kittens were her special secret. Her barnyard babies.

Not real babies. Not like the ones she would have had if William had lived, but they had mewed and wiggled and clawed their way into her heart. They were so helpless. They needed her, as she needed them. Even more than she knew.

A sudden noise made her look toward the ladder. Someone was coming up.

Chapter Twelve

Adam's head appeared in the hayloft opening. Emma's heart sank. Her secret wasn't a secret anymore. Now he and everyone else would know how foolish the old maid, Emma Wadler, had become.

"What are you doing here?" she demanded, masking her embarrassment with annoyance.

In the light of the single lantern, his hat cast a dark shadow across his eyes. She couldn't read his expression. After a moment of silence, he said, "Your *mamm* asked me to help you with chores so we can get going to the auction. Now I see why you've been coming up here so often. How many kittens are there?"

A blush heated Emma's face and neck but at least he wasn't laughing at her. "Four."

He climbed up to sit beside her. "What a cute bunch. How old are they?"

"About six days, I think."

"How long have you been taking care of them?"

"Five days."

"What happened to their *mamm?*" He lifted a gray one from her lap and cuddled it close to his chest.

Her nervousness began to fade. "She was run over on the

street in front of the house. I didn't even know she'd had kittens until I went to the stable later in the day and heard their mewing."

The kitten he held began making pitiful cries. "It must have broken your heart to hear them."

"It did."

Even knowing the odds were slim that they would live, Emma had soon found herself armed with a hot-water bottle, a box with high sides and a kitten-size baby bottle with cat-milk formula and a round-the-clock routine.

Raising the kitten to face level, he said, "They look healthy. You are a *goot mudder,* but why not take them into the house?"

"*Mamm* is highly allergic to cats."

"Oh, no." He started to laugh.

"It's not funny," she chided, but she felt like laughing, too.

He quickly grew serious. "Show me what to do and I will help."

She looked at him in astonishment. "Do you mean that?"

"Of course. You can't be scurrying out here day and night. You have a business to run. I will help during the day."

The idea of taking a break sounded wonderful, but could she trust him to do a good job with her babies? She didn't want all her hard work to be undone by his carelessness.

Apparently, he read her indecision because he said, "You should watch me the first few times to make sure I'm doing it right."

For some reason she did trust him. She demonstrated how to swaddle them inside a piece of cloth, how to get the bottle into their mouths, even how to burp them and clean up after them before returning them to their box. She fed one more so he could observe and then he fed the other two.

When they were done and the kittens all returned to the box, he said, "We'd better hurry or we will be late for the start of the auction."

Spending the day in his company—in public—suddenly became a frightening prospect. She rubbed her hands over her arms. "I don't think I'm going to go."

Chapter Thirteen

Adam saw his plans for the day unraveling before they got started. The picnic basket and thermos of hot chocolate under the front seat of his buggy would stay where they were. "What do you mean you aren't going?"

"I have work to do here."

"Naomi said she can run the inn while you are gone."

"I know she can, but I have the kittens to think of, too."

She walked past him and began to descend the ladder. He followed, feeling their closeness draining away. What had he done wrong? "The Yoder farm isn't that far. We can come back to feed them and then return to the auction."

"It's silly to make so many trips. I'm staying here. You go on." She pushed open the barn door and walked out into the crisp morning sunshine.

"I was only going because Naomi asked me to drive you. I'll go patch that hole in the dining room wall."

Apparently, the connection he'd felt between them went only one way. From him to nowhere. His disappointment was as sharp as the kittens' claws.

She spun around. "I forbid you to work today. You are to go to the auction, eat good food, visit with your friends. Your cousins are going, aren't they?"

The auction would be one of the biggest social events of the winter. The weather was cold but the sun was shining brightly. Families would come from miles around, English and Amish alike, to support the Yoder family and have the chance to pick up a bargain. Even his father might be there.

She took a step closer. "You should go."

Sucking in a quick breath, he said, "I would like to go, but only if you go with me. Please, Emma."

Her eyes softened; he could see her wavering. Before she could reply, her mother came bustling out of the house, a large box in her arms. She made straight for his buggy. He had no choice but to rush over and open the door for her.

Naomi said, "*Danki.* You two should get on the road. Emma, I've decided I want you to bid on the ice cream maker and on the pressure cooker."

She laid the box on the floor of Adam's buggy and held out her hand. "Here is the money."

When Emma didn't move, Naomi pressed the bills at her and began pulling her toward the buggy. "If you don't hurry you could miss the household items. Oh, I can't be out in this cold for long. It makes my bones hurt. I'm so glad you're going for me, Emma. And thank you for driving her, Adam. I won't worry about her a bit in your company."

Adam climbed in and extended his hand to Emma. For a second, he thought she was going to refuse, but suddenly Naomi began sneezing. Emma sprang into the vehicle and closed the door between them.

With a hidden smile, Adam slapped the reins against the horse's rump and sent him trotting down the street.

Chapter Fourteen

At a loss for words, Emma could only stare at Adam. Had she misunderstood him? He couldn't possibly think of this outing as a date. How could a man like Adam be interested in her?

She jumped like a rabbit when he asked, "What's in the box?"

"A quilt and some of my jam. We are donating them to the sale."

"Is your jam as good as Grandma Yoder's? If it is, I'll have to buy all you have."

Lifting out a jar, she held it up for him to see. "I am Grandma Yoder."

He turned to look at her in surprise, then burst out laughing. "Well, Grandma, I love your gooseberry jam. Why not use your own name?"

"A jar of Emma Wadler's jelly doesn't sell as well as one with Grandma Yoder on the label. Tourists are funny like that. They want things that look and sound like the Amish names they're familiar with. Since the recipe is one handed down from my mother's mother on the Yoder side of the family, I have no qualms about using the name." She put the sample back in the box.

"You are a good cook. You should open a café."

She looked up sharply. Was he making fun of her? "The inn is enough work."

Giving her a sidelong glance, he said, "I have an idea about that. Want to hear it?"

He seemed serious. She nodded. "Sure."

Eagerly turning to face her, he said, "I could cut a door to the outside in the dining room and build some booths along the back wall to give you more seating. You already cook for the guests so why not cook for more? The town is growing. The English like to eat out. It could give you a steady income, especially in the winter. You could call it the Shoofly Pie Café. What do you think?"

Surprised, Emma mulled it over. What he said made sense. Finally she nodded. "It is a good idea. I will think on it, but you may be sorry you suggested it."

"Why?"

"Because then you'll have to pay for the cinnamon rolls you eat in the mornings."

He grinned broadly and clicked his tongue to get the horse moving faster. Looking at Emma, he said, "Your mother called you a treasure and she was right. I'm glad you decided to come with me today."

Emma discovered that she was glad, too. A tiny spark of happiness flickered in the gloom that had become her life. Settling back against the buggy seat, she breathed in the cold morning air, feeling more alive than she'd felt in years.

After a few minutes of silence, he said, "Tell me about yourself, Emma."

"I'm boring."

"No, you aren't."

"If I tell you my life story you will fall asleep and the horse will run off the road."

"Seriously, how did you come to own the Wadler Inn?"

That she could talk about. "A cousin of my father first

bought the place fifty-five years ago. He never joined the Amish church. I started working for him when I was fifteen. He treated me like the daughter he never had. When he passed away suddenly, I decided to buy the inn and run it myself."

"Did you ever think about marrying?" Adam asked softly.

She stared at her hands as her oldest heartache returned. "Sure, but it didn't work out that way for me. The man I planned to marry died."

"I'm sorry."

"It was *Gotte wille*."

"If the right man came along, you could still marry. It's not too late."

She glanced at his handsome profile against the blue sky. Did she dare believe him?

Chapter Fifteen

Adam turned the buggy into the Yoders' lane. They'd arrived in plenty of time to bid on the items Naomi wanted. Since the quilts wouldn't be auctioned off until after lunch, they were free to wander the grounds and seek out other bargains.

Within an hour, Emma got the ice cream maker, but the pressure cooker went for more than she was willing to pay. He bought her a hot pretzel at midmorning as they watched the horses being sold, and was rewarded with a genuine smile. Why had he ever thought she was plain?

Everywhere around them were the sounds of voices raised in greeting and laughter. He and Emma both ran into relatives and friends. What he had at first assumed was standoffishness on her part proved to be shyness. It seemed Emma had many layers. He wanted to explore them all.

"Having a good time?" he asked as she retreated from a group of her mother's friends.

"I am," she admitted with a touch of surprise and that tiny smile that so intrigued him.

"I am, too." He stood close beside her, not touching her, but wishing he could hold her hand or caress her cheek.

She said, "If you want to stay, I can go home alone and

take care of the kittens. They are my responsibility and I'm sure they're getting hungry."

"I said I would help and I meant it." They rounded the corner of the toolshed on the way to the buggy and came face-to-face with his father.

It took a second for Adam to find his voice. When he did, he nodded. "*Guder mariye,* Papa."

He looked for any sign of softening in his father's eyes and thought he detected it when his father's gaze lit on Emma. They were saved from the awkward silence by the arrival of three of Adam's cousins. David, Lydia and Susan all carried plates with hot pretzels on them.

After greeting everyone, Adam said, "I'm sorry but I must go. I have promised to take Emma home, but we will be back later. Perhaps we can meet up then?"

His cousins exchanged pointed glances, but it was David who replied, "Sure. We'll be here all afternoon. The cattle aren't going on sale until three o'clock."

"Great. We'll see you there." As Adam walked away, he thought he heard the girls snicker behind him, but when he glanced back, they had turned away.

Emma was quieter than usual on the ride back to town. As he pulled up in front of her house, she turned to face him. "I'm sorry to be a wet blanket, but I don't think I'll go back with you."

Instantly concerned, he asked, "Are you ill?"

"Just a headache. Anyway, you will have more fun without me."

He tried not to let his disappointment show. "I won't, but I will feed the kittens for you while you go lie down."

She stepped out of the buggy. "That's not necessary. I like the quiet time with them."

"As you wish," he answered.

Turning away, she paused and looked over her shoulder. "I had a very nice morning."

"Me, too." He waited, but she didn't return his smile. As she walked away he felt he'd somehow landed back at square one.

Chapter Sixteen

After taking care of the kittens, Emma entered the house with lagging steps. Inside, she was surprised to see her mother sitting in the rocker by the stove. She held her Bible in her hands.

Looking over her glasses, Naomi said, "You are home early. Where is Adam?"

"He's gone back to the auction. I was feeling tired."

And like a fifth wheel among his family and friends. She didn't know how to fit in.

"I imagine you are tired, what with getting up every two hours through the night to feed those poor motherless cats."

Emma's jaw dropped. "Who told you?"

"I may snore, but I'm still a light sleeper. When a daughter starts sneaking out of the house at night, a parent wants to know what is going on. I could see you didn't want to tell me about them so I didn't say anything."

Plopping into a chair, Emma said, "I'm sorry if I worried you. I couldn't let them die without trying to save them. They were so helpless."

"If you can put that much effort into saving four kittens, can't you put it into saving yourself?"

Emma frowned. "What's that supposed to mean?"

"I think you know. You were seventeen when William was killed. I know you loved him but he is gone. You are still here. You used William and that inn as an excuse to avoid being with people your own age. You have built a wall around your heart higher than the fireplace. When your father died I felt the same way. Perhaps that's why I let you wallow in your grief. After a while, I didn't know how to make you see you'd shut yourself off from life."

"I've made the best life I can with what God gave me. I'm not pretty, I'm not witty. I'm dull and plain."

She thought she had accepted her lot, but Adam had her thinking about all the things she'd never had—a home of her own and a man to hold her and love her.

Naomi shook her head sadly. "This is not what God wants for you. It would not be what William wanted for you. Life is passing you by, Emma. When I saw those kittens, I knew you felt it, too."

Tears blurred Emma's vision. "I don't want to feel that pain again, *Mamm*."

"God will help you bear any pain that comes your way. Trust in Him. Please stop passing up all the joy life has to offer out of fear. Do you like Adam Troyer?"

"I do. I do like him."

"I can see that he likes you. All you have to do is smile at him and he will do the rest. Give him some encouragement, or sit in that chair and grow old without a husband and children and nothing but cats to love."

Emma bit her lip as she listened to her mother's harsh but true words. Could she take the chance? What if it didn't work out? Would she be worse off than she was now?

Naomi drew a deep breath and blew it out in a huff. Rising to her feet, she said, "I believe I want to go to the auction now."

Emma gathered her courage and stood. "I will go with you."

Chapter Seventeen

David Troyer clapped Adam on the back when he sat down beside his cousin. "I thought I was seeing things this morning. There was my cousin, escorting the homeliest old maid in the county around this auction."

Lydia giggled. "When I thought of all the pretty English girls Adam used to chase I could barely keep a straight face."

"Me, too," Susan added. The girls, eighteen and nineteen, were always laughing at something. Or someone.

Seated on the wooden risers at one end of the cattle pens, Adam listened to his cousins' remarks with growing unhappiness. Finally, he said, "Emma Wadler is not homely. She is a devout, hardworking woman with a kind heart. You don't know her the way I do. I'm thinking of courting her."

Lydia and Susan flashed a scowl at each other. Then Susan asked, "Are you serious?"

"*Jah,* I am." He hadn't known Emma very long, but that was what courtship was for. To talk and make plans, to discover if they were right for each other. In his heart, he knew she was the only woman for him.

David nodded toward Adam's father seated a few rows away. "Are you sure you aren't rushing into this for another reason?"

Adam clenched his jaw. "I don't know what you're talking about."

David shook his head. "You think if you quickly settle down and start planning a family your father will welcome you back with open arms. That isn't fair to a woman."

"If that happens I will be overjoyed," Adam admitted. Like David, he thought it would take more than an Amish girlfriend to convince his father he had mended his life. None of that had to do with the way he felt about Emma.

After the cattle were auctioned off, the gas-powered tools were brought out. David and the girls left. Adam made his way up to the tools to look them over. From the corner of his eye he saw his father talking to the auctioneer beside the gas skill saw Adam intended to bid on. To his surprise, his father beckoned him over.

His *dat* said to the auctioneer, "This is my son. He has a gift for fixing things."

Adam glanced sideways at his father. "What seems to be the problem?"

The auctioneer said, "We are trying to make the most money we can for this family. A working machine brings more money than a broken one."

"I will see what I can do." Removing the cover, Adam got to work. Within a few minutes he had the gas motor chugging away and the saw buzzing.

Delighted, the auctioneer asked, "How much do I owe you for the repair?"

Adam shook his head. "Nothing. It is my gift to the family. I was hoping to buy this, but now it may bring more than I can afford."

He started to turn away, but his father stopped him by grasping his arm. "You did a good thing for this family."

Adam smiled at his father. "From the time I was little I

was taught to think of others first. I wasn't a very good student, but I had a good teacher."

His father smiled. "Maybe you weren't as bad a pupil as I thought."

Chapter Eighteen

Emma stepped eagerly out of the buggy when she arrived back at the Yoder farm. The auction was still in full swing. She looked about for Adam, but didn't see him in the crowds of Amish and English bargain hunters. The sunshine was warm enough to start turning the snow to slush, but no one seemed to mind.

She looked at her mother. "What would you like to see first?"

Adjusting her bonnet, Naomi said, "It should be time for the quilt auction. I will go and see what my quilt fetches. I might have to bid up the price if it goes low."

"Careful, or you'll be stuck buying back your own work."

"What are you going to do?"

Emma glanced around. "I think I'll go look at some of the tools."

Naomi patted her daughter's cheek. "I pray you find the perfect thing to mend your heart there."

Emma smiled broadly. "I believe I may."

The women parted and Emma set out to find Adam. There was much she wanted to say to him, but mostly, she wanted to be near him. To hear his deep voice and happy laughter. He had brought sunshine into her life after a long, dark winter.

Suddenly, she caught sight of his cousins. Susan and Lydia walked ahead of her into the large barn. Perhaps they knew where Adam had gone. Hurrying to catch up with them, she paused inside to let her eyes adjust to the dimmer light, then spotted them looking at a collection of lanterns.

Walking that way, she had almost reached them when she heard Susan say, "Look. There is *Onkel* Daniel and he's talking to Adam."

A thrill danced through Emma at the sound of Adam's name. She tried to see where the women were looking.

Lydia said with a smirk, "I can't believe it. All he had to do was tell his *dat* he's dating Emma Wadler and that smoothed things over?"

Susan crossed her arms. "Guess it was a *goot* plan. *Onkel* Daniel wants him to marry and settle down."

"Do you think he will actually marry her? Can you see them together for a lifetime? He's so handsome and she's so plain."

Susan picked up a lantern to study it. "She does own her own business, and Adam doesn't have two cents to rub together. No…you're right. Why would he settle for her?"

As the women walked on, Emma stayed rooted to the spot. The question echoed through Emma's shocked mind. Why would Adam, a man who could have any woman, settle for her? Why would he?

The answer was as clear as the sky outside. He wouldn't.

Chapter Nineteen

Adam was so happy he was humming as he climbed up to Emma's loft. She was there before him, holding the kittens piled in her lap. "*Guder mariye,* Emma. How are the little ones?"

"The smallest one won't eat. I think he is sick. The vet told me they would likely die. I should have listened to him and let him put them to sleep without suffering."

Her tone was so sad it almost broke his heart. She wouldn't even look at him. He sat down beside her. "*Nee,* do not say that. You have given them days of love and care. Do not give up now. We will take him to the vet and see if there is medicine to make him better."

She looked at him then, her eyes empty and red-rimmed as if she'd been crying. "Some things can't be fixed, Adam. Don't you have work to do?"

"I thought I would help you with the kittens first."

"I don't need help."

He took her chin in his hand, forcing her to look at him. "Emma, what's wrong?"

She pulled away and replaced the kittens in the box. "Nothing is wrong. I got my hopes up and that was my fault.

I'm a foolish old maid, but not so foolish that I can't learn from my mistakes."

Something wasn't right. She wasn't talking about the kittens. "It isn't foolish to hope, Emma. I have hopes and dreams, too. I dream about finding a woman to share my life, about raising a family together and making a home filled with love and faith."

Would she understand what he was trying to tell her?

"Good luck with that, Adam." She scrambled to her feet, put the box under her arm and descended the ladder.

Confused and worried, he watched her leave the barn. What did he do now? Maybe he was rushing her.

Rising to his feet, he dusted the straw off his trousers. Patience was what he needed. He would show her how important she had become to him in little ways and wait for her affection to grow.

Leaving the barn, he walked through the garden gate to the inn. The morning sun gleamed off the snow on the roof and the long icicles decorating the edges. They were pretty, but they were proof that the gutters were blocked. The unusual weather was the culprit. The heavy snow followed by warmer days and freezing nights was causing the problem. When the sunshine began to melt the snow, the water that couldn't run off could seep under the shingles and might damage the walls inside. Emma couldn't afford any more trouble.

It was an easy fix. He knew exactly what to do. All he had to do was climb a ladder to the roof.

He would, as soon as his hands stopped shaking.

Chapter Twenty

Empty box in hand, Emma sighed as she walked home. In spite of all that had happened, she refused to go back into the darkness where she had lived for so long. Life held hardship and disappointment, but it held joy, too.

Like the joy of finding out the vet's daughter was eager to take over the care of the kittens, and the sick one needed only a dose of antibiotics to make him better. Knowing they would be well taken care of lightened Emma's heart. Yes, from now on she would look each day for the unexpected joys God granted everyone.

It would be hard, because she had believed Adam was one of those joys.

After putting her box in the barn, she walked toward the gate. When she pulled it open the first thing she saw was Adam high on a ladder against the side of the inn. He leaned out to lay something near the downspout and the ladder slipped.

Emma's heart jumped into her throat as he clawed at the frozen shingles. Terrified that he would plummet to the ground and be killed, she raced toward him screaming, "Hang on, Adam!"

Grasping the heavy ladder, she stabilized it and leaned against it to hold it still. "I've got you. Come down."

Breathless, he descended the rungs. "*Danki.* You saved me from a nasty fall."

Her racing heartbeat slowed from its wild gallop. He was safe. "You need someone out here to keep you from breaking your neck."

When his boots touched the snow-covered grass, he let out a sigh and smiled at her in spite of her scolding. "God put you here to keep me from harm."

"This time. What about next time?"

"That is up to God. Are you busy? I could use your help for another fifty or sixty years."

She gaped at him.

Stepping closer, he pulled off his gloves and cupped her face in his hands. "I wanted to take it slow, make you see how much you mean to me, but I can't. I must tell you now that I've fallen in love with you, Emma Wadler."

"Why would you settle for a woman like me?"

"You mean someone who is smart, someone with compassion and a deep faith who has beautiful eyes? A woman who is full of grace and can cook better than my grandmother? I don't know, Emma, why would I settle for someone like that?"

"Because it will help you mend things with your father." She waited to see his reaction.

He gave her a puzzled look. "My father and I have already mended things between us. That has nothing to do with why I love you. I want to marry you, Emma, but I will settle for courting until we know each other better. May I court you?"

Her heart tumbled over and poured out the love she had been hoarding for years. She smiled broadly at him. "Yes, Adam Troyer, you may court me."

Before she knew what was happening, he kissed her. It

was a kiss full of warmth, hope and the promise of many joys to come. As his arms encircled her, she knew it was a kiss that would mend her broken heart at last.

* * * * *

INSPIRATIONAL

Wholesome romances that touch the heart and soul.

Love Inspired.

celebrating
15
YEARS

HISTORICAL

COMING NEXT MONTH
AVAILABLE MARCH 13, 2012

THE COWBOY COMES HOME
Three Brides for Three Cowboys
Linda Ford

THE BRIDAL SWAP
Smoky Mountain Matches
Karen Kirst

ENGAGING THE EARL
Mandy Goff

HIGHLAND HEARTS
Eva Maria Hamilton